STEVE ALLEN

MURDER ON THE GLITTER BOX

ZEBRA BOOKS
KENSINGTON PUBLISHING CORP.

ZEBRA BOOKS

are published by

Kensington Publishing Corp.
475 Park Avenue South
New York, NY 10016

First Zebra Books paperback edition: July, 1990

Printed in the United States of America

chapter 1

"**S**on of a bitch!" cried the lady. "It's Steve Allen!" Tessa Moore, a wild glint in her eye, was bearing down on me in the lobby of the Beverly Hills Hotel. She had two young men in tow, one on either side, creating a sort of flying wedge with Tessa in the lead. People stepped aside for her and quite honestly I would have escaped too if I could have. Since that was impossible, I put on my most amiable smile.

"Well, snookums, how are you?" she asked.

"Mr. Snookums to you," I told her, "but I feel fine, thanks."

She kissed me energetically on both cheeks and was aiming for my mouth, but I stepped back. The perfume she wore was so strong I had a feeling that if I inhaled too deeply I might suffer permanent brain damage. Tessa was dressed in the oddest way: a white silk shawl that mostly covered pink tights and a tiger-striped leotard underneath. You might suppose she was on her way to an aerobics class except for the diamond necklace, matching earrings, and assorted bracelets and chains. Her blond hair stuck out in all directions, almost like a punk rocker, God bless the mark. With the

5

jewelry, the effect was a bizarre combination of *haute couture* and New Wave Trash.

Tessa is a comedienne, of course, if feminists will forgive the suffix. She works hard to be eccentric; I don't think it comes naturally to her. You'll probably remember *The Tessa Moore Show* of a few years back. It was canceled after two seasons, but she still has a loyal following who stay up to catch her on the late-night talk circuit. Her fans marvel at her tomahawk nose, her sharp tongue, and one of the foulest mouths in town.

We spent a few minutes telling each other how marvelous we looked—Hollywood people do that a lot—while her two young escorts hovered at a polite distance. Somewhere along the way, Tessa managed to take hold of my right hand and pull me closer.

"I hope Jayne's keeping you on a tight leash, you heartthrob you." Tessa's slang was invariably twenty years behind the times.

"Jayne's in Hawaii for a few weeks doing a picture while we're having our house repainted," I told her, probably unwisely. "We decided it was best to get out of the workmen's way."

"Ah, so you're here all by your lonesome?"

So help me, Tessa was trying to be seductive, which is not easy when you look like that. I did Groucho eyebrows and suggested we have dinner some night. I was just being playful, you understand. Polite. Actually, I hate for women to feel rejected so I tend to comedy-flirt a bit. My wife understands.

"We'll have to tango one of these wild evenings," she suggested. "Blindfold the orchestra, sort of thing."

6

She pulled me closer, making me fear my politeness had gone too far. "How did you do it, Steve?"

"Do it?"

"You can't fool me," she chided. "Tessa hears everything, you know. You're taking over Terry Cole's TV show—aren't you?"

Somehow we had moved from make-believe sex to serious business, not an unusual move in this town. Still, I was taken aback. *Me* take over *The Terry Cole Show,* currently the number one late-night TV talk show in America? It was a pleasant idea, in a way, but not true—though I *have* been a guest on the show countless times and three years ago was the host for one fun-filled week while Terry went to the Bahamas to celebrate his divorce, if that's the right verb. As you may know, I invented the talk-show format back in the pioneer days of television and put in twelve years of duty at it. While I wouldn't want to go back to it, I admit the idea of a grand return for a few wild weeks had a certain allure.

"Darling, tell Mama the truth."

I smiled and made a vaguely Italian gesture with my hands and shoulders.

"You can tell me," she said. "I won't blab."

I just kept smiling—a cunning smile, designed to deceive. Of course you're wondering why I didn't simply come out and tell Tessa *no,* I am *not* taking over Terry's show, nice as it would be—but then you don't know Hollywood, a town where rumors count. In the land of make-believe, careers can rise or fall on mere whispers over lunch in the Polo Lounge or the Palm. So while this rumor unfortunately was untrue, it didn't hurt me one bit to have it gossiped about town—and Tessa would take care of that.

So there it is: I smiled mysteriously where I should have said no. In retrospect, I realize I should have said a hundred times no. I should have run from Tessa Moore as though she were the Black Plague and left instructions for no one to mention Terry Cole or his damned television show ever again. But I was feeling young, innocent, and hell-bent for glory.

"Promise you'll remember your good friend Tessa," she cajoled. "I can be awfully funny late at night."

I thought of a funny answer, but it was dirty so I withheld it.

"And about that tango," she began, flashing her somewhat reptilian eyes at me in a predatory way, but thank God, she was unable to complete her offer. One of her polite young men stepped forward with a slightly pained expression, pointing to his wristwatch.

"Darling, it's almost two o'clock," he said.

"Oh, damn, I must dash!" cried Tessa. "I'm doing a dog-food commercial across town with Lassie."

"Tell her I said 'woof-woof.' "

"Ciao," she said.

"No," I said, "Lassie is a collie."

Tessa laughed, waved, and started walking across the lobby to the front door. Before she reached the door, however, she turned and called to me in a voice loud enough to unsettle the San Andreas Fault.

"We'll have to boogaloo in your bungalow, darling, one night real soon!"

People turned to stare. I concentrated on not blushing, though the tips of my ears tingled like a niacin rush. I told myself Jayne would understand. After all, this was only Tessa Moore and not to be taken seriously. Like most comedians, she thrived on attention. All she wanted was center stage, all the time, any way she could get it.

Don't we all?

chapter 2

As I'd told Tessa, I was living at the Beverly Hills Hotel while our house was being repainted. Actually, it was more complicated than that. The reason the house needed a new coat of paint was that the hillside behind it had turned to mud in last winter's rains and had come oozing down across our lawn, filling the swimming pool and settling inch deep in the living room before coming to a halt. Such are the perils of Southern California hillside living. Months later we still had not entirely managed to get rid of the layer of brown dust that had found its way into every nook and cranny. To repair the damage, we began by refinishing the hardwood floors and buying new carpets, but once Jayne gets started it's hard to stop her. Somehow the new carpets made the old furniture look shabby, and once there was new furniture there was an obvious need to add that extra guest room we'd always wanted. Before I knew it, I had agreed to a new kitchen with skylights in the roof. Jayne said it would all be a good investment. She's the only woman I know who can spend thousands of dollars and end up convincing me we're saving money.

When the different crews of workmen came, I said: "Sweetheart, why don't you accept that invitation from the Jack Lords in Hawaii? It's going to be hell around here for a while." Actually, I was afraid if I didn't get her away from the remodeling, the house would be so changed I wouldn't be able to find it when I drove home at night. Fortunately, the Lords—Hawaii Five-O, remember?—own a sprawling condo on a perfectly white, mud-free beach. I could see Jayne's eyes light up. And, as if on cue, a call came through from her agent, Tom Korman, telling her that the producers of an NBC-TV film starring Bob Hope were offering her a good part in the production, one sizable enough to require her to spend at least two weeks in the islands.

"But I can't leave you to deal with all this yucky mess," she objected.

I gave her my martyred look. "It's all right, dear. You go to Hawaii—you get tanned and relaxed for the two of us. I'll just check into some depressing hotel somewhere."

So Jayne left and I moved into a bungalow at the Beverly Hills, which is hardly some depressing hotel somewhere. There are glitzier places, like the Century Plaza, and more expensively exclusive hotels, like the Bel Air, but the Beverly Hills has an old-Hollywood charm all its own. You go backward in time as you enter the door, back to a more romantic, pre-television day, the time of Gable and Flynn and Hedy Lamarr, whose ghosts still seem to linger in the pastel hallways.

The old town has changed, of course; the skyline here has turned commercial, but the Beverly Hills Hotel remains an island of nostalgia, a pink palace set in its well-tended grounds, with the muffled hiss of traffic from Sunset Boulevard on one side and the quiet residential mansions of the surrounding neighborhood on the other.

I love this hotel and have certain semi-rituals when I stay here. Generally I allow five or ten minutes just to cross the lobby, since you're apt to run into friends, old and new, and might even be willing to sign an autograph or two. In fact, after I left Tessa, I gave my signature to a charming young couple from Des Moines, Iowa, where I spent my freshman college year, and learned all about their parents who used to listen to me on the radio. I also said hello to a producer I hadn't seen since the Emmys and agreed to write a song and play it at the piano at a screenwriter's daughter's wedding that was coming up in a few weeks. Crossing the lobby of the Beverly Hills is not a bad way to stay in touch with the ebb and flow of what the columnists call Tinsel Town. Sometimes I fantasize that when I retire I'll just park myself comfortably in the lobby here and simply greet people. There could be worse ways to spend one's twilight days—though Jayne has pointed out that comedians never retire, and she's right.

"Hello, dear," I said to the young woman behind the reception desk. "Any messages?"

"Oh, yes, Mr. Allen," she said, handing me two pink message slips along with my key. The first was

11

from Sonny Melnik and had come in at ten-fifteen that morning. The message said: "Please call back." The second was also from Sonny Melnik and had come in just a few minutes earlier. It read: "Urgent, please call."

Well, well.

I drifted away from the main desk and started walking, somewhat absentmindedly, out of the hotel, past the sun-drenched swimming pool and along the flower-trimmed paths to my bungalow in the rear. Sonny Melnik, I should explain, is the producer of *The Terry Cole Show*. He's also one of Terry's oldest friends, and the man you had to get past if you had almost any business with Terry. His messages, coming in so quickly after Tessa's bit of gossip, were intriguing. Entertainers and actors, you see, are in a way like old fire horses. As soon as we hear the alarm bell, our pulses quicken, and if there are no competing distractions at the moment, a sort of gravity pulls us toward accepting the offer, whatever it is. You can't conduct a career on that basis, needless to say. A thousand-and-one details have to be soberly considered—money, the amount of your time required, travel factors, if any, billing, other performers involved, the production umbrella under which you'd be operating, etc. So what often happens is you end up talking yourself out of an offer that originally seemed attractive.

At that moment I didn't know whether I wanted to respond to the alarm bell. I did know that on a full-time, long-term basis my vote would be a no-thank-you. But again—for a few weeks, booking some of my favorite comics and jazz players as guests—I could visualize having a ball.

I guess I was getting carried away. I walked right past my bungalow and followed the path in a circle back to the swimming pool before I realized what I had done. A little boy in the pool was looking at me like I was an idiot. I felt foolish as I turned around and made my way back to the bungalow.

The bungalows that belong to the Beverly Hills Hotel have a colorful history. Secret deals have been plotted in these cozy little cottages, deals that have resulted in the rise and/or fall of great studios and stars. Sad to say, the bungalows have also served as places of assignation, to put it politely: world famous celebrities have been known to use these back paths for many a rendezvous. Actually, this was what was going on in the bungalow next to mine at that very moment. I had just seen a couple arrive disguised in floppy hats and dark glasses—one nose was somewhat familiar, but that's about all I could see. I looked away, not gazing too directly. It was all very well to greet your friends in the hotel lobby, but here among the back paths it was mind-your-own-business time.

My bungalow consisted of a living room, bedroom, and small dining area. There were two full bathrooms, for some reason, both equipped with telephones. Outside the bedroom wall was a small, fenced-in garden, all my own. The furnishings inside were posh art deco, understated, with colors that tended to be soft pastels. There was a small stone fireplace along one wall in the living room, and I had moved a sofa to make room for a rented spinet piano. I'm addicted to playing the instrument.

I sat down at the piano and began to noodle around the keys in a distracted manner. I found myself playing

"There's No Business Like Show Business." I had stuffed pillows and blankets up against the soundboard to mute the sound but wondered if I was entertaining the pair in the suite next door.

I stopped playing and began to pace restlessly up and down the living room. I kept coming back to Sonny Melnik and *The Terry Cole Show*. I looked at the pink message slips a few more times to see if I could read any more nuance into those words, "Please call back," and the more interesting, *"Urgent.* Please call."

I knew I should not return Sonny's call until the next morning at the earliest. Game playing is important in this town—it would be a mistake to show I was unduly interested. If I called back too soon, Sonny might begin to think I was *too* available, which would mean I wasn't hot right now, and if I wasn't, he wouldn't want me.

A couple of hours later, as I picked up the phone, I had an odd feeling, a foreboding I tried to shake off. My fingers hesitated on the touch tones, and it wasn't just wondering if I was playing the Hollywood game right. I felt like a sailor heading toward wild and uncharted seas.

chapter 3

"**H**i-ho, Steverino! What's happening?"

"Same old stuff," I told him. "How're you doing, Sonny?"

"Wunnerful, wunnerful," he said, half singing. I think he was doing a Lawrence Welk imitation, but with Melnik it was hard to be sure. For an important producer, the man was strangely klutzy, given to weird imitations, malapropisms, and *non sequiturs*, sometimes all in a single breath.

"Well, who'd 'a' thunk it?" he asked, emitting a staccato laugh.

"Who'd 'a' thunk what, Sonny?"

"You being in town, just when I was thinkin' of you—wondering what my old bosom buddy was up to these days. I mean, speaking of coincidentals!"

"I have all their albums," I said.

"Whose albums?" asked Melnik, never a great straight man.

"The Coincidentals," I said. "Never mind." Conversation like this could make you numb.

"And Jayne?" he inquired. "How's your lovely spousarino?"

15

"Spousari*na*," I corrected.

I told him about our house and the mud slide and Hawaii and all. He told me about *his* wife's having a hysterectomy. Probably you're thinking that a top television figure like Sonny Melnik and a prominent entertainer should be having a more scintillating conversation. What we were doing, I suppose, was pretending there was nothing special on our minds. Then suddenly Sonny began to approach the point.

"Hey, you ever been to Rio?" he asked, seemingly apropos of nothing.

"Years ago," I told him. "I love the music."

"Yeah, Rio de Janeiro," he said with a sigh. "Terry's going there for a few weeks. This is confidential, Steve. Frankly, I've been urging him to take a vacation. You know how hard the guy works. It's time he cools it a little, enjoys the whatever of his labor—know what I mean?"

"Yours of the 14th received and contents duly noted."

He chuckled, being accustomed to so responding to Terry.

"He did look a little tired on last night's show," I said. "So when's he going?"

"Tomorrow."

"Tomorrow?" You don't leave an important nightly TV show, for which you're rumored to receive three million dollars a year, with less than twenty-four hours notice, not even to go to Rio.

"Such a wild and crazy individual." Sonny was chuckling. "He just had a sudden whim to go Carnival it up. Real spur of the minute."

"Sonny, I have to tell you, Carnival was over two months ago."

Expert con artist that he is, Sonny didn't bat an eye. "Listen, Steve—with Terry, he makes his *own* Carnival, know what I mean? Anyway, I was saying to myself, 'Who's as funny as Terry Cole? Who has the wit, the presence, the late-night *joie de vivre* to take over the show while he's gone?' And do you know who I came up with?"

"Dan Quayle," I told him.

"You," he cried. "Right-o! Who else but Steve Allen? It would pay twenty grand a week for two weeks."

"Well," I said, playing by the rules, "I can't give you a yes or no right now. I have to—"

"How soon could you give me a yes or no?"

"Well," I said, "if you'll forgive me for sounding like Ronald Reagan with all the *well*'s, I have to discuss the deal with my agent, and off the top of my head—which is beginning to lose a lot of hair, I might add—the twenty thousand doesn't exactly rush me into a state of rapture. That would mean that Terry was making a hell of a lot more for not even showing up."

"Oh, that could be discussed, I suppose," Sonny said. "You remember, of course, that the last time you filled in for Terry for a week you got only five."

"Ah, yes, I remember it well," I said, singing the line from the Lerner and Loewe classic. "And while we're on the subject, I've never figured out how you bastards got away with paying Terry's replacement hosts only a thousand a night."

For the first time Sonny's laughter seemed genuine. "We got away with that," he said, "the same way we got away with paying guests minimum union scale.

17

But listen, what the hell does the money mean to you anyway? You're independently wealthy."

"That's right," I said, "and asking questions like this is how I got to be independently wealthy. Actually, I'm hip that your offer of twenty means going through the roof compared to the usual steal . . . er, deal."

"Listen," Melnik interrupted, "maybe we can sweeten the pot with a few extras."

"Extras?"

"Like Terry's own dressing room—not the phone booth the network usually provides for the guys that fill in. And listen," he continued, his voice taking on a dreamy quality, as if he were thinking of himself enjoying what he was offering me, "what if we keep your refrigerator stocked with the best smoked Scotch salmon in the world, specially flown in from Harrods? Now visualize a wet bar stocked with every kind of booze you can think of—"

"Sonny, I don't drink."

"Oh, yeah, I forgot. Well, just in case you get the urge to entertain. And we might even be able to cover your tab at the Beverly Hills, you know, like when we fly a guy out from New York we have to put him up somewhere, right? And I know you like to have your dressing room supplied with fruit juices, fruit baskets— we'd cover that too. Hey, we could also send over to the hotel the best-looking young masseuse in town— you know, just to help you relax."

"Is she Swedish or Oriental?"

"How does one of each sound?"

"Both at the same time?"

"Hey," Sonny said, "you're turning me on."

"All right," I said. "You've talked me into it. I'll

take the money, the fruit juice, the expenses at the hotel, everything but the Swedish and Oriental girls."

"Why turn that down?" he asked. "I understand you like a nice relaxing massage."

"I do indeed," I said, "and once a week Jayne brings in a German woman—in her late sixties, and about fifty-five pounds overweight."

chapter 4

I find the back seat of a limousine awfully lonesome. Generally, I sit up front with my driver, Jimmy Cassidy.

"Tell me about Sonny Melnik," I asked as our burgundy-colored stretch Caddy edged up Highland Avenue toward the freeway. Cass knows a bit of everything about this town.

"Sonny? I drove him once or twice. A real son of a bitch—I'd watch out for that guy."

"Why do you say that?" I've known Jimmy Cassidy for over twenty years and his opinion is something I value.

"Well, he's real smarmy, you see, with people he needs to impress. For instance, does he ever kiss Terry Cole's *tochas*!" Cassidy's Irish, but everybody connected with show business speaks at least a little Yiddish. "No, really, it's embarrassing to watch. He just about cuts up Terry's food for him. But if you're just a worker or a guest trying to get on the show, somebody who's not so important—or a driver, for chrissake—someone he doesn't need, well, I guess he takes his revenge for all the crap he gets from Terry. Passes it down the ladder. Me, I won't drive for him anymore. I don't need that kind of treatment."

Cass spat out some chewing tobacco onto Highland Avenue to emphasize his point. With most people, chewing tobacco can be fairly disgusting, but with Cass it seems only normal. He's a failed actor, I suppose, a cowboy from Wyoming who came to Hollywood to make it in the Westerns, but Westerns went out of fashion just after he hit town. That was a bad break, but Cass is a true believer and I don't feel sorry for him a bit. He's fifty-five years old now, but he keeps the faith that Westerns are going to swing back into style and make him as famous as John Wayne. I think he visualizes an Academy Award out there waiting for him like some Holy Grail. He refuses to sink into despair. Meanwhile, waiting for his big break, he's a hell of a chauffeur.

A few years back, I was able to get Cass a walk-on and a few lines in a film that was a spoof of old Westerns. To my surprise he was terrible—stiff and unnatural—not himself at all. Soon after that, I bought him this burgundy-colored stretch limo because *I* was getting worried about how he was going to make ends meet, particularly since none of us are getting younger. Cass has a lot of cowboy pride though; the gift is supposedly a loan, and—what the hell—the car was secondhand. He pays off a little of the capital each year and theoretically will be the sole owner of this splendidly glitzy crate somewhere in the year 1999. Until then, he drives me around Los Angeles when I'm in town, at a reduced rate—which I try to make up in the tip.

"Did I tell you, Steve? I'm auditioning next week for a big magazine layout, a Marlboro ad. I'm going to be one of the Marlboro man's sidekicks, standin' around the campfire while he smokes his cigarette."

"Great!" I told him. Actually, I *could* imagine Cass as the Marlboro man's sidekick, especially if he didn't have to open his mouth and speak. Cass has the right kind of weathered, handsome face, lean build, and watery blue Anglo eyes.

We talked about this for a while as we drove along the freeway toward Burbank. Cass, eternal optimist, was already spending the money from the series of fantastically successful magazine ads that was about to come his way. He might open up a dude ranch in Palm Springs. There would be live entertainment in the lounge, of course—maybe I could do a night now and then. I have to admit that Cass made the whole thing seem so real that we started working out a routine we'd do, a comedy version of "Don't Fence Me In." We pulled up to the security gate at the mammoth Burbank TV studio singing in two-part harmony, with me playing an imaginary guitar.

It would be safe to say that neither Cass nor I have ever completely grown up. I've simply turned endless childhood into a good living, where Cass has not.

The security guard looked first into the roomy interior of the limo's rear and, finding no one there, returned his gaze to the front.

"It's Ste-e-eve Allen!" we sang in harmony. "Here to see Sonny Melnik!"

The guard didn't even blink. These guys have seen everything, and then some.

chapter 5

Melnik sat behind the largest desk I'd ever seen, a chrome and glass affair, monstrous, with Sonny in a high-back chair trying to look equally grand.

"Hi-ho," he greeted. "Long time no visit."

I had to stretch across the desk to shake hands. "You could land a helicopter on this thing," I told him.

He grinned immodestly. Sonny himself was short and round. Imagine a stocky body, stubby legs, no neck, and a pear-shaped face with small, paranoid eyes. Cover this body with pink madras-striped slacks, a white Ralph Lauren Polo shirt, a gold chain around the stubby neck, and you have Sonny Melnik.

He introduced me to his assistant producer, Sol Zukor, and the show's director, Lawrence A. Washington, an aristocratic-looking black man impeccably dressed in a white linen suit. Everyone said how glad they were that I was going to guest host the show for a couple of weeks. I told them I was happy to be aboard.

"Golly, Solly, why don't you tell Steverino about some of the wunnerful guests we have lined up for him!"

Sol Zukor was middle-aged with a sad, basset-hound face. He sagged in every direction. Being Sonny Melnik's personal assistant was not the easiest job in the world. He told me about some of the fascinating individuals I would be interviewing in the next few days. There was a TV evangelist who had just published his autobiography, *From Sin to Stardom*. He would be sharing the couch with a former prostitute turned crusading feminist, a rock star who was speaking out against drugs, and a star of action and revenge films by the name of Hal Hoaglund, who was very hot this year. Hal was plugging his new movie, *Kill or Be Killed*. This was just the lineup for Monday. From Tuesday on, we had politicians, comics, singers, a famous model, a transvestite, a porn star (I insisted she be canceled) and various celebrities with books they had just written telling all about the *real* them—their insecurities as well as all their triumphs; all their confessions that were fit to print.

Everyone, of course, had something to sell. Par for the course, but it had to be kept under control. We'd let them show film clips and the covers of their new books in exchange for either scintillating conversation or some actual entertainment. They'd have to sing for their supper, so to speak.

Sol handed me the questions for the first night's

guests, a talk-show staple since the days of the original *Tonight* show. Since the early 1950s all talk shows have a few people on staff who phone guests, usually three or four days before they appear, and ask what *they'd* like to discuss.

"Do we have bios, too?" I asked. In addition to having a few questions to prime the interview pump, I also like to read a bit of background material before a show. The better staff people will also provide a host with any recent magazine or newspaper articles about barroom brawls, arrests, divorces, exposés, slanders—all the lovely reality that years ago used to get you run out of the business and now, so solidly have Oswald Spengler's predictions been borne out, are more likely to get you an extra million dollars for your next picture.

To tell the truth, I'm that thorough when I'm starting a new series, but after a few weeks things are generally running so smoothly that I need only glance at the prepared questions before the show and simply wing it from that point on. It also helps that I personally know a good many of the people I interview.

Perhaps I should explain, at this point, that the easiest gig in the history of entertainment—go back as many thousands of years as you want—is hosting a talk show. So simple an assignment is it, in fact, that talent is simply not one of the requirements. For readers who don't think clearly, perhaps I should explain that I did *not* just say that talk show hosts have no talent. Some of them do. They may have a talent for comedy, or for singing. But others, let's say in category *B,* have no talent whatever, in the traditional sense of that word. But it turns out they're just as good at conducting the simple business of a talk show as the people who do have ability.

I was speed-reading through a couple of the guests' bios when Lawrence Washington made an interesting slip. "It's great to see you being so thorough," he said. "When Terry gets well again it wouldn't be a bad idea if he did this kind of research himself."

Sonny Melnik shot the director an immediate and enraged look.

Lawrence added quickly, "Of course, Terry's such a genius he just *knows* the right question. It's like he's on automatic pilot after all these years."

Sonny's piggy eyes were ablaze with fury. I had a feeling that if I hadn't been present, there'd have been a lot of shouting going on. What interested me most was not whether Terry Cole researched his guests, but Lawrence's unguarded comment. On the phone yesterday, Sonny had said nothing about Terry's being sick.

"So, any problems with the guest list?" Sonny asked, changing the subject. There was still a hint of a snarl in his voice.

"Now about Reverend Cash," said Zukor, then stopped.

"Yes?" Sonny asked sarcastically, then turned to me with an exasperated smile. "It's hard to get good help," he whispered.

"What about the reverend, Sol?" I asked gently, trying to be encouraging.

Cash was the TV evangelist with the new book.

"Well, I'm sure you're aware, Steve, how sensitive this could be. For some of our viewers down South,

25

Cash is the next best thing to Jesus Christ. What I'm saying, you might want to tread carefully."

I told Sol, fundamentally speaking, that the Reverend Cash would not be crucified by me. A cagey smile touched the corners of Lawrence A. Washington's mouth. "Actually, Steve, I think our problem child Monday night is going to be Hal Hoaglund."

"Why's that? Hal's been an enormous star for nearly three months now. The girls in the audience will probably jump on stage and molest him."

"He stutters," Lawrence said.

"Stutters? Are we speaking of the major sex symbol of the moment?"

"We are. Without a script he stutters," Lawrence insisted. "And I mean st—st—stutters. He's terrified of appearing on talk shows."

"I should think so. I'm surprised his agent is allowing him to do it."

"Well, he's memorized his lines, answers to just about any question he knows you'll ask him. As long as he has lines, he's all right. He was able to get through Phil Donahue this way a few weeks back, but I'm afraid we could have some trouble. I mean, this guy could really die."

"Don't worry. I'll get him relaxed," I said.

"Steve's a genius at getting people to relax," Sonny Melnik said belligerently.

"Well," I said, "no one has ever died on one of my shows."

chapter 6

I was in a Gershwin sort of mood later that evening, sitting at a grand piano at the house of my friend, Rip Rawlings, in Brentwood. I'm a bit of a bore at most parties, I'm afraid. As soon as I see a piano, I'm out of circulation, deep in my own inner jazz land, gazing into nowhere with a dreamy smile while my mind savors the genius of Gershwin, Porter, Berlin, Kern, or Rogers.

Rip and his wife, Vera, live in a California ranch house built on one level, horseshoeing around the swimming pool. It's a relaxed sort of place. Rip is a screenwriter. Some writers in Hollywood go about with a sour, misunderstood expression—they're trying to tell you they wish they lived in a time and place where the written word was appreciated, rather than in this neon land of sunny illiteracy—but Rip has no such problems. He cheerfully came to Hollywood thirty years ago from New York, a best-selling novel to his credit, and began churning out screenplays as if it were easy to do so.

The crowd tonight was mostly over the age of forty: writers, agents, mostly former New Yorkers. Some of these people have lived in California for decades and still behave as if they're exiles. They stick together, subscribe to *The New York Times* and talk about New York food. Right now they seemed pleased to be hearing Gershwin rather than the latest rock and roll.

After giving them a few selections from *Porgy and Bess,* I launched into "They Can't Take That Away From Me," which always makes me think of Fred Astaire and Ginger Rogers gliding around a dance floor. I was making the tune swing, for laughs playing it in Errol Garner's style. I was just coming up to the last eight bars when I heard a resounding baritone voice singing in my ear: "No, no, they *can't* take that away from me!"

I turned and couldn't believe my eyes. "My God, Winston Dane!" I cried, stopping the piano solo in mid-measure. "I haven't seen you in ten years!"

"More like twenty, Steve," he said wistfully. "Time flies when you're having fun." For some reason, show people enjoy stock lines.

Winston Dane was one of the pioneers of early television, belonging to the same period as Oscar Levant, Arthur Godfrey, and Dave Garroway. He had been regarded as an intellectual, which was probably the kiss of death. He had hosted one of the first late-night talk shows in America until he was fired in 1963. Terry Cole took over his time slot and made it into a whole new ball game, not to coin a phrase. Terry was sharp and clever, but no one ever accused him of being an intellectual.

"You look great, Winston," I told him honestly. For someone who had to be in his early seventies, Dane hadn't really changed that much since I'd known him so many years ago. He still appeared tall, spry, and twinkly eyed. His hair and mustache had always been a distinguished silver color—I think he'd been born that way—and he seemed very trim.

I stood up from the piano. "So what have you been doing with yourself?" I have to admit, I hadn't even thought of Winston Dane for years.

He was beaming. "Oh, I've been living the good life, actually. In Rome mostly these days. I have a nice little house on the Appian Way."

"No kidding, the Appian Way," I repeated. As often happens with old friends who have not seen each other in years, our conversation felt a bit awkward. "You doing any television?" I asked and immediately regretted it. Maybe TV was a sore subject, after the way he had been treated.

"Oh, no!" he said with a laugh. "I don't miss it at all. It's splendid to be a civilian."

"I'm sure," I said, probably smiling too much.

"No, honestly, Steve, I love being retired." The painful edge to his voice belied the statement. "In Hollywood people think once you're out of *their* business, you might as well be dead. But there's a big, interesting world out there outside of New York and L.A."

"Listen, I'm envious," I lied, taking his arm. "Most of us just fantasize about getting out of this rat race. You, you've made the grade. Boy, Rome!" I sighed, shaking my head in wonder at the thought of living in the Eternal City.

"Well, I was ejected rather brutally, you know, from network TV, but it's worked out for the best. Right now, I wouldn't change my life for anything."

"That's great, Winston." I was wondering if he'd

ever married, or if he was living in Rome alone. I had once greatly admired the man, but at the moment I was conscious of running out of things to say. "How long are you in town for?" I asked feebly.

"Only a few days. I'm passing through, on my way to Tahiti."

"Tahiti!" I enthused.

"You see, I'm planning to make my way across the South Pacific to Australia, then up to China by Christmas."

"China at Christmas! I'm envious."

"Naw, not you, Steve. You're an old workhorse. You'd be lost as a man of leisure. By the way, what are you drinking?" he asked, taking my arm and leading us both toward the bar. This seemed like a good idea.

"I usually tell the barman to surprise me," I admitted.

"That must lead to interesting situations."

"It does." I was telling Winston the truth. Most people have a favorite drink that must absolutely be prepared in a certain way, but I really don't. Basically, all booze tastes the same to me, and I can take it or leave it, depending on my mood.

"How about a Kamikaze?" Winston suggested.

"Damn the torpedoes," I agreed, but settled for a Perrier when it turned out our hosts' bar did not include such exotic fare. Winston had a glass of *"vino bianco,"* as he called it. We touched glasses.

"I hear you're taking over Terry Cole's show for a while," he said just as I was about to take a sip. The rumor mill in Hollywood must be working overtime, I thought. Winston saw the look in my eye and the way my glass hesitated. "I've had a chat with Kathleen this morning," he told me, lowering his voice. "Play your cards right, Steve, and you might have that show a lot longer than two weeks."

I had to stare at Winston in dumb amazement. Kathleen Cole is Terry's ex-wife, but I was not at all certain what kind of inside knowledge she would have these days about Terry. They were not rumored to be friends exactly.

"How *is* Kathleen?" I asked cautiously.

"Rich, bitter, and usually in heat," he told me. "As ever."

"Ah . . . and Terry—I understand he's going to Rio for a while, just a short vacation?"

Winston was grinning wickedly. "They didn't tell you, did they?"

"Tell me what?"

"About Terry."

"What about him?" I asked, not certain it was a good idea to be discussing this.

"He's over the edge," Winston said. "Bonkers. Nutty as a fruitcake. Beyond the fringe into the Twilight Zone of the Fourth Dimension." Dane always did have a way with words.

"Well, perhaps in television that's an advantage." I was trying to be fair.

"We're not talking a *little* cuckoo here, Steve. Let me give you an example: last week in his opening monologue, Terry started doing an Elvis Presley imitation, but he just couldn't stop. He was Elvis for the rest of the show. Wouldn't snap out of it. He went home that night and he was *still* Elvis. Right now he probably thinks he's living in Graceland, getting ready

31

to do a remake of *Blue Hawaii*. They didn't air the show. Ran a repeat at the last moment."

"That *is* serious," I agreed, honestly shocked. "You're certain of this?"

"It's what Kathleen told me. She should know."

I wasn't so sure. Kathleen and Terry had been divorced for three years and she had an ax to grind. After all, she was only awarded twenty-five thousand dollars a month in alimony payments after asking for fifty thousand.

Under the circumstances, I thought it unwise to change the subject. "Winston, you know what I'm thinking? How about your coming on the show next week, as a guest?"

"Oh, no. At this late date, I'd be terrible."

"You'd be great, Winston. And the public would love to see you again."

"Steve, they wouldn't even remember me. But thanks for the thought. I'd just as soon leave television in my distant past."

"You sure? Not even one short five-minute segment?"

"Thanks, no."

The thought of returning to television, even briefly, seemed to agitate him. A friend of mine, singer Ann Jillian, came up to say hello at that moment, and when I turned to introduce Winston, I saw he had fled.

Later in the evening, I noticed him standing in front of the avocado dip looking pensive and down. *Damn it,* I thought, *a retired comic is a sad sight.* I decided I'd try again to get him on the show. It would be good for Winston Dane to be seen again.

chapter 7

Rip and Vera's party was on Friday night. I spent the rest of the weekend sleeping, swimming, and sunning, albeit covered with sunscreen, saying no to two cocktail parties, an award ceremony where foreign journalists got to pick their favorite stars, and an offer from Tessa Moore, who had wished to rendezvous with me around midnight in my bungalow but was probably kidding.

I was getting serious about next week. Sol Zukor had kept his promise and had sent over all the material he could muster on the guests. Besides the various summaries to read, there were one autobiography, two novels, and volumes of press clippings from which I learned about assorted depravities.

Because I hadn't done talk-show duty in some time, I felt like an athlete getting ready for the big game. On Sunday morning I read the New York and L.A. papers, looking for material for my monologue. Actually there are times when the news straight seems to be a better parody of itself than anything I could create.

Around noon on Sunday, I worked out a bit where I'd pretend to be a ghetto teenager, a multimillionaire crack dealer who drove a Mercedes and was flunking out of high school. But no—drugs in the inner cities had become a more terrible problem than ever. I could imagine a flood of angry letters.

After that, I stood in front of the mirror and worked out a fair Margaret Thatcher imitation; at least *I* laughed. But a California audience probably wouldn't get it. England was too far away; they wouldn't know or care.

I went back to *The New York Times'* "Week in Review." What other topic could I find? The ongoing conflict in the Middle East? Forget it. How about *apartheid?* Now *there's* a funny subject. I spent half an hour working out a sidesplitting confrontation between Bishop Desmond Tutu and the South African Minister of Law and Order—I played both parts—until sinking onto my sofa in despair. Maybe I should get the flu and cancel out. Suddenly my throat *was* feeling a little sore. I called room service and had them send over an emergency ration of fresh orange juice and hot tea.

Jimmy Cassidy arrived late in the afternoon, feeling blue because he hadn't gotten the job in the magazine layout playing the Marlboro man's sidekick. Cass flopped down dejectedly on one of the chairs. We made a swell team: an unfunny comic and a failed cowboy.

"Hey, Cass, what's Irish and stays out all night in the backyard?" I threw at him, trying to cheer him up.

"Paddy O'Furniture," he told me sadly. "I heard you do the line on the radio recently."

"Oh, sorry."

"You know, the thing that kills me is I was trying so damn hard," Cass said suddenly. "I mean, I even wore a suit to the damn interview, can you believe it? I wanted 'em to know I was responsible, for God's sake, not just some redneck flake.''

"A suit? But they were looking for a cowboy."

"Damn it—*anybody* this side of Jackie Mason can be a cowboy. What was I supposed to do, ride a horse into the office? I wanted to show 'em I could be a real good spokesman for the product, see—maybe travel around the country making personal appearances in shopping centers, that sort of thing. But those guys got no imagination.''

I nodded. There wasn't much to say. Jimmy Cassidy had a genius for the inappropriate. When he should wear a suit, he generally could be found in old Levis and dusty boots. And now, here was a part tailor-made for him and he screwed it up by trying to be something he wasn't: cosmopolitan. It was enough to break your heart.

Fortunately, Cass bounces back. Within a few minutes he was on the phone ordering up his idea of breakfast from room service: steak and beans, coffee and whiskey. The kitchen at the Beverly Hills Hotel must get some very strange requests, but they always manage to come through. In this case, Cass drank the whiskey and I had the coffee.

"Oh, almost slipped my mind," he said, getting more and more comfortable on my couch. "I found out what's wrong with Terry Cole."

"Oh?"

"Yeah, I had a job driving these dudes yesterday, see. Some big-shot TV guys. They were talking about Terry Cole in the back seat there, saying he was in some clinic to kick his cocaine habit. Said he had a two-hundred-thousand-dollar-a-year habit. Can you believe that? All that money up your nose?"

"Terrible," I agreed. My mind was far away. At this point, I didn't care much if Terry Cole believed he was Elvis, had a two-hundred-dollar-a-year habit, or had gone off to party in Rio de So-what-o. What was important right now, I finally knew what I was going to do for my opening monologue: *me*.

I owed it to Cass, thinking about how he would have had much better luck with his audition if he'd simply been himself. It's a cliché, of course, but easy to lose sight of in Hollywood where you're always being tempted not to be yourself but to imitate whatever's currently successful.

So for my monologue, I was going to be *me*. I'd tell the audience about the Bishop Tutu and Margaret Thatcher and teenage millionaire ideas and my despair at realizing none of these things would work.

They'd love it, I was certain of that, because the best laughter is usually built on truth and perhaps each person out there would be able to sympathize with my predicament. The more I thought about it, the more certain I became that I was on the right track.

Cass eventually passed out and spent a good part of the day snoring softly on my couch. I hate loud snoring—who doesn't?—but the soft, purring kind, perhaps for some primitive, atavistic reason, I'm able to interpret as vaguely comforting, as if a large animal were sleeping peacefully in my cave. It was evening by the time Cassidy aroused himself and left, giving one last shamefaced look at the level of the contents of the whiskey bottle.

As for me, I called it an early night and woke up

Monday morning with a sense of resolution and confidence. Perhaps I should explain that I don't perceive myself as particularly intelligent, but somewhere up inside my skull there's a portion of my brain that works like mad. All I have to do is get the hell out of its way. Quite often I go to sleep wrestling with a problem and with no further conscious effort the solution is quite nicely mapped out when I awaken, more or less in the same way that a hotel bellman delivers a fresh morning paper to your door right on schedule.

The hour spent poring over *The New York Times* had been wasted. All the news-of-the-day subject matter wouldn't be needed at all. I'd revert to my old standby, providing ad-libbed—and, I hope, funny—answers to actual questions written by the studio audience. I called Zukor, told him that was my decision, and asked that he have his staff people pass out the question cards to the audience visitors while they were still standing in line so there'd be plenty of time to pick up the questions and deliver them to my dressing room.

The actual taping of the show is done at six in the evening and almost always starts right on time. Cass drove me to the network about three-thirty and I had one final meeting with Sonny Melnik and the show's dapper director, Lawrence Washington. Then I dressed in a charcoal gray pin-striped suit, which I'd brought along in a black nylon clothing bag, topping it off with a pink shirt and burgundy tie. I then lounged around Terry's sumptuous dressing room, the refrigerator of which was well stocked with orange juice and smoked salmon. With an hour to kill, I relaxed by reading a few chapters of Mortimer Adler's *Ten Philosophical Mistakes* (don't laugh—it's a great way to clear your mind of mundane concerns) to the accompaniment of some old Chet Baker audiocassettes in the background. That emotional, teenage voice of his and the beautiful, soft trumpet tone always relax me and make me smile, although I'm not sure what I'm smiling at.

A little later the makeup lady came in, removed a few years from my face, darkened the old sideburns, and at last I was backstage waiting with that odd itchy excitement, the adrenaline working up my heart and soul, ready to go out and convulse all those people in the studio and around the country who didn't have sense enough to be watching Ted Koppel.

chapter 8

The band whipped crisply into my theme song, "This Could Be The Start Of Something Big," instead of Terry's, the standard opening credits were given, and the announcer, Jimmy Langford, in a semi-imitation of Ed McMahon's singsong introduction of Johnny Carson, said, "And *now*—hee-ee-ere-s Steverino!"

I stepped out from behind the curtain to thunderous applause. In some settings that might have appealed to my ego, but on The Terry Cole Show it meant absolutely nothing because, after being warmed up for twenty minutes, the audience would have applauded as heartily for Attila the Hun, Jack the Ripper, or Adolph Hitler. They applauded at a similar hysterical volume, in fact, for Terry Cole himself, for all his replacement hosts, for all his guests, and probably would have done the same for any stagehand who walked on with a broom.

It took my eyes a moment to adjust to the bright lights but I had no trouble heading for the correct camera.

"Good evening, Latvians and Germans," I said. It's a line I sometimes use to gauge an audience's readiness to laugh. Sometimes, believe it or not, they think they've heard the words "ladies and gentlemen" and don't laugh at all. But this was a good crowd and the line got about a 32 on a 0-to-100 scale, which is all it deserves. So we were off and running. "As you've already been told, Terry's not here tonight"—mock groans—"but we hope he'll be back soon. Apparently he's feeling a little under the weather. What he's feeling for down there I have no idea, but I'm sure you all wish him well.

"And when he climbs up *out* of the well, we'll dry him off and—" The audience was getting better all the time, laughing at all sorts of stream-of-consciousness nonsense lines that weren't even jokes.

"You know," I said, "I had the pleasure of meeting a few of you out in the parking lot a bit earlier, and as individuals I have the impression that you're the salt of the earth. But," I said, withdrawing from my inner jacket pocket a dozen or so light blue question cards, "as a group, to the extent that I can judge by these questions you've asked me, you're a little on the flaky side."

More squeals and giggles, this time a bit self-conscious.

"In any event," I said, "I'll just read some of your questions and see what answers we can come up with. The first is from a Mrs. Johnson. I see you're from Vancouver, is that right? Okay. Mrs. Johnson's question is, 'When are you coming up to God's country?' "

The answer had already occurred to me, but I pretended to take a moment to think of it. "When I drop dead," I said.

After that it was a few more questions and then the floor manager signaled that it was time for an opening musical number by pointing to the piano. The band's rhythm section gave me a little jazz-style walking music so I moved over and sat down at the shiny grand that had been provided.

"What would you like to have me play?" I asked.

"The piano," somebody shouted, getting an enormous laugh.

"I'll handle the jokes," I said, using another stock line. "But seriously, is there any selection you'd like me to play?"

This led to expressions of extreme consternation on the part of Bobby Winger, the bandleader, the announcer, and Mr. Melnik, the producer, since we had planned and rehearsed "Satin Doll."

"Honeysuckle Rose," someone else called out.

"Thank you for that request," I said. "I'm not going to honor it, but— No, seriously, here's a great Duke Ellington classic, which is exactly what I'd planned to play anyway. Who cares what you people want?"

The arrangement I'd brought along, done by Bill Holman, one of the best, is a real showstopper and you'd have to be a pretty bad piano player not to sound great supported by that kind of chart and a good orchestra. I did a lot of Basie right-hand tenths in the plink-plink manner, a couple of fake descending *arpeggios*, actually done with the back of the right-hand thumbnail on the black keys, and all in all fooled the people down to their socks. Again the audience cheered like crazy, but why not? A sign that said "Applause, Applause, Applause" was blinking right at them.

A moment later, sitting behind Terry Cole's desk, I chatted briefly, as is the custom, with his announcer, who said, "Say, it was very nice of you to come down at the last minute."

"And it *is* a comedown," I said, doing one of those plays-on-words to which I am so given. Jimmy, for his part, laughed it up, as all such announcers must.

After answering a few more of the audience's questions and getting a few more laughs, we jumped into the first commercial break, which gave us a moment to catch our breaths. On stage the bright television lights were partly dimmed, providing a bit more repose.

The set itself was classically simple: a desk where the hosts have sat since time immemorial and a long, comfortable couch for the guests. Behind us were a few potted palms and a fake window that looked out onto an abstractly glamorous nighttime Hollywood scene—what you might see if you were standing on top of the Hollywood Hills, rather than inside a studio in Burbank. The floor manager helped me get comfortable in

Terry Cole's high-back swivel chair behind the mahogany desk. One of the sound men had to readjust the miniature microphone on my lapel.

As I looked down at it I noticed a small refrigerator at my feet underneath my desk. It was well concealed from the audience and cameras.

"What's this?" I asked.

Langford grinned. "Mr. Cole sometimes requires a little inspiration," he said.

"Ah!"

I opened the refrigerator and saw a single bottle of something called Cajun vodka. There seemed to be a pepper floating on the bottom. "Hey," I said, "this looks like serious stuff."

Langford had a sly, sarcastic smile. I was getting the feeling he didn't like Terry Cole at all. "Terry sometimes needs a *lot* of inspiration," he explained. "How about you? They've got everything backstage: mineral water, soda, juice, beer, wine, opium—you name it."

There were two coffee mugs, I saw, on an inside shelf near the refrigerator, so that any of these substances could be ingested without the knowledge of the viewers. "Maybe I'll try a drop of the vodka in my orange juice, but not now."

Time was running out. Langford returned to his chair and I prepared myself to go back on the air.

The lights on stage came back up. The floor manager had his earphones on and was quietly counting down the seconds to airtime. "Ten . . . nine . . . eight . . . seven . . . six . . . five . . . four . . ." The last three seconds are done silently, by hand. The orchestra started playing, the audience cheering.

We were off again.

chapter 9

My first guest was the Reverend Dion Cash, whose autobiography had already reached the best-seller list. The Reverend was tall and distinguished with silver hair and a white silk suit that must have cost fifteen hundred dollars. He wore a diamond ring on the little finger of his right hand, a smile big enough to swallow the state of Alabama, and he had small, shifty eyes. Personally, I wouldn't have bought a used car from him.

"Howdy, Mr. Allen!" He was as easy as could be—actually quite likable—waving at the audience as if they were old friends, then lumbering down onto the couch. We joked around a while. Even though he was a clergyman, he seemed determined to show everyone he was a good sport. He was also determined to show the cover of his book, which he held in his lap and flashed toward the camera whenever possible.

"Reverend Cash, I read part of your autobiography over the weekend and I have to tell our viewers—some of it is pretty racy stuff!"

The comment made him turn very grave. "Well,

43

Steve, before I opened my heart to the Lord, I was tossed around upon the sea of depravity."

"The Sea of Depravity! You make it sound as real as Lake Tahoe."

"For those of us who almost drowned in it, it is, Steve. It is."

We talked for a while about St. Paul and St. Augustine, how they, too, had been sinners before their conversions. Jesus loves sinners, Cash reminded us. And Dr. Cash seemed fairly fascinated by sin himself.

"Do you mind if I read a paragraph from your book, Dr. Cash?"

"Please do," he said, smiling.

"This is a description of your first amorous encounter, when you were twelve: 'We lay down in the long grass behind the barn. Mary May was three years older than I was and although I was very naive, I remember thinking that she seemed to be deliberately provoking me, tempting me to a sort of sin that was foreign to my experience. In all honesty I cannot say that I resisted the temptation. The part of me that is purely animal succumbed to Mary May's sweet face, her firm, ripe flesh, the delicate aroma of her body in the heat of the summer afternoon.'"

At that point I closed the book and was about to address a question to Dr. Cash when a wise guy in the audience yelled, "Don't stop now, Steve!"

It got a big laugh, needless to say, although neither the reading nor the laughter fazed the Reverend in the least.

"I suppose we've all had such experiences in our youth," I said, "and please understand I'm not pointing a moral finger at you here, certainly not from any position of my own superiority. But has it occurred to you that in writing this sort of account—and, as you know, there's a good deal more erotic detail provided in that chapter—you might be inciting impressionable young people to the very sort of behavior that you yourself now say was sinful."

Dr. Cash smiled in that gentle, patient way—somewhat reminiscent of Jerry Falwell's friendly mask—as if he were explaining something to a not very bright child.

"You see, Steve," he said, "I did wrestle with that very problem. And so, for that matter, did St. Augustine himself, in his famous *Confessions,* describe certain of his early sins in such a way that a sensitive person might be aroused by the reading. And who's that Catholic priest—a very fine writer—who has written a number of novels about life in the modern world—"

"Andrew Greeley?"

"Yes," he said, "that's the gentleman. He, too, in some of his books, has included scenes of that sort, and in some quarters Catholic priests are considered to take an even narrower view than do representatives of other Christian churches on these same questions. But I think if anyone reads my entire book"—he flashed the cover again—"they'll understand that I did not include that passage, and a few others like it, as a way of being provocative or sensational. The point is that the Lord led me *away* from such a behavior pattern—and, believe me, it wasn't easy."

The next guest was a singer straight from Harrah's Club, who did a rock number, though one in which you could actually understand the lyric. Then it was on to the next guest, a former prostitute turned feminist who was now running for political office. To be precise, she wanted to be Mayor of Beverly Hills.

Well, everyone was having fun. At one point, I thought I saw Reverend Cash eyeing the former call girl. What my guests do after a show, of course, is none of my business, as long as they're consenting adults, though one retains the right to disapprove.

The future Mayor of Beverly Hills even offered me an honorary spot on the city council. I told her that for me it was President or nothing.

Everything was going just fine—until Hal Hoaglund came on.

chapter 10

I knew we were in trouble right away. Even in makeup, Hoaglund was as pale as a ghost. There were beads of perspiration on his forehead. He tried to smile as he came out onto the stage, but the smile came off as a weird grimace. The man was nearly catatonic with nerves.

Physically, Hoaglund made Conan the Barbarian seem like a wimp. He was well over six feet three, with massive shoulders, legs like tree trunks, and arms whose muscles bulged even beneath his carefully tailored blue suit. On top of this gargantuan body sat a bullet-shaped head that was styled with a military haircut, an honest-to-God crew cut. In the film before his current masterpiece, Hal portrayed an android who fell in love with a beautiful woman. This was the picture in which he made his mark. An android, for those who may not know, is a mechanical human, a glorified robot, who can do all kinds of superhuman things, presumably even in bed. As Hal came out onto the stage, a few women in the audience actually moaned a little. (Personally, if I were a woman, I'd be into the suave, intellectual, piano-playing type with glasses.)

Poor Hal Hoaglund did not look happy. Within that android body of his lurked a sensitive soul. I knew from his bio, for instance, that he played the violin. After bodybuilding, in fact, that was his major interest. He actually aspired to take a chair with the Boston Pops one day. This sensitive side of Hal—the *real* Hal Hoaglund, if you will—was perhaps what left him tongue-tied in front of his adoring fans.

"Sit down, Hal," I said as he kept pumping my arm. "Easy on the sofa," I warned humorously, but he looked aghast at the thought, as though sofas *had* been known to crumble when he was around.

He was opening his mouth to speak. I waited, encouragingly.

"Ha—ha—*hi*, Steve," he managed.

"And hi to you," I replied. "Now, Hal . . ."

"I'm very ha—ha—*ha*ppy to b—b—*be* here tonight."

Now *I* was beginning to sweat. So far, the audience assumed he was doing an imitation of either Mel Tillis or his famous android, and I thought I'd better play with the latter possibility.

"You . . . like . . . earth women?" I asked, one robot to another.

His eyes expressed great sadness. "B—b—"

"*Beau*tiful earth women, yes," I finished for him, though I had no idea what he was trying to say. "Yes, earth women make it worthwhile being rich and famous and a movie star and all."

"I—I—I—"

"You play the violin, don't you, Hal? This man, ladies and gentlemen, is not merely the gentle giant you see before you, but a musical prodigy. Isn't that right?"

"Wh—whu—"

This gave me an idea. "Why don't we play something together? Okay? A little spur of the moment thing?"

"Na—na—*no,*" he said quite definitely.

"Well, then," I continued cheerfully, "let's talk about your new blockbuster, *Kill Or Be Killed.* In this film you play a . . ."

"Fuh—fuh—"

"A *foot*ball player, whose wife is raped by the quarterback of the team you're going to play against in the Superbowl. So the film is about . . ."

"Re—re—"

"Revenge," I enunciated as though I were a speech therapist. This was getting bad. The audience had caught on that there was something quite wrong with Hoaglund, and they were getting nervous. Actually, there are few things more uncomfortable than watching someone on stage embarrass himself. You just want to slink down in your chair and disappear. I was able to finish Hal's sentences for him and joke around, delicately, as though this were some nifty routine we had worked out, but I sensed that the show was on the verge of collapse.

I was never so happy in my life to see Melnik rise from his off-camera chair and signal the half-minute warning to station break.

"We'll be right back after a word from our sponsors," I said optimistically. The APPLAUSE light went on and the audience dutifully complied. The orchestra started playing, the stage lights faded, and we were mercifully off the air. Melnik came rushing forward to my desk, whispering.

"Listen, Steve, this is a disaster. My apologies to Mr. Hoaglund," he said quickly to Hal, then turning back to me, he added in a lower tone, "but this guy's gotta go."

"He's right, Mr. Allen. I think I'd just better leave."

I looked at Hoaglund in astonishment. *His voice was as normal as could be!* Not even a hint of a stutter.

"You can speak," I said.

"I only have a problem in front of a TV camera," he said with a sigh. "I don't know what gets into me."

The poor guy looked miserable. There was something about this sweet, bumbling giant that tugged at my heartstrings. He really did have a sort of King Kong charm. Suddenly I got an idea. I opened up Terry Cole's secret refrigerator and pulled out the bottle of Cajun vodka.

"Look, Hal—how about a good stiff shot? There's really nothing wrong with you. A lot of movie people

49

get *very* nervous when they're put in front of a TV camera. Maybe all you need is to relax.''

"Really, Mr. Allen? Gosh, you seem *so* relaxed.''

"That's because I've been doing this for years and years,'' I lied, smiling. "Now trust your Uncle Steve.''

I was pouring Cajun vodka into one of Terry Cole's coffee mugs, doing it under the table so that nobody could see. Melnik gave me a worried look, but I waved him away. "This is going to be just fine,'' I told him, then reiterated what I had told Hal: "Trust me.''

Melnik returned to his side of the cameras and Hoaglund took the coffee mug. "Golly, Mr. Allen, I don't really drink, you know. I had a sip of champagne once, and boy, did it ever go to my head!''

"Down the old hatch now! *Chin-chin!* All in one gulp, yes, that'sa boy. And call me Steve, Hal. This is Hollywood, man, where people don't even have last names.''

Hal downed the coffee mug full of Cajun vodka as he must have drunk countless health-drink concoctions, like medicine. His face turned bright red. He gave one mighty exhale, like a fire-breathing dragon, then a rumbling sound emerged from deep in his throat. "Holy God,'' he said.

I took the mug underneath the table and filled it one more time. I also poured a drop or two for myself; being a talk-show host was more stressful than I remembered.

"Here's sediment in your eye,'' I said. "Come on, take your medicine,'' I ordered when he seemed to hesitate, "like a good boy.''

Hal *was* a good boy: he did just what I said and downed that second mug of Cajun vodka as quickly as the first. His eyes were watering and he was breathing hard. Out of nerves I was about to hit the vodka myself—what the hell—but the floor manager had already begun counting down with his fingers, and before I knew it, the lights were up and we were on the air.

"Hot damn, it's great to be here, Steve!" Hal cried, raising his coffee cup in a salute to all America. "This is the best show I've ever been on!"

Yes, there was a remarkable change to Hal Hoaglund. It would be funny if now I couldn't get him to shut up.

"Hal—"

" 'Scuse me, Steve, but I just want to say how privileged I feel to be here tonight with a clip from my new film *Kill Or Be Killed*—and I want to thank my agent, Kelly McGuire, and my director, Bobby Vito, and my mother and father for encouraging me, and really the whole friggin' bunch." I rang my ever-ready no-no ding-bell.

On the far side of the cameras, I could see Melnik chewing his fingernails. Fortunately, the audience was eating it up.

"Hal, now that you're a big star, you must have lots of women wanting to go out with you . . ."

"Oh no, sir! *No*, sir! I send 'em away. Between my bodybuilding and my acting career and my violin lessons, I don't have time for no foolin' around."

"So marriage is not in your immediate future?"

"Ma . . . ma . . . ma . . ."

I was afraid he had begun stuttering again, but I realized he was probably joking about the idea of getting married. Hal had become quite the kidder. He began choking, too, and getting red in the face. The audience thought this was a riot. We were all laughing together when Hoaglund fell face forward from the couch onto the floor.

The audience cheered and whistled at this brilliant sight gag. What a stuntman. As for me, I was beginning to get a very bad feeling.

"We're going to break away for a moment to allow our local stations to identify themselves," I said to the camera.

Melnik was looking at me as if I were crazy, pointing to his watch: it wasn't yet time for a station break. I nodded at him—*oh yes, it is!*

"So stay tuned and we'll be right back."

Belatedly, the orchestra began to play. In the booth Lawrence Washington managed to get us off the air. I heard later that some stations had about ten seconds of empty screen before a commercial came on the air to aid people in their endless battles against halitosis, body odor, ring-around-the-collar, and irregularity.

I wasn't looking at the monitor. I knelt down by Hal's prostrate form and turned him over onto his back. I was feeling terrible that I'd made the man fall down dead drunk, but when I turned him over, I felt worse.

Hoaglund wasn't dead drunk. He was just dead.

chapter 11

Half an hour later, I was sitting in the tenth row of the empty theater feeling numb. The audience was gone, quickly ushered out of the building when it became obvious the show could not go on. At eleven-thirty tonight, the insomniacs of America would *not* see Steve Allen but a rerun of Terry Cole—who might not be able to play the piano, but at least people didn't drop dead in the middle of his interviews.

I couldn't believe this was really happening, though if I needed proof I only had to look up on stage to where the police were milling about. There seemed to be dozens of officials, two in white jumpsuits, measuring and photographing everything in sight. Sonny Melnik arrived back on the scene just as the coroner's team was removing the body. He was dressed in jogging attire—metallic gray with red stripes down the sides of the pants. Perhaps he thought being a TV producer was like an athletic event, the survival of the fittest. At this particular moment, Sonny seemed to be losing the race. He was out of breath, red in the face, and waving his arms about.

"Do you know how much this is costing me?" He

pointed to his watch as though we should see dollar bills escaping into the void. "I mean, I'm as devastated as anyone here—that poor bastard signing off like that—but in ten minutes my entire crew will be on overtime!"

Sonny was all heart. "We won't keep your crew longer than necessary," said one of the LAPD people. "Just a few questions and then they can go."

Sonny wheeled about to glare at the man. "And who the hell are you?"

"Detective Sergeant W.B. Walker, sir."

"Well, Detective, I should tell you I'm goddamn bosom buddies with your chief of police, so you'd better be giving me some consideration here or you'll be beating the walk back in South Central like some rookie—get my drift?"

While I had never envisioned that Sonny would be presented with an award for Dignified Behavior Under Stress, I was nevertheless surprised to see him revert to the level of a complete jerk. In fact, as little original empathy as I had had for Melnik, I was literally embarrassed by his outburst.

"Walking the beat, sir."

"What?"

"You said, 'beating the walk.' But other than that, yes, sir—I could get your drift a mile away."

Sonny seemed to stop breathing. Was he being mocked? His lips twitched. Finally, close to apoplexy, he stormed off the stage, mumbling, "We'll see about this. Oh, yes, we'll just fucking see about this!"

Detective Sergeant Walker sighed. He was short, roundish, and wore a brown suit almost as shapeless as a pair of pajamas, a wide, brightly colored necktie,

54

and an expression that suggested an exhausted pessimism about the human race. Still, there was something about Detective Walker that made you take notice. Despite his size and wrinkled appearance, he had a certain Napoleonic stature. It was clear that he was the man in charge.

When Hal Hoaglund's body had been removed on a stretcher, the detective began examining the stage. He narrowed his eyes, frowned, and to my surprise went over to my chair, sitting down behind the desk I had so recently vacated. He leaned back and appeared almost dreamy for a moment. Perhaps he was imagining the alleged glory of being a TV personality. He actually closed his eyes and I briefly imagined he might be drifting off to sleep. All in all, it was fascinating watching him. I had never seen a police investigation in progress before.

After what seemed a long time, the detective opened his eyes and noticed the two coffee mugs that were still in place on the desk. He stood up, leaned over my cup, sniffed, and recoiled sharply. He took a handkerchief from his pocket, picked up Hoaglund's empty cup, and sniffed it as well.

He walked to the edge of the stage and looked into the empty theater. "Mr. Allen? Are you with us?"

"Here," I answered, rising from my seat.

"Would you mind coming up here a moment?"

I walked up onto the stage and shook Walker's meaty hand. He seemed to be regarding me carefully from beneath heavy-lidded eyes.

"Mr. Allen, I was wondering if we could go over some details. I understand there was something unusual about Mr. Hoaglund's behavior?"

"He was extremely nervous, Sergeant. Actually, it's not so very unusual for movie people to be intimidated by the talk-show format. In movies, they have their lines all written for them. If they make a mistake, they can redo the scene forty times. Here they're on their own, sink or swim. They have to ad-lib and be themselves."

"Hmm, be yourself with millions of people looking on," mused the detective sergeant. "That's quite a proposition."

"For some people it's impossible. Others of us are just natural-born hams."

Sergeant Walker didn't seem amused. "Now, Mr. Allen, had you ever met Mr. Hoaglund before tonight?"

"Never," I replied. "I didn't even speak to him before the show began because he arrived late and was in makeup when I came out of my dressing room."

"So you had no relationship, not even indirectly?"

"What do you mean?" I asked. Actually I knew exactly what he meant: he wanted to know if I had any motive for wishing Hal Hoaglund dead.

"Maybe you had some business dealings through a third party, for instance. Maybe you knew his girl-friend. Anything like that?"

"Sergeant, I never met Hal before tonight, we had no business dealings, and I certainly never met his girl-friend—if he had one, which I doubt, since Hal was so busy with bodybuilding, his film career, and learning the violin."

The detective raised an eyebrow. "How do you know he played the violin?" he asked softly, almost in a whisper.

"I read it in the bio his PR people sent over," I said, unfortunately raising my voice. I didn't like the tone of these questions, especially after all I'd gone through.

"Ah, I see. Now, Mr. Allen, do you generally get drunk with your guests?"

I sighed. "Look, Sergeant, as I told you, Hoaglund was extremely nervous. I happened to find a bottle of vodka in the refrigerator beneath the desk and during a break I suggested that he have a few shots, though I'm not much of a drinker myself. I thought it would help him to relax."

"Please show me this refrigerator, would you?"

I leaned over the desk and was about to open the refrigerator door, but the detective stopped me abruptly, holding back my arm. "Don't touch anything, please," he said courteously. Detective Walker took his handkerchief and used it to open the door. The bottle was where I had left it.

"Mmm, now what's this stuff floating near the bottom? Very interesting," he said.

"That stuff, as you put it, is pepper. This is Cajun vodka, something of a specialty item."

He shook his head at the wonderment of something so exotic. "Cajun pepper vodka. My, my! Is this a favorite of yours, sir?"

"Of mine? Sergeant, this bottle doesn't have anything to do with me. I simply found it here—that's the extent of it. I assumed it must belong to Terry Cole."

"Was the bottle unopened?"

"Well, the seal was broken, I think—but it seemed more or less full."

"Uh-huh. So Mr. Hoaglund asked you for a drink?"

"Well, no, I suggested it," I replied. "As I keep telling you, I thought it would get him relaxed."

"I'm only trying to get this straight, Mr. Allen. I gather you poured the drink yourself?"

"Yes."

"No one helped you?"

"No."

"No one other than you handled the bottle, correct?"

"That's right."

"And you poured the vodka into coffee mugs so you could conceal what you were drinking?"

The detective made the word *conceal* sound sinister. "Yes," I admitted. "You don't want your viewers to know you're boozing it up on the air. Coffee cups have been used that way for years on TV."

"I see. Now you poured a glass—or should I say a mug—for yourself as well. Did you drink any of it, sir?"

"No. I was about to, but we'd been talking during the commercial break and I'd lost track of the time. All of a sudden I saw we were back on the air and I had to put the mug down."

"Now let me get this straight—you were the only one to touch the bottle. You poured the vodka, the deceased drank, but you did not drink yourself. Correct?"

"Absolutely," I replied impatiently. The repeated questions were getting to me, though I knew he was just doing his job. I had by now been made so ill at ease by Walker's questions that I probably would have flunked a lie-detector test.

"You, er, think there was something in the vodka?" I asked cautiously.

Detective Sergeant W.B. Walker shrugged. He was a man who had seen the worst that human beings could do to one another. "We'll know soon enough," he said philosophically. "Maybe it was a heart attack. Maybe something he ate. Maybe he was murdered; we really can't be sure yet."

"That's terrible," I said with a sigh, shaking my head. "Poor guy." I stared sadly at the spot where Hal Hoaglund had fallen to his death.

"Where are you staying, Mr. Allen? We might need to talk with you again."

I gave him my bungalow number at the Beverly Hills Hotel, which he wrote down carefully on a pad and put away inside his wrinkled brown jacket. "You can go home now, sir. Get yourself some sleep."

I nodded and began shuffling off toward my dressing room.

"Oh, Mr. Allen?" he called softly.

"Yes, Sergeant?"

"Please . . . I wouldn't leave town if I were you. Not just yet."

chapter 12

At exactly eight-thirty the following morning there was a knock at my bungalow door and the cheerful call, "Room service," in some sort of not easily distinguished foreign accent. I had placed an order, the night before, for the sort of breakfast that was common in my earlier years but now rarely enjoyed—strong coffee, scrambled eggs, bacon, not too crisp, fried potatoes, buttered rye toast with strawberry jam and marmalade on the side, orange juice to start the ritual, and a glass of ice-cold milk. It is breakfasts like this, indulged in year after year, that have already helped put millions of Americans in their graves, but as the old saying goes: all things in moderation, including moderation. I'd never have been able to get away with it had Jayne not been out of town, since she's as strict as Nurse Chambers, the character she used to play on the TV series *Medical Center,* about my daily diet, and quite properly so. After years of personal involvement with the Pritikin health-care program, she had finally talked me into it, with the result that I've taken off fifteen pounds and cut way down on my cholesterol level, blood pressure, and general loginess. Ordinarily at home I'd be having something like oat-bran flakes and fresh fruit served with skim milk, half a glass of fruit juice, some hot herb tea, and, just for a bit of extra fruit-sugar energy, a few dates. But Jayne was out of town, I was having a little trouble sleeping, there was the damn police investigation going on, and—what the hell, I permitted myself this moderate binge.

Living in a first-rate hotel has some consolations for the weary traveler.

I put on my red short-sleeved nylon robe and went to the door. On the path outside the bungalow, I found Detective Sergeant W.B. Walker standing over my breakfast cart, reading my newspaper, and apparently inhaling my bacon.

"You look hungry," I said.

"You're a mind reader," he said, seemingly a bit more friendly than the evening before.

"No problem," I said. "Jump in."

The detective smiled innocently and helped the young Filipino waiter wheel the cart inside my living room. "This brings back old memories. I worked as a waiter when I was a kid in Tennessee. Coffee?" he inquired.

"Oh, thank you!"

He ignored my sarcasm. The sergeant, I noticed, was wearing the same brown suit I'd seen him in last night, now even more wrinkled. His hair was tossed and he had actually neglected to shave. Perhaps he had driven directly from bed to have breakfast with me at my bungalow. I noticed a second coffee cup on the cart. How very thoughtful. Sergeant Walker poured each of us a cup, dropping three cubes of sugar into his own, then enough cream to make it overflow onto his saucer. He sat down on my sofa with a contented sigh and began to drink with an occasional quiet slurping noise. I was rather fascinated by his movements. I wondered where this man had come from to torment my life—but I supposed, philosophically, that people like this were likely to appear when guests dropped dead of mysterious causes on one's TV show.

The sergeant was studying me between slurps. "Rat poison," he said.

"You don't like the coffee?"

"It was rat poison that killed Hal Hoaglund. It was concealed in the Cajun vodka. We don't know the brand yet, but the lab should have the information in a couple of days."

I suddenly felt strangely guilty again. "So it was . . ." I couldn't quite finish the sentence.

"Murder," he agreed. "Yes, indeed."

"I don't believe this." I sighed as I stood up to pace the room. "*I* almost drank that vodka, too." It was astonishing how close I had been to not being here this morning in my nice bungalow at the Beverly Hills Hotel watching Detective Sergeant W.B. Walker eat part of my breakfast. My next thought was that I had done this: *I* had killed Hal Hoaglund by giving him the Cajun vodka. I sank down on the corner of my piano bench feeling my legs would no longer hold me.

"Well, I suppose you're going to arrest me now. Aren't you supposed to read me my rights or something?"

"Whatever for?"

"I was the only one to handle the vodka. I gave poor Hal the fatal drink."

"There's no law against offering someone a drink,

Mr. Allen. As long as you didn't know there was rat poison in it.''

"No-o," I said hoarsely, shaking my head. "I didn't know. You do believe me?"

The sergeant was pouring the runover coffee from his saucer back into his cup. He graced me with a small smile. "It's not up to me to believe you or disbelieve you, Mr. Allen. I'm only trying to establish the facts."

I was feeling fairly shattered. "The bottle was just there in the refrigerator, looking cold and tempting. I've no idea where it came from."

"Well, this might interest you—I've learned that Terry Cole drank Cajun vodka. He used to be a martini man, but that had lost its kick for him recently. Cajun vodka was his latest find. He liked to sip it on his show."

"So maybe . . .''

"So maybe someone was trying to kill Terry Cole. Yes, that's a possibility. A person could have left the bottle for him last week, a deadly little gift, but then Mr. Cole went on an unexpected vacation and you took over the show and ended up giving it to Hal Hoaglund."

"But who would want to kill Terry?" I wondered. This was all inconceivable to me. I was, after all, a mild-mannered type. "You're certain about the rat poison?" I asked, hopelessly wishing there were a mistake here, and an innocent reason for Hal Hoaglund's death.

"I assure you, there was enough poison in that vodka to kill a dozen people. It was quite clever—the pepper disguised the taste. Now we need to know who was the intended victim. And from that, perhaps, we may learn who did the deed. By the way, your eggs are getting cold. I imagine you've lost your appetite."

The sergeant had already finished my bacon and toast. It was sensitive of him to ask about the eggs.

"Why don't you have them," I suggested. "No sense in eating just half a breakfast."

"Thanks." He took the plate, covered the eggs with catsup, and attacked the food as if he had not eaten in a week.

"Mmm, better than the bacon," he told me. He wiped his mouth, with an odd daintiness, with the back of his hand. "Tell me about Terry Cole."

"Terry? Well, he's a bit of a maniac, I suppose. Driven to succeed. As you probably know, he got his start on a small station in Iowa back in the beginning days of television. He still manages a boy-next-door quality, but people who work with him think he's a son of a bitch."

"Then he has enemies?"

"I'm afraid so. The guy's a real autocrat. He once fired his writers just for trying to speak to him when he was trying to think up a joke himself."

"Can you give me names of anyone who might have wished Terry Cole dead?"

I shook my head. "I can't imagine."

"What about his ex-wife?"

"Kathleen? She certainly got enough money from Terry—twenty-five thousand a month in alimony, as well as their beach house, which is supposedly worth six million. I can't understand what she would feel bitter about. Terry certainly took care of her financially."

"And the producer, Sonny Melnik? What about him?"

I shook my head. "Sonny and Terry go way back. They're almost like brothers. Sonny's been producing the show for more than twenty years. He must be nearly as rich as Terry by now."

Sergeant Walker stood up, put his empty plate down on the room service cart, and wiped his hands on his suit. "Well, I guess we'll be looking into all this for some time, Mr. Allen. Thanks for breakfast. I'll be in touch."

I was too depressed to rise and walk him to the door. I sat on the edge of the piano bench studying the carpet.

The sergeant turned to me before he left. "One more thing, Mr. Allen."

"Yes?" I actually laughed, thinking of Columbo, but did not explain.

"There's a possibility Terry Cole was not the intended victim. You see what I mean?"

"Not really."

"Well, for all we know, the intended victim could have been Hal Hoaglund," he said brightly, "or, more likely, *you*, sir."

"Me? Someone wanted to kill *me*?"

"Interesting thought, eh?"

He gave a small salute, as though this were all quite humorous, and then he was gone, leaving me with much to ponder.

chapter 13

The *intended victim* was a phrase that somehow masked the true horror of the act of murder. I sat for some time after Detective Sergeant Walker left, staring at the pillaged remnants of my breakfast, trying to absorb this inconceivable new twist my life had taken.

Any way I looked at it, I could come to only one conclusion: *I* had killed that poor kid. I kept seeing him with the damned deadly coffee cup in his hand. In my imagination, the trusting look on his face took on a mournful, accusing quality.

Down the hatch, Hal . . . Trust me, kid.

Well, I certainly had taken care of Hal Hoaglund's nerves, and the responsibility weighed heavily. The sergeant had suggested that I might have been the intended victim, and I spent one guilty moment almost wishing it had been me. There had been a vulnerable quality to Hal, a shy, bumbling android who lifted weights and wanted to play the violin. How could I live with the fact that I had caused his death, however unintentionally?

My thoughts were tumbling round and round. Was it possible someone had wanted me dead, as the sergeant had suggested? I couldn't believe it. I've always had a long and happy honeymoon with the human race. There were some people who didn't laugh at my jokes, perhaps a few who envied my easy good luck, but I honestly couldn't think of a single enemy. Oh, hell, I'd shot my mouth off over the years about the Mafia, the Ku Klux Klan, the Nazis, Joe Stalin, the Ayatollah, and any number of other professional bullies, but such people are despised by millions so it was unlikely that any of them would have singled me out from the sea of critics that quite properly surrounded them. No, I couldn't think of anyone who might put rat poison in a bottle of vodka for any reason whatsoever. Perhaps I was naive, but the act of murder was beyond the deep end of my usually active imagination.

The morning newspapers had arrived with breakfast. I put them off as long as I could but eventually got the nerve to see what they said. The headlines were worse than I had feared. "THE HUNK DIES ON TALK SHOW" screamed from the *Herald-Examiner*. Even the dignified *L.A. Times* featured prominently in the lower right hand side of the front page: "FILM STAR COLLAPSES ON *TERRY COLE SHOW.*"

The old ego felt irrationally uncomfortable with that. Couldn't they have mentioned *The Steve Allen Show?* Then I felt a wave of guilt at even considering such a thing at a time like this.

I found only one cause for optimism in the morning papers. The police had not yet given out the information concerning the rat poison. At this point, the papers were speculating that Hal died from cardiac arrest or other natural causes. I had a grim feeling that when the word *murder* crept into the accounts, I was going to get more media attention than I wished.

The phone rang as if on cue. It was a reporter from *The New York Post* who had managed to track me down at the Beverly Hills Hotel. He didn't know about the poison but wanted to know all the juicy details of Hal's death. I was polite but evasive. This was followed by a call from *Hollywood Reporter*'s Radie Harris asking the same thing. After I managed to put her off, I called the front desk and told them not to put any more calls through to my bungalow till further notice. Then I called Jimmy Cassidy and asked him to come rescue me. He and his limousine were not far away, at the Beverly Wilshire. Cass was about to take an Arab sheik on a shopping tour of Beverly Hills, but he sent a message to the sheik's penthouse suite that he would just have to buy up Beverly Hills without him. Cass is a real friend. I suppose he could hear the desperation in my voice.

Hotel residents trying to avoid the press can leave the bungalows by a small side gate rather than going through the hotel lobby. I put on my largest hat and sunglasses for the occasion and probably looked as furtive as the lovers next door. When Cass pulled up to the side exit, I darted from the bushes and got in beside him.

"You look like a fox coming out of the henhouse," he said.

I sighed and slunk down in the seat as we pulled past the hotel onto Sunset Boulevard. "I feel more like a dead chicken than a fox."

I told Cass about the rat poison and my morning visit from Detective Sergeant W.B. Walker. Cass is a great listener. He absorbs what you say and then just looks back at you with his watery blue eyes, which is generally comment enough. From his look today, I knew I was up the creek without a fishing license.

"Well, boss, where are we going?" he asked finally. We had been driving slowly around Beverly Hills in a loose circle.

"Let's go to the beach," I suggested. "Somehow or other I've got to get myself together to do a TV show tonight."

"They're going to let you try it again, huh?" Cass seemed surprised.

"Of course," I told him irritably. "It's not my fault someone left a bottle of rat poison in Terry Cole's refrigerator."

"No, not your fault, not one bit," he agreed.

I was in a sour mood. Here was this lovely opportunity to have a lot of laughs on a big TV show and a guest has the bad manners to drop dead, poisoned, on my first night. How tacky!

"I've sure never seen you act so depressed-like, man," Cass told me as we were driving down the last curves of Sunset toward the sparkling blue ocean.

"I've never killed anyone before," I said sarcastically. "It takes a little getting used to."

When we hit the beach highway, I told Cass to drive north. It was a lovely day, a clear blue sky with just a few whitecaps on the sparkling ocean. The ocean generally clears my head and helps me put things in proper perspective. I had Cass drive me here thinking I might sit on the beach and work on tonight's monologue—but now that I was here, a comedy routine seemed the least important thing I could imagine.

Somewhere north of Malibu, I came to a decision. I am not a passive individual; I don't take life's adversities without a struggle.

An almost fiendish smile came to my lips. Damn it, I was going to solve this crime myself! For the first time all day, I felt strong, captain of my own limousine, so to speak. No one was going to poison a guest on *my* show and get away with it.

"Let's drive to Trancas, Cass," I told him softly. "I think it's time to see a rich divorcée."

chapter 14

Trancas Beach is a fifteen-minute drive past the Malibu Colony, about as far north as the Hollywood crowd likes to go. I've always considered it the jewel of the L.A. beaches, sitting as it does on a wide, serene bay with great stretches of perfectly white sand that seems specially sculpted for the very rich. The waves break way out and seem to roll in forever. The southernmost part of this bay is called Zuma and is open to the public. Trancas, on the north, is about as private and exclusive as you can get.

Cass pulled off the Pacific Coast Highway onto Broad Beach Road and drove along the back of a row of beach houses whose architecture was everything from tasteful Cape Cod to less tasteful Glass 'n Glitz. I was looking for Kathleen Cole's sunny mansion on the sand. I hadn't been in the area for years, not since Terry and Kathleen had lived here together, throwing folksy little barbecues on Sundays for a very in-crowd of status worshipers that the Coles liked to collect around them. Personally, I find it exhausting to act famous on my days off.

I had to ask Cass to slow down since I wasn't sure I'd recognize the house again after so much time. As a matter of fact, I wasn't even certain Kathleen would be home or inclined to see me. I didn't have her unlisted phone number and coming here was really only a sudden impulse.

"Is that it? Stop a moment," I said. We had arrived at a cubist monstrosity—very modern—all glass, with strange boxlike shapes sitting on top of each other. It looked familiar but I wasn't sure.

After scratching my chin for a moment, I decided I'd simply go in and ask.

Actually, this cubist mansion turned out not to be Kathleen Cole's—the fair plunder of her divorce—but the home of a very nice old woman with white hair who recognized me on her security video monitor and invited me in for tea. She was a very nice rich old lady, as a matter of fact, telling me that television had been in a sad decline since I had stopped doing my regular show. When I mentioned I was trying to find the Cole residence, she was able to direct me three houses down.

Kathleen Cole's house was also the last word in modern: strange shapes, cubes and jutting rectangles, and walls of tinted glass. I found it a cold sort of place, more like a museum than a house. There was a court-yard in front with a piece of abstract sculpture in the center that reminded me of a five-car pileup on the Hollywood Freeway. I stood in front of a vast white door—beneath the lens of another closed-circuit TV camera—smiled cheerfully, and rang the bell. From deep inside the house there came the sound of a low, melodious chime. After a moment, I rang again.

At last there was a voice coming from a small speaker by my hand. "God Almighty! It's Steve Allen! *What* a surprise!"

There was a soft buzz and the door clicked open. I stepped onto a cement rectangle from which a series of landings and stairways went off in all directions, up and down, like the geometric illusions of an Escher drawing. From where I stood, the entire house looked like one great room without sides, with many hanging plants and the tinted glass walls open to sky, sun, and sea. It was a striking sort of place. I could imagine a spaceman living here, or some timeless Aztec queen.

All this, but not a human being in sight.

"Kathleen?" I called hesitantly. "Hello?"

"I'm out on the deck, Steve," she called back. Her voice seemed far away.

Deck, schmeck, I thought. "Is that upstairs or down?"

I heard a silvery laugh. "Up," she summoned. "Up and along the ramp, walk in the direction of the beautiful sea . . . and"—to the melody of *"Over The Rainbow,"*—"there you'll find me."

Had Theseus ever followed so golden a thread? I followed her directions, walking along a skyway that

72

passed above the living room and led me out onto a sun deck that looked down upon the ocean below.

Kathleen Cole lay reclined upon a deck chair. She was nude except for a whisper of bikini pants, languidly lying there with only a casually folded arm to cover her breasts. I wasn't sure where to look, but since I pride myself on being a world-weary sophisticate, I did my best to appear blasé.

"Steve, darling, how splendid to see you!"

"I seem to be in a better position to do the seeing." Whoever first said, "You-see-one-you've-seen-them-all," was a very unreliable philosopher.

There came the silvery laugh again. "Oh, naughty boy!"

Kathleen Cole was a stunning woman, with or without clothing. She had to be past forty, but you would never guess it from the vibrancy of her long, auburn hair—or the honey-colored, lithe body displayed before me. Older women are looking better longer these days. Kathleen had a golden tan that covered her evenly from head to foot, almost like a suit of clothes, though I had a feeling if I looked too closely I might see the nip and tuck of the surgeon's tools.

"It's been years, Steve, hasn't it?"

"Well, I've been busy, Kathleen."

"Ah, yes, playing the piano, writing songs and books, always on the radio and TV. Do you ever sleep? And how long have you been married to Jayne?" she cooed.

"Thirty-four years now."

She rolled onto her side and looked up at me with large hazel eyes. "However do you manage to stay married? I was always so bad at it myself. There's always so much temptation in our business, don't you find, to sample other goodies?"

Playfully she wetted the top of her finger with her tongue just in case I didn't know what temptation was.

"Jayne and I have been very lucky," I said. "Ever since we first fell in love, I've—"

"Love?" she answered dreamily, as if trying on the word for size. "Me, I'm always so restless. Sometimes I lie here in the sun and feel the breeze caress me, and I wonder . . ."

She gave me a meaningful, long-lidded look. I swallowed hard.

"Kathleen, I dropped by today because something ghastly happened on Terry's show last night."

"Ah, yes, that poor Hal Hoaglund dropped dead. How very sad."

"It was more than sad. The L.A. police say it's murder. Someone put rat poison in Terry's Cajun vodka—"

"That he kept underneath his desk," she finished. So she knew about that. "*Rat* poison!" she cried, eyes blazing. "How perfect that would have been for the son of a bitch. But why would someone poison poor Hal?"

I shrugged, miserable. "Hal drank the vodka by mistake," I told her evasively.

"Rat poison," she said again, seemingly fascinated by the idea. She hugged her knees girlishly, further obscuring her breasts.

"Kathleen, I feel terrible about this. I'm trying to find out how it happened. That's why I've come here."

For a moment it seemed she had forgotten I was there. She even forgot to pose seductively. I had to repeat my last request. "Can you tell me why anyone would try to poison your ex-husband?"

Her eyes focused on me from somewhere far away. "Poison?" she asked. I was beginning to fear Kathleen had become unglued. "Why, Terry's the ultimate rat, of course. Rat poison would only be logical, don't you agree? But such a pity that lovely young stud drank it instead."

"You already said that."

I could see this wasn't going to be easy. "Tell me more about Terry. I always thought he had, well, a kind of charm," I lied. "Sort of a sly and elfish sense of humor."

Actually it had been years, many of them, since I had trusted charm as we all do in our youth and sometimes, foolishly, to the grave. If only good people were charming, what a wonderful world it would be. But a high percentage of the real schmucks and crooked bastards I've met, or learned about, have had it. Hitler, for example. That monster not only appealed to the German people's passions and fears, he also charmed them. Most of the Mafia guys I've met, in Vegas or—sometimes—in the living rooms of Beverly Hills mansions, have had a certain kind of charm. Almost all of the most hideously ruthless executives in the entertainment industry have tremendous charm. A few of them don't have a hell of a lot else. Not a few politicians are long on charm and short on intelligence and principle. Gypsies always charm their victims before they rob them. So do all the con men in the world, not to mention the leaders of the cuckoo cults that have hoodwinked so many pitiously gullible young people in recent decades. Hell, the point of the play and movie

Amadeus was that Mozart, though a genius, was the biggest jerk in town, for all his combined charm and glamour. So, yes, Terry Cole did have a certain kind of charm. He'd also had a modest gift of wit. He'd never have made the grade if he'd had to compete in big-league comedy competition, but he had lucked out in working as a talk-show host, without question the easiest gig for a comedian in the history of the business.

Kathleen interrupted my train of thought. "Oh, yes, charm," she said. "That's the part he plays in public. Terry should get an Academy Award for absolute fraud, my love."

"And in private?"

"In private, he's a vicious little worm. A spiteful son of a bitch mother fucker scum-sucking rat, darling."

Despite my four decades in the business, and long personal acquaintance with its denizens, I'm always shocked when women, particularly attractive women, use gutter language.

"So he's not too popular, then, with his inner circle," I said.

"Popular!" she shrieked. "They've published a list of his enemies. It's called the Los Angeles phone book!"

It would have been too cruel to ask why she had married him in the first place. And anyway, I knew the answer. Cole had his personable side—the side he showed in public. He was famous and a multimillionaire. Obviously she had learned only gradually of the ugly nature of the man. At first she would have been exposed only to his charm and the glamour of his position.

"But of course the person who placed the poison in

the bottle had to know about Terry's secret refrigerator underneath his desk. That would narrow down the field of suspects.''

Kathleen did not seem impressed by my reasoning. ''The booze in the coffee cup routine was an open secret to everyone on the show. Terry's been hitting the sauce pretty heavy in recent years. Even some of his guests were hip to it.''

''What about the Cajun pepper vodka? How long has he been into that?''

''I haven't the faintest, darling. Last I knew, he was a committed believer in the old Stolichnaya. I suppose his taste buds have been getting more jaded. You know, younger women, stronger vodka, that sort of thing.''

''Let's go back to people who might wish him dead.''

''The Screen Actors' Guild, all the agents in town . . .''

I chuckled, if only because she expected it. ''But if you had to make a list, Kathleen, who would you put at the top?''

She thought about this for a moment.

''Sonny Melnik,'' she said at last. ''If ever there was a man who might lust for murder, that's him.''

I was surprised. ''Sonny? I thought he was Terry's oldest friend.''

''Compared to what?'' she said with a sneer. ''Oh, sure, they go way back to the time when Terry was doing a crummy little radio show in Cedar Rapids, Iowa. Sonny was running a small-time agency, probably out of his hat, in Chicago in those days, booking dumb little acts around the Midwest. Somehow Sonny heard about this brash, sarcastic young wiseass beginning to make a name for himself in Cedar Rapids, and then in Des Moines, I think it was. Terry, of course, sent him some tapes and that's how it started."

The rest of the story I was generally familiar with. It had been Melnik who had brought Terry to Chicago and gotten him a local morning jokes-and-traffic reports radio show. After that the transition to television had been so easy as to be inevitable. In those days, you see, there was so much demand for people in the new medium that literally hundreds of us were drawn into the vacuum. Some of us were talented, some not, but in those days it didn't seem to make any difference. Any no-talent with a glib line of patter, three suits, and a reasonably attractive face could become a game-show host, a TV weatherman, a newscaster, or what have you. Ratings weren't particularly important in those days, and compared to today's hectic pressure, TV work was pretty easy duty.

Although Terry enjoyed some modest early local and regional success, he was nationally a total unknown until he started his talk show. In less than a month, he became a capital-C celebrity.

Overnight fame, with all its blessings, is always a shock. On Monday you are just yourself, unknown to the world at large. You are an anonymous figure in crowds or public places. Paying bills is a struggle. You know that there are beings on your planet such as Marilyn Monroe, Elvis Presley, Marlon Brando, Barbra Streisand, The Beatles, presidents, prime ministers, Popes, great artists, authors, scholars, or athletes, but they seem a breed apart from humanity in general. Tuesday morning you wake up to learn that you are now, quite officially, one of that rare breed. The suddenness, the sharpness of change in your life—of many changes, in fact—is breathtaking. Your former financial difficulties have vanished in the instant, and you have no way of knowing that money problems of another sort loom in the distance. Thousands of people who on Monday would not have given you the time of day, on Tuesday want to give you all sorts of things, including a great many that you do not want to be given. People invite you to dinner in their homes. They introduce you to their daughters or sons. You are suddenly sexually attractive to women, or men, who before your celebrity would have considered your own advances impertinent if not revolting. Strangers keep running up to you with pieces of paper on which you're expected to sign your name. You can no longer enter a restaurant or other public building in the normal way but are now expected to stand for a few moments— even in rain, snow, or sleet—while bystanders photograph you. As they often put it, "My wife wouldn't let me in the house tonight," or "My mother would never forgive me if some physical evidence of having made contact with you was not brought home." You are suddenly considered a subject for interviews. A week earlier, had you tried to tell any of the disc jockeys, radio announcers, journalists, or TV newspeople what you customarily eat for breakfast, how you and your wife settle arguments, how—physically—you went about writing your songs, or jokes, you would have been insulted, then reported to security personnel. Now the very same, and often dull, answers you would have given earlier are considered utterly fascinating. You are exactly the same person. You are not a whit more handsome or beautiful, wiser, more virtuous, more talented, or superior in any way. Except, that is, the one way that in the modern mind counts for more than anything else. You are now famous. You ought not to be deluded, incidentally, that it is your talent—if any—that is suddenly of such interest, although it may be to a few sensitive individuals, mostly those in the theatrical profession. What is profoundly fascinating is your fame. It is a truly magical factor, which makes everything about you glow with a new light.

So Terry Cole went through all of this and began the transformation from adorable fellow to schmuck. His meanness, his pettiness, his tendency to plagiarism, his dog-in-the-manger attitude toward the long list of established performers he would not permit to be booked as guests on his talk show, all of this certainly complicated the life of Sonny Melnik. The poor man put up with Terry Cole's tantrums and insults and catered to his whims for three decades because without Cole he would lose his own dearly won fame and riches, an unthinkable alternative.

But I still had trouble trying to imagine Sonny Melnik as a poisoner. I couldn't stand the man—who could?—and pinning the murder on him had a certain appeal. But there was a major obstacle: Sonny knew Terry's schedule better than anyone. If he was trying to kill Terry, he would not have left poisoned vodka in the refrigerator at a time when Cole was off for two weeks. As I thought about this, it occurred to me that the person who tried to kill Terry had to be a semi-intimate: close enough to know about the refrigerator, but not aware of the details of his daily schedule.

"How about someone outside the show?" I asked. "Are there any old girlfriends, business associates he screwed over?"

Kathleen graced me with her predatory smile. "Well, there's Tessa Moore," she said.

"You've got to be kidding."

"Believe it or not, they had an affair—of sorts—six months ago. Tessa thought she might get a regular spot on the show, maybe replace Terry on one of his nights off. Terry, of course, wasn't even attracted to her—who would be, poor dear?—but he went to bed with her, maybe to make a fool of her. *Then* he told her no way. Terry's like that, you see. He really seems to go out of his way to make people hate him."

"I'll add Tessa's name to the list," I told her. "Who else can you tell me about?"

Suddenly, Kathleen blushed slightly and looked decidedly uncomfortable.

"Well," she said, purposely fluttering her eyelashes in a comic way, "since you seem to have cast yourself in the part of Nick Charles, I suppose you suspect little ol' me, too."

I replied in that marvelous clipped, whiny, gentlemanly diction of William Powell's, "Well, Nora, I must say I never would've suspected you, my dear. Actually I'd had my eye on Asta, our faithful dog, since I'd learned that he considered Terry Cole little more than a piece of meat."

Kathleen laughed.

"Hey, listen," she said, "if all you have to do to get on the list of suspects here is despise Terry, not only should my name be included, it should be at the very top. My secret ambition is to make passionate love on the bastard's grave."

"Is that an invitation?" I asked, just playing the game, of course. Then—playfully—as William Powell,

I inquired, *"Did* you put the poison in the bottle, my dear?"

She grinned wickedly but shook her head. "I wish I'd thought of it, but I didn't. Why don't you sit closer, dear? You're so horribly far away, with the sun in my eyes and all."

I tried to keep the conversation on the business at hand. "Where *is* Terry, by the way? Sonny told me Rio de Janeiro, but I've been hearing stories of him being sick and crazy and messed up on drugs."

"Terry's all those things and more," she said. "He's gone to a clinic in Santa Barbara, a lovely little place called The Happy Valley Tranquility Center. They've put him back together before—when dear Terry starts getting too outrageous and the network starts to fear he's no longer America's cutest and oldest little boy."

"Amazing," I told her. I was thinking of the sharp differences between the public and the private Terry Cole.

"Do you know what would be even more amazing?" Kathleen whispered. "If you took a swim in the pool with me. You know I've always found men with glasses so terribly sexy."

I found myself suddenly looking at my watch. "Whoops, look at the time! I'd love to stay, dear, but I have the show tonight and—"

She took my hand. "Don't go, Steve. To hell with television—we'll drink champagne and swim together and come back up here and . . ."

"Gosh, that sounds marvelous, Kathleen. If only I could."

I was on my feet and beating a nervous retreat.

"We'll have dinner sometime when Jayne's back in town. Maybe catch a movie."

I fled back along the skyway above the living room floor, to the landing, and out the front door—where I quite literally ran into the arms of Detective Sergeant W.B. Walker.

chapter 15

A soft *whoomp* was the sound we made.

I was fleeing from the house, not looking where I was going. We met chest to chest, danced around in each others' arms off balance, until we managed to separate. The detective sergeant gaped at me in furious surprise.

"What the hell are *you* doing here, if I may ask?"

"Bumping into you at the moment."

I pulled away and tried to give him my innocent, first-day-of-school look. He was having none of it.

"Mr. Allen, you didn't tell me you and Mrs. Cole were friends."

"We're not," I said, blushing. "We just . . . uh . . . know each other."

He gave me a disgusted look. "I think we'll have to do some more talking, Mr. Allen. If you'll be kind enough to wait, I have just a few questions I want to ask Mrs. Cole first.''

He was reaching for the doorbell, but I held his arm. "Sergeant," I said, "I have to tell you something."

"Yes?"

"It's about Mrs. Cole," I admitted.

"Please continue." The sergeant's face had taken on a quality of bland expectancy. He seemed ready for a confession.

"Well, if you go in right now you'll probably see that Mrs. Cole isn't dressed to receive you."

"You mean she's naked?" he translated.

"Substantially, but it's all quite innocent," I assured him. "Mrs. Cole likes to sunbathe, you see. I wouldn't want you to get the wrong idea. After all, I'm a happily married man."

He didn't seem convinced.

"I get to meet lots of happily married men," he told me, "in my profession."

"Sergeant, you must believe me. I know this looks awkward. But I've only met Kathleen Cole three or four times in my life. I was simply in the neighborhood, so I thought I might drop by and . . . uh . . .''

"And *what?*"

"Ask her a few questions."

The cherubic face of Detective Sergeant W.B. Walker had a look of weary pessimism. He seemed to take it amiss that I might be cavorting with the probably intended victim's unclad ex-wife.

"I think we should have our talk right now," he decided, pointing me out of the courtyard toward Broad Beach Road. His unmarked car was parked behind Cass's limousine. Cass, I could see, was stretched out in the backseat watching television. The detective sergeant and I got into the front seat of his police car, which was not nearly so comfortable.

"Well, Mr. Allen? What are you up to?"

"I thought I should come by and . . . uh . . . speak with her about the murder last night."

"Why?"

"After you left this morning, I tried to settle down to work and found I couldn't. I mean I did kill Hal Hoaglund. I didn't know there was poison in the vodka, but I gave it to him. The whole thing keeps replaying itself in my mind. I realized I'm never going to get a decent night's sleep again if I don't do something."

"And do what, exactly?"

"Help the investigation. Maybe find the rat who put the poison in that vodka and made a killer out of me."

Sergeant Walker sighed. "Sir, the police department doesn't need help from amateur detectives. You should go home and let us take care of this."

We were looking at each other pretty hard. "Sergeant, I'm sure you're tremendous at your job. But in this case, I have one advantage over you."

"What's that?"

"I'm an insider. I know these people. I work with them. They'll talk to me more freely than they'll talk to a cop."

He gazed out his window at the brown hills above Trancas. His bushy eyebrows were knit in thought.

"So what did she tell you? You said you came here playing detective, so tell me what you got out of her."

"All right. I learned who's at the top of the Terry Cole Hate Club, a rather large group, by the way."

"Okay, who?"

"Sonny Melnik," I told him smugly.

"His producer? I thought they went back all the way to Kansas."

"Iowa. Apparently it's an unhealthy relationship. Sonny's been Terry's toady for thirty-odd years now, taking more abuse than most men could put up with. Obviously the resentment has been building over the years."

"From what I hear, Mrs. Cole herself is not overly fond of her ex-husband."

"That's right, but she says she didn't try to poison him."

"She'd say that, of course, but maybe she had a partner, the help of a boyfriend, for instance," the sergeant conjectured, eyeing me again in a speculative way. "What else did you and the naked lady talk about?"

I recounted what Kathleen had said of Terry's short affair with Tessa Moore, and how—from her point of view—there were dozens of ex-friends and staff who might wish him dead as well. For reasons I didn't fully understand, I left out a few parts of our conversation: Kathleen's low-key flirtatiousness and the present whereabouts of Terry Cole. The former was slightly embarrassing, and the latter—well, let's say that I enjoyed having a slight edge on Detective Sergeant Walker. After all, he was offering me no information. He nodded gruffly at everything I said and finally stepped out of the car.

"Okay. If you insist on playing Philip Marlowe, when you start asking questions among the crew on the show tonight, you might inquire whose daily job it was to put the vodka in the refrigerator," he tossed out casually as we were walking toward my limo. "I tried to find out last night but couldn't quite nail it down."

I grinned triumphantly. I was getting the official go-ahead to join the investigation. Walker's decision gave me an absurd amount of pleasure. I had a momentary vision of myself in fedora and trench coat.

"One thing. Anything you learn, you come directly to me, understand? I don't want any hot dog going off on his own and screwing up my case."

"Do I look like a hot dog?" I asked.

He made a grumpy sound and was about to leave but turned back with one final thought.

"Remember, Mr. Allen, there's an actual killer out there. He—or she—may have had you in mind. You may think of playing detective as an amusing parlor game, but I can assure you—death lasts a long, long time."

chapter 16

"And he-e-e-re's Steverino!"

Once again I came out fake-dancing to the strains of "This Could Be The Start Of Something Big" with three television cameras tracking my movements, the wash of bright lights in my face, and the live audience cheering. It was hard to adjust to the fact that with everything else going on, I had a show to do as well.

Unlike yesterday, I was totally unprepared. I even arrived twenty minutes late and had to rush through makeup, which isn't like me at all. Still, being prepared hadn't helped too much yesterday and ad-libbing answers to audience questions had always worked.

Somehow I got through the routine. Everyone was laughing so it must have been okay. If you want to know the truth, I can't even remember what I said. I simply opened my mouth and started joking around and it all seemed to work.

Guests tonight were a football star who had just finished his first movie, a teenage actress who was a pivotal member of that odd group known as ''The Brat Pack,'' a singer, and a comedian who had contracted AIDS. It was a fascinating group, as always, and the show went fairly well. I asked the right questions and pointedly didn't offer anyone a drink. In fact, I did my best not to even look downward in the direction of Terry's hidden bar. As for the rest, I was on automatic pilot. My thoughts were concentrated on the crew as much as the guests.

As a matter of fact, the crew of *The Terry Cole Show* was unlike any I had ever encountered. Generally, the stagehands, propmen, electricians, the audio and camera men—all those names you see in the final credits that roll by so quickly—are relaxed, gregarious, hardworking souls ready to share a laugh with one and all. Usually, I have fun with the behind-the-scenes workers. I actually respect what they do. But the crew of *The Terry Cole Show* seemed nervous, unwilling to look

88

me in the eye. There were no backstage jokes before the show, no laughter, no friendly grins. I thought at first they were angry at me for committing the *faux pas* of poisoning a guest on my first night out. Eventually, I began to think that Terry had simply trained them to be terrified.

I tried to make friends with the curly-haired kid who pinned the microphone to my lapel during the break after my monologue.

"Hi," I said. "Been working here long?"

"No, sir." His eyes shifted away. His hands seemed to tremble slightly as he adjusted the mike.

"Call me Steve," I said jokingly. "Hell, we'll be working together for two weeks. That's a long time in this business."

"Yes, sir." The kid didn't smile. He looked as if he wanted to get out of the conversation.

A pleasant-looking young black man hurried over to my desk.

"Is everything all right, Mr. Allen?" He also had a subdued look, as if I might start sending people out to join the unemployment lines at any moment. I held out my hand. "Hi. Who are you?"

He hesitated to take my hand but finally returned a timid shake.

"My name's Steve Linder, Mr. Allen. I'm assistant director."

"Great! Can't be enough Steves in the world, I always say. Now, Steve—"

But before I could ask him what I wanted, Lawrence A. Washington was giving us a fifteen-second warning, and the young man hurried off.

This was the damnedest thing! In all my years in the

business, I had never seen a depressed crew. Sometimes they're almost arrogant—they seem to know that stars will come and go, but they'll remain, the support team for all our glory. I thought about this with half a mind throughout the next segment of the show—with the other half, I was interviewing the teenage queen of The Brat Pack, who seemed to have only half a mind as well, so our conversation worked out all right. At the start of the next commercial, I rose from my seat and went over to the wings where young Steve Linder was standing. He seemed startled to see me.

"Man, everyone's awfully jumpy around here," I told him.

"Mr. Cole keeps us on our toes, sir."

"Yes, I've heard that."

"We have strict orders never to bother him by trying to speak to him."

"My God."

"Oh, yes, sir. A trumpet player was fired just for joking with him outside his dressing room."

I shook my head. "Well, man, that's not my style. As far as I'm concerned, the more people who joke with me the better. As a matter of fact, I could use a few friends on this set, especially after what happened last night."

Linder laughed. "I wish you were here all the time . . . Steve," he managed, though it seemed to pain him to say my first name.

"It might be fun at that," I replied with a grin.

We were getting someplace. I went back to my desk, got hooked up to the microphone—they didn't use the more common desk mike—and dealt with the comedian who had AIDS. That exchange, of course, had to be handled straight. The poor guy himself obviously wasn't in the mood for laughs, though he smiled gamely a few times. Personally I'd never even known the guy was gay. Come to think of it, I still don't. Two commercial breaks later I casually made my way over to Steve Linder once again. He flashed me a V and said I was doing a great job.

"Steve," I said, "I was wondering if you could help me find out a few things." The young man instantly looked wary but I went on. "As you can imagine, I feel terrible about what happened yesterday. I'm trying to figure out *how* it happened."

He nodded gravely.

"You must be aware of Terry's drinking habits, and the refrigerator under the desk?"

"Oh, yeah. Pretty much everyone here knows about that, though it's supposed to be a secret."

"Does Terry bring his own booze? Or does someone do it for him?"

Linder laughed at the thought of Cole's doing anything for himself. "The vodka's Mr. Melnik's job."

"Sonny? Seems kind of demeaning to ask the producer of a show to take care of housekeeping."

"Well, that's Terry Cole for you. He's a genius at finding ways to insult people. I used to hear Mr. Melnik grumbling about it when he'd come to stock the refrigerator."

"This is always done *before* Terry comes out onto the set, right?"

"Oh, yes. Mr. Cole gets into a tantrum if things aren't done just the way he wants. Actually"—he looked around to make certain we were alone. "Actually, Mr. Melnik was rebelling a bit. Can't say I blame the guy. He was having *his* assistant, a guy named Bobby Dyer, take care of the vodka recently. Mr. Cole doesn't know about this."

"You're saying someone else put the vodka in the refrigerator yesterday?"

"I don't know about yesterday. Probably that particular bottle was left over from the show Friday night."

"But it wasn't Sonny who put it there?"

"No. Bobby's been taking care of the booze the last few months. No one was supposed to know."

"Why was it so important that only Sonny Melnik handle the vodka?"

"I guess Mr. Cole wanted as few people as possible to know about his drinking, which is a joke. We all know. And then of course, a little chore like that—it was probably a way to keep Sonny in line."

"But Sonny rebelled," I mused. "Can you point out this Bobby Dyer for me? I'd like a word with him."

"Oh, he's not here tonight. He called in sick."

"How about last night?"

"He wasn't here then either. The last time I saw him was Friday."

It didn't take any great detective work to find this a mite suspicious: the man who apparently put the poisoned vodka in the fridge being absent these last two nights? I put my arm around Linder's shoulder.

"Can you get me Bobby Dyer's home address, Steve? There must be a staff list hanging around someplace."

"Sure. I got one in the production office. I can give you the address after the show."

I finished the last two interviews feeling a bit smug about my detective work. The last two were more successful than the first two—no one dropped dead to-night—and I finished the show at the piano with a medium-tempo version of "Ain't Misbehavin'."

Bobby Dyer's address was waiting for me at my dressing room, placed on the makeup table.

chapter 17

Dark rain was coming down hard by the time I left the studio. I had watched the clouds rolling in over the ocean on the drive back from Trancas that afternoon, but still the change of weather seemed sudden and dramatic. Southern California is a stark sort of paradise, a natural desert subject to earthquake, fire, and flood. I thought vaguely about the hillside behind my house, hoping it would not slide down again into my pool.

Cass pulled the limo right up to the studio door, but I got soaked making the dash into the front seat.

"The gods must be angry," I said to Cass.

"There ain't no gods in L.A.," he said.

I gave him Bobby Dyer's address, which was on a street neither of us had heard of. Cass found a map of Los Angeles in his glove compartment and we spent the next ten minutes looking up the street in the index, getting the map coordinates—L7—and then trying to find Dixon Way among the hundreds of tiny lines on which millions of men, women, and children spend their lives. L7 was an area comprising half of Hollywood and part of the foothills. Dixon Way turned out to be a short curlicue not too far from the Hollywood Bowl, off a road that wound up into the hills. Cass circled the spot with a pencil, certain we'd never find it again otherwise, and we set out through the stormy night.

It was not a good night to go calling on an associate producer who may or may not have planted a bottle of Cajun pepper vodka seasoned with rat poison in Terry Cole's secret refrigerator. On the freeway coming from Burbank, we passed a bad wreck: a sports car had somehow jumped the center divider to crash head-on into a BMW. Emergency lights flickered through the gloom. The hazy orange smoke of flares rose from the ground, making the freeway disaster look like a scene from hell. Besides the highway patrol, there were fire trucks and an ambulance. We had a glimpse of a body covered by a white sheet lying on the ground. Cass and I drove on in silence more carefully than before.

Our headlights penetrated the wet, sad night. As we came off the freeway at Highland Boulevard, Hollywood seemed awash in a blur of multicolored neon. If I were to put this scene to music, I'd score it with the lonely muted trumpet of Miles Davis. All I needed was a trench coat and a cigarette dangling out of the corner of my mouth. It was definitely a film *noir* evening, and Detective Allen was feeling moody. I fantasized quitting show business and becoming a private eye. I'd need a gun, of course, a seedy office, a proper hat—

well, I could use my letters-to-the-editor fedora, without the *press* sign—and a few loose women hanging around, but these things could be arranged.

"Do I turn here?" Cass asked.

I was holding on to the map with a small pocket flashlight in hand, supposedly navigating our course.

"Where are we?" I asked.

"Jesus, Steve! Pay attention."

Does *your* chauffeur speak to you like that? Cass was perfectly right, of course. I'd been goofing off. I managed to find where we were on the map and directed him into a residential area of small old houses, each with a little plot of front lawn. None of the streets ran in a straight line in this part of town. They meandered along the foothills, often coming to an abrupt end. The rain did not help our progress. We must have spent twenty minutes getting lost and finding ourselves again before I was able to lean out of the window and shine the flashlight up toward a street sign that was partially obscured by an overgrown palm.

"This is it," I announced. "Dixon Way."

The house we came to must have been built in the twenties, which is about as old as things get around here. It was built to resemble a small medieval castle, complete with turrets shaped like wizards' hats. A place like this could have been built by some eccentric actor of the silent era. There was not a light on anywhere inside. Beyond the dim street lamp on the corner, everything was utterly dark.

Cass reached way back into the glove compartment.

"Whad'ya got there, a gun?"

"What's got into you, man? *No,* I don't have a gun.

95

For a wet night like this, what I got here is even better."

"An umbrella?"

"No, sorry."

He pulled out a silver flask, raised it to his lips, and took a long swallow, then wiped it and passed it to me.

"I'd prefer a chocolate shake."

He didn't laugh.

"Go ahead, boss. You need a little shot. Trust me."

Where had I heard that line before? I sighed, prepared myself for eternity, and pretended to take a short swallow. This particular brand of rat poison tasted very much like Remy Martin, V.S.O.P. Jimmy Cassidy has good taste in friends and booze.

We left the car and were uncomfortably wet before we reached the shelter of the doorway. What had once been a single castle had been divided up into little castlets—four separate apartments that were now probably condos, for all I knew. Bobby Dyer lived in the one marked *D*—for *Dungeon?*—which was downstairs and around back, with an entrance near an overgrown garden next to the ancient swimming pool that had only a few inches of ugly water on the bottom. There was a doorbell and I rang it. There was no answer, so I rang again. Finally, I knocked loudly on the door with my fist.

"What do you think?"

Cass shrugged. "No one home, except maybe a few ghosts." He took out the flask from his hip pocket, took a swig, and offered me a shot. Rain was slanting off the roof and pouring down on our heads. I could see why some detectives took to drink.

"I got an idea," I told him.

"Mmm?"

"Let's break in."

"Man, you've been watching too much TV."

I grinned. "Listen, there's nothing to it. I know a nifty way to undo a lock with a credit card. We'll get in, look around a bit, split, and no one will be the wiser."

I don't know what had gotten into me. This was an absolute first for me, breaking into a stranger's house, and on a stormy night to boot. I gave Cass the flashlight while I fumbled in my wallet for my American Express card—I don't leave home without any of my credit cards. I slipped the card into the crack between the door and the frame, moving it upward into the lock. The card touched against something solid and would move no further. I tried to force it. For a second I thought the door was about to give, but actually it was my American Express card that gave, snapping in half.

I swore a little and tried the lock again, this time with Visa.

"Steve, I'm not sure about this."

"Damn it, I got Diner's Club, Mastercard, and Bullocks. I tell you, I'm going to get in this door."

The Visa card had no more power to open doors than American Express. My credit rating was going downhill fast. I was going for the Discover card when Cass held back my arm.

"Steve, I've got a better way."

"I'd like to see that, Cass," I challenged. "I really would."

We each took another draw on the cognac. Then he removed his jacket, rolled it around his fist like a glove, and lightly smashed through the glass window at the side of the door.

"Simple, huh?"

"It lacks finesse, but it'll have to do."

Cass got the window open, climbed inside, and came around to open up the front door. He was about to turn on a light, but I warned him not to.

"Let's be discreet. Use the flashlight."

"Discreet!" He giggled. "That's a sissy word."

There was glass all over the living room floor. Apartment *D* was decorated in an old-fashioned way. There was a rocking chair, a couch, a television set, a sideboard with some good china on it. None of the furniture was expensive. Basically, this was a room your aging grandma could be happy in except for one thing: a variety of dumbbells and muscle-building equipment scattered around the floor. There was a physical fitness magazine on the dining room table showing an incredibly muscle-bound man with blond hair and a leopard-skin bikini, apparently having a physical fit.

We left the living room and came to the kitchen, which was when I first noticed a strange smell—like food gone bad, but worse.

"Ugh. This guy's no great housekeeper," Cass said.

"Maybe he hasn't been home for a while." The place really felt dead: unloved, untouched, unlived-in. I looked in the refrigerator. There were a few dismal leftovers from some long-past meal. We moved down the hall, beyond a bathroom, to the bedroom. The rank, spoiled smell in the air was getting worse. I think this was when I got my first inkling of the disaster ahead.

"There's something about this smell," Cass was saying. "It reminds me of—"

We saw the body as soon as we opened the bedroom door.

There was a man lying with his head propped up against the bed, staring at us with vacant, horrible eyes. He was wearing nothing but bikini briefs, which made his marble white skin look more dead somehow. The flashlight dropped out of my hand, sending a crazy beam of light cascading across the bedroom.

Cass moaned. I picked up the flashlight and tried to get up enough nerve to look at the corpse more closely.

"Steve, let's get out of here."

"Just a minute."

I played the light over the dead man. He had been shot several times, at least twice in the chest and once in the head. There was a great deal of blood on the floor. I fought down a sick feeling in my stomach.

I judged the dead man to have been in his early fifties. He had a broad face with closely cut, graying hair. His shoulders and arms were enormous, presumably from pumping iron. Big muscles had not helped him much against bullets. There was a surprised look on his face. He looked as if he had been stepping backward to get away from the person with the gun, falling back toward the bed to die. I don't know how long Cass and I stood there staring at the dead man. Fascination alternated with horror.

"Bobby Dyer?"

"I think so," I answered. "We'd better call the cops."

There was a phone in the living room, but I suggested we use the one in the limousine. I didn't want to disturb any evidence. Probably it was ludicrous to start worrying about this now, after breaking a window and leaving our prints all over the living room and kitchen, but I suddenly couldn't get out of that apartment fast enough.

I was ahead of Cass going out the door. A hand grabbed my arm out of nowhere and held on fast. "Holy Christ," I shouted, frightened. I felt the muzzle of a gun pressed against the side of my head, knocking my glasses lose. Behind me, Cass walked right into me before he knew what was happening. "What the fuck—" he said.

"Don't move, either of you," came a hard voice. A light shone in my face. "Mother of God," said the voice. "It's Steve Allen!"

Where had I heard that voice before?

chapter 18

It was Detective Sergeant W.B. Walker and he did not seem amused. He shone his flashlight from my face to Jimmy Cassidy's, then back to my face again. I concentrated on looking as innocent as I could under the circumstances. I was greatly relieved when he put away his gun.

"You *do* get around, Mr. Allen," he observed dryly, a good trick considering that he was rain soaked.

"Ye-e-es," I replied. "I thought I'd pay a late-night call on our associate producer, Bobby Dyer—but the conversation was kind of stiff."

You say things like this, I swear to God, when you get into a film *noir* situation. Sergeant Walker for his part was wearing a very forties-style trench coat, the collar turned up against the rain. It made him look like a short, fat Dick Tracy. The beam of his flashlight moved across the front door to the window where the glass was broken.

"Great," he said sarcastically. "B and E." The flashlight returned to my face. I tried to smile. We were standing under the overhang of the porch, mostly protected against the rain except when the occasional gust of wind sent spray against our legs. Sergeant Walker let the beam of light fall on Cass's chiseled face.

"And who might you be?"

"Jim Cassidy, Officer—Mr. Allen's driver." It was the first time Cass had called me "mister" in years. I had a feeling he was trying to distance himself from me as far as he could.

"You guys stay right here," Sergeant Walker told us. "I mean, don't move a fuckin' inch, you understand?"

"Absolutely, Sergeant."

He flashed me a bitter look and went inside the apartment. Cass passed over the flask of cognac. It was quite a bit lighter than it had been earlier. We stood silently listening to the rain beating against the trees and ground. I could hear Sergeant Walker moving slowly through the living room and kitchen, much as

101

we had done. When he came to the bedroom, there was absolute silence for a minute or two. Then he came charging out of there with his head lowered and a scowl on his face.

"Congratulations, Mr. Allen. Two guys murdered in two nights. You're a dangerous man to get next to."

"Sorry," I said idiotically.

He seemed very disappointed in me. "You guys come with me," he ordered, not as polite as he had been. He took us around the side of the house where his unmarked squad car was parked in the driveway. He opened the door for Cass and me to get into the backseat, while he slid into the front. The next thing he did was to radio in the fact that there was a murder victim on Dixon Way. At least, I assumed this was what the sergeant was up to on the radio. What he actually said into the microphone was not so much English as a garble of codes and numbers. When he finished, he turned around to me with a heavy sigh.

"Okay, Mr. Allen, what are you doing here?"

"Just a little amateur detective work," I told him modestly. "I know this looks bad, but it's really quite easy to explain."

"I'll bet."

I told him about Steve Linder, my new namesake friend, the production assistant, and how I had learned about Bobby Dyer's being in charge of providing a fresh bottle of vodka each night to Terry's refrigerator, and how I had come here hoping to solve the mystery of Hal Hoaglund's sad demise.

"You just broke in?"

"Well, we got a little carried away," I admitted. "It was the thrill of the chase."

"A *little* carried away?" he said, rolling his eyes upward to whatever gods look after short, fat police detectives. "I could arrest you two for B and E. Probably obstruction of justice as well. Whatever gave you the idea you could just smash a window and walk into some guy's apartment?"

"It was the frustration," I tried to explain, "after breaking two credit cards trying to jimmy the lock."

"Tell me this—did you touch anything in there?"

"Sort of," I told him.

"Sort of *what?*"

"Sort of everything . . . at least in the living room and kitchen. But nothing in the bedroom. Isn't that right, Cass?"

"We were too damned scared to touch anything in the bedroom," Cass said.

"I'll bet you were."

I could hear sirens coming our way, getting louder all the time.

"By the way," I said, "what are you doing here, Sergeant?"

"I learned about Bobby from Sonny Melnik. He was only too happy to pass the buck to someone else. Believe it or not, you ain't the only detective around here."

Two cop cars were pulling up, their blue and red emergency lights sending out a cascade of color. The sergeant left us in the rear of his car while he went to confer with his colleagues. He was back in a few minutes with a uniformed cop by his side.

"Officer Larsen is going to escort you gentlemen back to the Beverly Hills Hotel so you can get into something dry. I wouldn't want my two star witnesses to catch cold."

"How thoughtful, Sergeant."

"And, Mr. Allen—I want you to stay in your bungalow, if you don't mind. Don't go anyplace. I'll be over as soon as I finish here. I haven't decided what to do with you yet."

Both Cass and I looked as obliging as possible. W.B. Walker gave us a disgusted look and joined a squad of uniforms that were moving around the side of the house toward the murder scene.

Officer Larsen said he was supposed to ride in the limo and stay with us until he was relieved. He seemed surprised when we put him in the back of the Cadillac and I rode up front with Cass. I told him he could watch TV or listen to the stereo, or even help himself to the bar. He was a young man, most sincere, and acted as if we were the very devils his momma had warned him about, trying to tempt him away from the straight and narrow. Riding through Beverly Hills, he sat very erect, keeping an eye on us.

I was beginning to feel cold and exhausted, now that I was over the first adrenaline shock of coming across a dead man. I considered how strange it was that Sergeant Walker had been following me all day—first to Kathleen Cole's and now to Bobby Dyer's apartment. His detection work was leading him along the same path as I: *only I had gotten to these places first!*

What a detective I was! Perhaps this was why Sergeant Walker had decided to honor us with a police escort.

Actually, it wasn't until we arrived at my bungalow and Officer Larsen grimly stationed himself by the front door that I realized his presence was no honor. He was no escort. He was, in fact, our guard.

chapter 19

By the time Sergeant Walker joined us from the murder scene, it was late, nearly two in the morning. Cass had fallen asleep in an armchair in front of the TV. He had changed out of his wet clothes into one of my shirts and a pair of trousers, which looked ridiculous on him since I am taller and—alas—somewhat wider in the waist. The TV was on to a rerun of an old *Magnum, P.I.* Officer Larsen had been trying not to watch, but I could tell he was following the story with rapt attention. As for myself, my eyes were staring at the tube, but my thoughts were far away.

We all sat up straighter when Sergeant Walker arrived. His trench coat was still dripping wet. When I took it from him to hang in the bathroom, I saw he had the same wrinkled dark brown suit on underneath.

"Don't you ever long for brighter colors?" I asked.

"I like brown," he grumped.

I was about to tell him that life was a rainbow waiting to be discovered, but he looked so out of sorts that I offered him a drink instead. He said he could use a cup of coffee. I could have made this myself—there was a small kitchen in my bungalow—but it's easy to be spoiled by the room service that's available twenty-four hours a day. When I got on the phone to the kitchen, the sergeant was hovering next to me.

"Think I can still get a sandwich this time of night?"

"Sure, Sarge. What will you have?"

"Something simple. I don't care."

He settled for a steak sandwich, well done, French fries, a salad, a pot of coffee, and a piece of apple pie. I had been feeding W.B. Walker pretty well today, which was fine with me. I figured as long as he was eating, he wouldn't be arresting me for murder, breaking and entering, or obstruction of justice, or a half-dozen other charges I'm sure he could think up.

"Are you married, Sergeant?"

"Why?" he growled. Then he sighed and plopped down on the sofa. "Who'd want to marry a homicide cop, for Chrissake?"

I decided there *was* something endearing about W.B. Walker. All he needed was about a month in the sun, people being nice to him, and no killings for a while, and he'd probably be almost human. When the food came, he told Cass he could go home. He sent Officer Larsen home as well. *"Some*body might as well get some friggin' sleep," he snarled.

The sergeant slurped his coffee and made little smacking noises with his lips as he gobbled up the steak. A bit of the catsup from the French fries ended up on his suit.

I was studying him, trying to imagine what made him tick, when his eyes came up from his plate and met mine.

"So how old do you think I am?" he asked, apropos of nothing.

I shrugged. His mouse brown hair was thinning, but there was no trace of gray. I had a feeling that W.B. Walker had looked middle-aged from the time he was twelve.

"Forty-five," I tried, being charitable since my real guess was older.

He snorted. "Thirty-nine! You see what comes from being a cop, Mr. Allen—you get old before your time. If I were you, I'd stick to comedy and leave murder investigations to unfunny people like me."

"Great," I told him. "Except Hal Hoaglund is dead because I gave him a cup of rat poison, and I'm never going to have another decent night's sleep until I figure out how it happened."

He slurped down some more coffee and then tore into the pie.

"May I ask you something, Sergeant?"

"What?"

"What does W.B. stand for?"

He blinked and sat back away from the room service table. "Thanks for the snack. I think it's time to get back to cases. Are you into bodybuilding, by the way?"

"Bodybuilding?"

"You know, build up the old pectorals and biceps. Impress the ladies at the beach sort of thing."

"No. What are you getting at?"

"Hal Hoaglund was a bodybuilder, you tell me, and so was Bobby Dyer, it appears. He had a lot of weights and exercise machines lying around his living room. It seems a large coincidence. Two guys dead, one right after the other, both of them into physical improvement like that. Now you're certain you don't go to a gym or something, Mr. Allen?''

"Well, actually," I said, "my wife got me going to Pritikin a few months ago. You know, their place in the Valley, at Fashion Square.''

"So you've become a muscle man?''

"No," I said. "I work out with the treadmill machine upstairs.''

"Has it done you any good?''

"Sure. When I started I was pretty wiped out after about twenty minutes on the machine. Now I can do an hour without thinking about it, at least if I've got earphones or a book in front of me. Exercise, all by itself, *is* boring, as you may have heard.''

"You look in fair shape," he said, eyeing me with his head turned slightly sideways. Then suddenly he laughed.

"What's so funny?''

"I was just thinking," he said, "when I was a younger guy I used to watch you on the TV. My family always thought you looked like Clark Kent.''

"Actually," I said, "the guys that do the Superman cartoon strip once ran a story for several weeks about my being mistaken for Kent. The story line had to do with our gang on the old *Tonight* show. You know, Steve Lawrence, Eydie Gorme, Andy Williams.''

"Who was your announcer?" he asked.

"Gene Rayburn," I said.

"That's right," he said. "I'd forgotten.''

"But what's all this got to do with the murder investigation?''

"What are you," he huffed, "a freak for relevance? I talk about all kinds of stuff when I'm on a case. You never know what you might stumble over, in idle conversation."

"I'll tell you something I've stumbled over," I said, "the idea that maybe we're all wasting our time and that there is no real murderer in the conventional sense. Obviously I'm not talking about whoever it was that killed Dyer, but maybe the poison in the vodka bottle wasn't meant for anyone in particular. You remember the Tylenol scare a few years back and the other things like that with the orange juice and the milk and all the rest of it? Some nut-case wants to get even with a pharmaceutical house or a grocery chain so he puts poison, in this case, in a bottle of Cajun vodka. Maybe we were simply unlucky enough for the bottle to come our way."

I could see from his reaction that Walker hadn't thought of that angle and he turned out to be honest about it.

"Does that make you feel like some pumpkins?" he asked. "Thinking of a possibility that hadn't occurred to me?"

"Well," I said, "there's nothing personal in this, but I think the idea is worth looking into."

Walker interlocked his fingers and stretched his arms in an odd way. "Your idea," he said, "ain't worth doodly-squat. The bottle had already been opened. If the seal had been unbroken, that would have been something else, but it wasn't. And then, as you were saying, there's Bobby Dyer to think about. He's down in a morgue right now with four nine-millimeter slugs in him. So we are looking for an actual killer."

"What if the two deaths are unrelated?" I tried. "What if Hal drank a tampered-with bottle that could have been meant for anyone—and Bobby was killed by burglars.''

"What if, what if," the sergeant said with a sigh. "I'll tell you what *I* think, Mr. Allen. It's possible Bobby put the poisoned vodka in Terry Cole's refrigerator and then someone killed him to keep him quiet.''

"But why would an associate producer, some little guy like Bobby Dyer, want to kill his boss?''

"My impression is that ninety-nine percent of Terry Cole's crew would like to kill their boss. But maybe Dyer was acting for someone else. He didn't necessarily have to have a motive himself.''

"Working for someone else," I mused, trying to imagine the cold-blooded person who would plan a murder. "You think someone hired him?''

"Sure. Someone knew it was Bobby's job to stock the bar. That person maybe gave him a funny bottle to put in last Friday. Maybe even Bobby didn't know there was poison in it—but he would have remembered afterward who gave him the bottle. That's probably why he was killed.''

We were both silent for a time. Sergeant Walker had finished his late-night snack and was beginning to look as if he could fall asleep on my sofa.

"What about fingerprints?" I asked. "On the vodka bottle, that is. *That* might tell us something.''

"Oh, it does," he told me with a sinister little smile. He rose heavily and began to move toward the door.

"Well?" I asked.

"Your fingerprints were on the bottle, and yours alone.''

I got the sergeant his trench coat from the bathroom and held it for him as he put his arms through the sleeves. While he was available, I thought I'd try one more question.

"So, what do the initials W.B. stand for?"

He smiled slowly. "Persistent, aren't we? Hell, you're such a fancy detective, why don't we see if you can find that out by yourself?"

chapter 20

Ward Bisbee, I considered judiciously. *Warren Bartholomew,* I tried, then rejected it as too upper crusty. Probably the name was an embarrassment to him. *Winnie,* I thought with a smile. How about *Detective Sergeant Winnie Bob Walker the Third*?

The morning sun was full on my face. I have a routine each morning at the Beverly Hills Hotel: I walk. This was what I was doing now.

It's a bit eccentric, I suppose. In the land of smoggy sunshine, where the automobile is worshiped above all things, people who walk are more than suspect—they are the enemy, to be stopped and carefully questioned by the police. Fortunately, the Beverly Hills police know me by now, and though I have been stopped a few times, the patrol cars generally wave me on or, better, ignore me.

I mention my morning walks because over the next few days they were about the only time I had to myself. Hosting the TV show each night was proving easy enough, though I like to do homework on my guests. Also I have been getting more ambitious with the piano as the years pass, and this week I was spending rehearsal time with the orchestra nearly every afternoon, working on some tunes I'd written. With one thing and another, there wasn't much time to think about Cajun vodka and Hal Hoaglund and Bobby Dyer with four slugs in his body and W.B. Walker's full name. Speaking of W.B., he had generally absented himself from my life, and for hours at a time I could forget about rat poison and other forms of violent death and concentrate on being a working professional trying to give people an intelligent laugh.

Friday morning arrived clear and beautiful and full of hope for an early spring. Birds were chirping expensively in the trees, the sky was blue, and the storm that had drenched Cass and me on Tuesday night now seemed a distant dream. I decided to walk further than usual today. I planned a course down through the residential flats of Beverly Hills, past the gaudy shops of Rodeo Drive to the Beverly Wilshire Hotel, where I thought I might enjoy a spot of breakfast before walking back.

What I like about these morning walks is that once I set my body in motion, my mind is free to roam. The last couple of days, it was the only time I'd had to devote to what I had begun to refer to as "my case." On this lovely Friday morning, I kept coming back to Sonny Melnik and how difficult it must have been to be the man behind the scenes all these years while someone else got all the glory. Terry Cole might be Sonny's meal ticket, but people sometimes bite the hand that feeds them. God bless the child that's got his own.

As far as I could see, Sonny was the person most likely to want to kill Terry Cole, but there was one problem: Sonny would have arranged for the poisoned vodka to have been in the refrigerator when Terry was the host of the show, not I. Every time I built up a convincing psychological portrait of Sonny as killer, I came to this frustrating dead end. If Terry Cole was the intended victim—as I believed he had to be—then whoever arranged to get the vodka into his refrigerator was not close enough to the inner workings of things to know that Terry was about to take an unscheduled vacation.

I tried to bend this around a bit. What if the poisoned vodka had been left last Wednesday or Thursday? Perhaps Terry had been starting to feel sick and had decided to forgo his usual on-camera treat. The untouched bottle would be left in the refrigerator over the weekend, and on Monday your obedient and oblivious servant would find himself playing barman to nervous film star, Hal Hoaglund.

This was a possibility—but why hadn't Sonny or Bobby Dyer tried to retrieve the deadly bottle? Surely they wouldn't have wanted a darling person like me or Hal to go blithely to his death?

I would have to think about this. I also had Kathleen Cole to consider, embittered ex-wife. I wondered why she hated Terry so much. After all, she'd got her money—an incredible, perhaps even unfair, amount—and her freedom. The more I thought about it, the more her bitterness didn't really make sense. I wondered about the provisions of Terry Cole's estate, if Kathleen had anything to gain by her ex-husband's death.

Yesterday, I had seen something quite peculiar at the studio: Kathleen Cole stepping out of Sonny's office. She was wearing a black dress and enormous dark glasses. She didn't see me, but I spent some time wondering what Kathleen and Sonny might have to discuss.

Could it be they were having an affair? When I was young, it used to puzzle me whenever I'd see strikingly attractive women dating, sleeping with, falling in love with and marrying remarkably unattractive men. It still puzzles me, but I guess I have more important things to think about these days. Suffice it to say that as unlikely a couple as Kathleen and Sonny might seem, I had seen many even more unlikely pairings.

Maybe they planned to get rid of Terry together, a cozy little murder. Anything was possible and, as you can see, my imagination was working overtime.

Thinking of conspiracies, I came up with a humdinger, although I've never understood exactly what a humdinger was. The entire crew of *The Terry Cole Show* had gone into this together, chipping in on the price of the rat poison for their boss! A ghoulish idea, but not entirely out of the question.

I thought round and round about dark, horrible passions and plots until my thoughts began to scare me. I came out of this reverie to find myself walking down the residential part of Beverly Drive. I had to laugh at myself, entertaining such indecent thoughts on this lovely spring day.

I lifted my face to the warming sun. High overhead, skinny palm trees were swaying in the gentle breeze. Palm trees always make me think of Fourth-of-July skyrockets—the long ascending line, then the explosive outcropping at the very top. On each side of the street, the impassive mansions of Beverly Hills stood serene and arrogantly confident, their well-groomed lawns stretching out to the sparkling clean sidewalk beneath my feet.

"Lighten up," I told myself. "Sonny's not such a bad guy, poor soul. And Kathleen's only a pussycat!"

I smiled at my folly and began to whistle a jazzy tune I'd just begun to create—hear, actually—in my head. That's when someone took a shot at me from a passing car and destroyed all my optimism.

Damn! Some bastard had actually tried to shoot me dead!

chapter 21

It happened too fast to comprehend. I had been marginally aware of the dark shape of a car pulling up alongside, but I was too involved in my thoughts to pay attention. The first shot sounded like a firecracker.

I turned toward the car, not quite believing what I

saw: a hand sticking out of a front window, and in the hand a nasty looking gun pointed my way. At that moment I wasn't looking where I was going and the tip of my right shoe caught against a tuft of grass in a crack of the sidewalk. I tripped, lunging forward just as another shot rang out. The accidental move saved my life. This time I could actually hear the whine of a bullet pass by close to my head.

My glasses fell off, hit the sidewalk, and bounced off into the grass. As I scrambled to retrieve them, I moved behind the palm tree to my right.

"Goddamn it," I shouted, "what do you think you're doing?" It became evident at once that whoever was firing at me thought the business of the moment was murder. I had expected him to drive off with a squeal of rubber after the first miss. To my astonishment the car had not moved. There was another deafening report and a bullet ricocheted off the pitifully thin palm tree behind which I had now risen to a standing position.

A quick glance left and right showed that coming to my aid was old Bert Williams's friend, Mr. Nobody. The block was deserted, as all areas of Beverly Hills seem to be at midday.

Shouting for help seemed reasonable, but I suddenly had trouble with dialogue. What the hell do you shout? I tried the word *help*, but it didn't sound right. *Police* felt no more reasonable. My third attempt was an inchoate "Hey!" None of it did any good. Neighbors, if they had not already been attracted by the sound of gunfire, were unlikely to be drawn by shouted pleas for aid. To my immense relief the killer's car began to move forward, but in a moment, when another shot rang out, I realized the son of a bitch had moved simply so as to get a better angle. Sideways, my shoulder to the palm tree trunk, I sucked in my breath, trying to make my one-hundred-ninety-five-pound form slimmer than the tree, and wishing fervently I had taken my Pritikin diet more seriously. The last slug went wild and smashed the window of a Rolls Royce parked in the driveway behind me.

"Now you're in for it!" I cried. It was clear that you might murder a poor pedestrian in Beverly Hills, but you cannot take on a Rolls Royce and get away with it. This is a town where property is sacred. The fuzzy black shape of the car leapt forward with the expected smoky spin of its rear tires and roared off down the street. I came out from behind my palm tree and ran into the middle of Beverly Drive, trying to get the license number. Quick thinking, but with my unaided eyesight I could not even identify the car's make.

"Maniac!" I screamed. "Somebody tried to kill me!" I said aloud to the silent houses that looked down on my tribulation. They didn't seem to care.

I strode up the path to a white colonial mansion that looked straight out of *Gone With The Wind* and rang the doorbell with an angry flourish.

"Right here in Beverly Hills, for Chrissake!" I mumbled to the closed door.

The door didn't open. Maybe the owners were in Palm Beach, Monte Carlo, or visiting their money in Switzerland. More likely, they were inside but didn't wish to get involved. Money is a way to shield yourself from the troubles of the street, and the citizens of Beverly Hills are not famous for their neighborly concern.

I suddenly felt inexpressibly weary. What got to me

117

was not so much that someone was trying to kill me, but the fact that no one had come to my aid. A morning like this can make you a cynic for the rest of the day.

I sat down on the steps that led to the stately Southern mansion, next to a metal statue of a liveried midget black holding a lantern in his raised hand. I was sure this would bring the police instantly, since any sign of vagrancy in this wealthy city is taken as the gravest transgression. But no cops came for me. I had become invisible.

After a few minutes, my heart had calmed down and I stood up again, now glad the police had not arrived. I had made a decision. I was now definitely going to get to the bottom of this. No one was going to try to kill me and get away with it.

I walked away quickly from the place of my near death, moving more carefully than usual because one lens of my glasses had been smashed and my vision was a bit distorted.

I had decided not to report the shooting to the police for one very good reason—I was afraid Sergeant Walker would use it as an excuse to end my new career as a sleuth. And there was no way I was going to let that happen, not now.

I trust you know me well enough to know I'm really a gentle type. Reasonable to a fault. Polite. Kind to women and hungry policemen.

But this goddamned black car and its driver had put an end to all that.

chapter 22

It was time to go right to the heart of the matter—
and the heart, it seemed obvious, was Terry Cole.
Hardly had I made that decision than a startling
thought occurred to me: it didn't seem to make sense,
but could Cole himself be the mastermind of the murder plot? He'd certainly be the last one to suspect, since
everyone would assume that the poisoned vodka had
been meant for him. Well, I didn't know, but I'd keep
the possibility in mind.

Saturday morning I called information for Santa
Barbara County and got the number for the Happy
Valley Tranquility Center. The name seemed odd. I
couldn't picture Terry in a lotus position deep in med-
itation. The woman who answered the phone had a
voice so soft and melodious you wanted to float off to
sleep.

"Tranquility Center!" she lullabied. "How can I
help you?"

"I would like to speak to Mr. Terry Cole, please,"
I baritoned back.

"Oh, I'm sorry," she told me—and she did sound
deeply sorry—"but here at HVTC our guests do not

receive phone calls. We have a policy of temporary isolation from the outside world."

"Like being shipwrecked on a desert island, eh?"

"Not quite. There are times when it's necessary to step back from the world in order to see the world more clearly," she lectured patiently. I had a feeling she might send me a bill for this nugget of wisdom. I pictured a blonde with glasses, a bit overweight. One of my children once had a kindergarten teacher like this.

"If you leave your name, however, I'll see that Mr. Cole gets your message before he leaves."

"No, it's not important, I just wanted to say hello. Thanks so much," I said quickly, putting down the receiver.

At least I had discovered Cole really was there at Happy Valley, just as Kathleen had told me. It seemed a strange place for him to be, though. I waited nearly an hour before trying to call Happy Valley again. I didn't want the receptionist to connect this call with the earlier one. This time I identified myself as Steve Allen, TV and radio personality suffering from exhaustion, stress, and strange bursts of melancholy.

"Can you help me?"

"Mr. Allen, we have helped many just like you," came the gentle, singsong voice I'd heard earlier.

"I can't go on," I said. "I have material possessions—but I've got no peace of mind, damn it."

"Peace of mind *is* everything, isn't it?" she said. She set up an appointment with me for later that afternoon. The initial forty-five minute evaluation would cost five hundred dollars, from which I gathered that peace of mind wasn't quite everything at Happy Valley.

Cass picked me up in the limo around eleven-thirty. Santa Barbara is ninety miles up the coast from Los Angeles. It used to be a rich and sleepy little town full of Spanish architecture and old patrician California families. In recent years, having grown, it has been infiltrated by a younger, sportier crowd. Now there are more condominiums than drowsy mansions, and oil platforms disturb the horizon when you look out to sea. This, we are told, is progress.

The highway to Happy Valley took us east into the hills beyond Santa Barbara. We drove along a gentle country road with overhanging trees, mostly eucalyptus and peppers, past large estates with well-kept grounds sitting neatly behind stone walls or white picket fences. Some of the people who lived here seemed the equestrian sort. We drove past a man and a woman in full riding regalia: black hats, red jackets, boots, and jodhpurs. I had a feeling that this part of Santa Barbara County would rather belong to New England than California.

The road was called Oak Manor Drive. It followed a musical little brook into a wild and peaceful valley. Eventually we came to a stone wall higher than the height of a man, topped not very discreetly with iron barbs. The gate itself was equally impressive: wrought iron, solid, with decorative spikes on top that would be impossible to climb over. Next to the gate, carved in stone—half covered with aristocratic ivy—was the inscription: HVTC. A video camera pointed down at us from a little turret near the gate. Tranquility, it appeared, needed to be protected from the crude outer world.

"Mr. Allen here for his appointment," Cass said into a speaker near his window.

"Please drive to the main building. There will be someone to meet you," came a soft, disembodied voice. The mammoth iron gate swung open ponderously and we were on our way. When the gate closed behind us, I had an irrational moment of feeling we'd been swallowed by some enormous beast.

Cass whistled when we turned a corner and saw the main house, an impressive English manor surrounded by acres of lawn. We passed some golf links and a swimming pool, and had a glimpse of stables that were sitting at the edge of a meadow. The sun was high in the sky, and indeed everything looked as tranquil as you could imagine.

As we pulled up to the house, I noticed a group of a dozen or so men and women in assorted acrobatic positions on the lawn. Everyone was wearing pink pajamas, except for the instructor—a lovely young woman—who was dressed in white pajamas. I suppose this was so you could tell the inmates from the playmates. I got out of the car and tried to see if Terry Cole was in this group. He wasn't.

"Are you interested in *T'ai Chi?*" came the melodious voice I had heard on the phone. I turned and saw she was as I had imagined: blond, fairly attractive, in her late twenties, with thick glasses perched on a pert nose.

"I'm more into Peking Duck," I told her.

She didn't think I was funny.

"Won't you come this way?" she suggested. "Your driver can wait for you here. My name is Doreen Hanson."

She led the way into the house. There was a large, old-fashioned hall that was two stories high with a great wooden staircase leading to the upper floor. The furnishings were very British, post-World War I.

"You could film *Masterpiece Theater* here," I told her.

"Oh, we'd *never* allow television cameras here, Mr. Allen," she told me primly. "This is a place where one can step out of the modern world and find one's inner rhythm."

She led me down a hallway paneled in oak to an office that reminded me of a grandmother's sitting room.

"Would you like some herbal tea?"

"No, thanks. Coffee, perhaps?"

"We don't serve products with caffeine at Happy Valley," she reprimanded.

"I should have known."

"Perhaps you should tell me why you've come to us for help."

"Well, Ms. Hanson . . ."

"Call me Doreen, Steve. We're informal here."

"Well, Doreen," I said, "it's a little hard to explain, but I'm terribly pressured by overwork, really. I'm behind schedule in delivering two books to publishers, currently working every night on a television show, I've just been asked to write the score of a new musical, I've got to go into a studio within the next couple of weeks to do a record album. Then I have some out-of-town concert dates. You know, comedy-and-music shows, and I—"

"I quite understand," she said sympathetically. "You must be under a great deal of pressure."

"That's it exactly," I said.

"Well," she said, "we've been able to be of help to a good many workaholics, if I may use the term. Here at Happy Valley, we teach our clients to get off the merry-go-round, to slow down, to linger, touch, sense, feel."

"Sounds wonderful," I said.

"Incidentally," she said, "there are far more service options available here than you might assume. For example, some of our clients derive dramatic benefits from a face-lift."

"I beg your pardon."

"In looking at you, Mr. Allen—Steve—I was just imagining you without that extra bit of flesh under your chin. You know, of course, that you can leave here looking fifteen years younger."

"Well," I said, "it's the sort of thing I'd have to think over."

"Certainly."

"So you folks do cosmetic surgery here as well as *T'ai Chi* and—"

"Yes," she said, "because we've discovered that if people look better, they feel better."

"That makes sense," I said.

"Well, I hope it all sounds like just what the doctor ordered. Did he?"

"Did who?"

"Did your doctor recommend us?"

"Oh, no," I said, for the first time slightly flustered, "but then you don't need a professional medical opinion on a question of this sort. If you're exhausted, emotionally drained, you know that sort of thing."

"Indeed you do," she said.

"That being the case," I said, "I wonder if I could

just look around the place a bit. See your facilities, perhaps meet some of your other . . . er . . . customers."

"Guests," she corrected.

"Exactly. So I'd like to go on the grand tour, meet the folks and decide if this is really the right move for me."

I was relieved when we started moving. Doreen showed me the library, the dining room, the kitchen, and one of the luxury suites on the second floor. There were no televisions, of course, or radios or stereos. As we walked, she went on at some length about an East-West blend of psychology, spirituality, and downright materialism that had made HVTC such a success among Hollywood burnouts. She described their approach as holistic, from which I believe they dealt with the entire human being: body, soul, and wallet.

We toured the medical center, which was in a modern building next to the main house. I saw the clean, sterile room where all my sags and creases could be shed. Then we were walking along a flowered path to a low, shedlike building where there were a number of classrooms. This is where I could learn a brand new attitude to go with my brand new face.

We sat in on a group therapy session where people were encouraged to shout at one another and let out their primal anger. It was very much like the streets of New York. Next came a lecture on Astral Projection— i.e., learning to take a walk outside of your body. I wondered if you could do this together with your dog, thereby killing two birds with one stone. All the while, of course, I was keeping a sharp eye out for Terry Cole.

The "guests" in their pink pajamas were primarily middle-aged and overweight, looking as if they had helped themselves to a few too many servings of the good life. Touring the music room, I recognized a TV actor who had once appeared on my show. He was playing New Age music on a synthesizer and looking spaced-out. I went up to him and patted him on the back.

"Son of a gun, Jim," I said. "Imagine meeting you here. Listen, have you seen Terry Cole, by any chance?"

"Hey, Steve," he said. *"Every*one's here, man. This is where it's happening."

Doreen led me away, outside again, to look in on the nude water polo going on in the pool. I was starting to feel discouraged. I had never seen Terry Cole without his clothes and doubted I would recognize him among all the pink and splashing forms.

After water polo, we strolled over to the Zen Archery range. A group of pink pajamas were practicing without bows and arrows. It looked strange, but Doreen assured me it was a wonderful way to tune up the concentration.

Just as I was beginning to lose confidence in my quest, there he was, Terry Cole, shooting invisible arrows at a target.

"Bull's-eye!" he cried.

I laughed so loudly that Terry looked over to inspect his new audience. "My God," he said, "Steve Allen!" He leaned his invisible bow against a tree before coming over to shake hands.

"It's good to see you." I was surprised, actually, at this burst of affection, since we had never been particularly close. No two talk-show hosts ever have been.

126

Cole didn't look very well. His hair seemed grayer than when we had last met, his elfish face pinched and drawn. He pulled me closer to give me a hug. I supposed Happy Valley had loosened up his inhibitions, but what he was trying to do was whisper in my ear.

"They're trying to kill me," he hissed.

"Me, too," I whispered back. "I thought I was done for Friday."

Terry pulled back from our embrace. His intense blue eyes were blinking rapidly. "Those fuckers from Pluto are after you, too?"

"Ah, no. My guys are in a black car, maybe a Mercedes."

He nodded savagely. Although Terry and I had never been close, this was looking like the start of a beautiful friendship.

chapter 23

Doreen didn't seem very happy with the blossoming of our sudden friendship. Probably she thought I was an un-tranquil influence from the nasty world outside.

"Now, Steve, we don't want to disturb Terry's archery practice." She had her kindergarten voice on again.

"But he got a bull's-eye," I said. "With an aim like that, why practice?"

"Listen, sugar. Me and Steverino gotta talk," Terry told her. He was a man used to getting his way, even here. "So bug off."

"Very well. A few minutes then," she said with a hurt air. Terry led me away from the Zen Archery range toward a bench by a small duck pond. There were no ducks that I could see. Maybe they too were invisible.

"I'd go crazy here," I said.

"Most people do," he told me, looking at me with wild eyes. "That's the name of the game."

"Terry, I have to ask you something."

"Shoot, kiddo. I'm a man with a lot of answers."

"What's the deal about Cajun pepper vodka?"

"The big hot flash?"

"Exactly," I told him. "How long have you been keeping that white lightning in the clever little refrigerator?"

"Too long," he said with a sigh. "You're talking about dark secrets now."

"Ah, a lot of people drink too much," I told him sympathetically. "I imagine you needed a shot when the guys from Pluto started getting too close, eh?"

"You flipping out? I keep the vodka handy so I can have a good stiff shot when some egomaniac jerk is giving me a hard time on the show."

Terry was looking at me as if I were crazy, which I felt was damned unfair, under the circumstances.

"I hate them, you know," he said calmly.

128

"Whom do you hate, Terry?"

"The guests," he answered. "Most of them, anyway."

I studied the invisible ducks for a while before answering. "It would be difficult to do a talk show without 'em," I suggested.

"You think so? Sometimes I wish the opening monologue would go on forever. Do you have any bread, by the way?"

"Does it have to be real?"

"No." He shrugged.

I handed Terry a loaf of invisible bread and he began to feed the ducks, doing soft imitation quacks.

"What I hate about guests," he told me, "is that they all want to talk about themselves."

"I see what you mean."

"Do you, Steve? I mean, never once do they ask about me. Hell, maybe *I've* just written a book. Maybe *I've* got a brand new film coming out. *I'm* opening in Vegas. But do they ask me?"

"It's heartless," I said, "when you think of it like that."

We were silent again. Our conversation didn't so much flow as jerk forward in sudden starts and stops.

"I can take guys from Pluto," he said. "Guys from Pluto are *nice*. It's guests I can't stand. Talk, talk, talking every goddamned minute, acting like they're the only people in the world with something to say."

"Thus the vodka," I suggested, trying to lead him along.

"A man needs a little relief."

"Don't I know it."

"I'll tell you, Cajun vodka can really blow your

mind. I mean, you look at things from a whole new perspective.''

"So you have Sonny give you a fresh bottle every night?''

"I pay that creep two hundred grand a year. He might as well do something useful for it.''

"But why a fresh bottle every night?''

He gave me a cunning look. "Virginity, Steve, is essential to my well-being.''

"Ah.''

"And how's Jayne?'' he asked, wildly disconnected. "You doing any TV these days, huh? Maybe you have a new book/movie/Broadway musical you're promoting? Okay! Fine! Here's your chance, Pops. We're all listening.''

"I wouldn't want to burden you with my life story, Terry.''

"No, go ahead. Burden me. Everybody else dumps on me; why not you?''

"Well, Jayne's in Hawaii,'' I responded, "and as for television, I thought you'd heard—I've taken over your show, just until you come back, of course.''

"What?" he cried, grabbing my arm in a clawlike grip. I repeated about Jayne's being in Maui and my doing his show, which I had assumed he'd known. I had assumed wrong.

Terry Cole turned the palest shade I had ever seen.

"My show?'' he moaned. "How the hell could you do *my* show?''

"Oh, it's just temporary—until you return.''

"Oh, it's temporary, all right! I can tell you that!''

"Look, Terry, someone had to fill in for you while you're . . . away.''

"Yeah? Wait till I get hold of that fucking Sonny Melnik! No offense, but *my* public doesn't want to see *you*, man. Understand? They want to see me!"

"Of course. Everybody has his own fan club, but—"

"You're trying to take over!" he screamed at the top of his lungs. Doreen heard the commotion and was bearing down upon us.

"Get this man out of my sight," Terry cried. "He's disturbing my goddamn tranquility!"

"You'd better come with me, Mr. Allen."

"It's only a misunderstanding," I assured her.

Two young men in white uniforms were hurrying across the lawn to see what the trouble was. They looked strong enough to throw me over the fence if necessary.

"I'm going to have to ask you to leave now, Mr. Allen," Doreen told me firmly. "I'm afraid Happy Valley is not for you."

And in this manner I was ejected from paradise.

chapter 24

ass and I drove in silence back toward L.A. I stared out the window at the endless traffic. Sometimes it's hard to believe how many people and automobiles are clogged into this part of the world. A little kid in the back of a station wagon stuck out his tongue at me. I put my thumbs to the sides of my head and made elephant ears at him. This gave me an idea.

"What if it were all an act?" I asked aloud.

"What?"

"Being crazy. Maybe there *were* no spacemen from Pluto."

He gave me a worried glance before returning his eyes to the road. "Steve, when's the last time you had a real vacation?"

"No, really, Cass—what if Terry were only faking being crazy? Maybe he wanted to drop out of sight for some reason. Maybe he wanted to give himself an alibi."

"An alibi for what?" Cass asked.

"That's a damned good question." My thoughts were spinning on the great merry-go-round of possibilities. Again, what if Terry Cole himself had put the poisoned vodka into his refrigerator? We could be looking at this whole situation backward. Terry could have left the poison and then disappeared to the safety of the Happy Valley Center.

Yet why would he do that? None of it made a lot of sense as far as I could see.

"This is one big mystery," I told Cass.

"No, this is the Beverly Hills Hotel," he corrected, pulling up the U-shaped drive from Sunset. "Want me to come in?"

"I want to be alone," I told him. "I need to think this one out."

"Call Jayne in Hawaii," he advised. "Tell her to hurry back here and take care of you."

"I'm all right," I muttered. I had talked with Jayne a few times since Hal Hoaglund's death, but I'd kept her in the dark as to the extent of my involvement in the case. If she knew what I was up to, she would probably insist I stop messing around in matters that should be left to the police. Women!

I was entering the lobby, heading toward the desk to see if I had any messages, when I noticed Winston Dane coming out of the corridor that led to the Polo Lounge. I changed directions and hurried to intercept him.

"Winnie! Just the man I need! But I thought you'd be halfway to China by now."

He was looking quite dapper and distinguished in a dark three-piece suit that seemed more London than California. With his silver hair, I thought he looked more like a diplomat than a former talk-show host.

"Oh, I've been having a fabulous time. This town! Such a carnival! I decided to hang around another few days, but next Thursday I'm absolutely off for Honolulu.''

I hadn't thought much about Winston Dane since I had run into him at the party at Rip and Vera's house in Brentwood. At this moment, he looked so elegant, old-worldly and non-Hollywood, that he seemed just the person to help me get a perspective on everything that had been happening lately.

"Winnie, let me buy you a drink.''

"I just had one, old boy.''

"You need another,'' I assured him. I took his arm and we reversed directions back toward the Polo Lounge. The room was dark and a low, rich murmur of conversation filled the air. One always had the impression that great deals were being made and unmade here, as well as the passing of often-spiteful gossip from ear to ear. A waiter led us to one of the semicircular booths and as we passed through the room, eyes darted up briefly to see who had just entered the lion's den. I waved at a few people I knew—a producer, an actress, and two agents. When we arrived at our booth, Winnie ordered "a small sherry,'' as he so charmingly put it. Thinking wistfully of Jayne in Hawaii, I ordered a virgin Mai Tai in her honor, all the juice but none of the hard stuff.

"Winnie, you know everything about this town.''

"Whoa. I *used* to know everything about this town, two decades ago. Past tense, Steve. And I'm glad to keep it that way.''

"But look around you. Has the Polo Lounge really changed? Not a bit! It's still the same old story.''

"A fight for love and glory?''

"A case of do or die,'' I agreed. We laughed just as

our drinks arrived, along with a bowl of potato chips, and we clinked glasses.

"What's on your mind, Steve?"

I told him what was on my mind, the whole saga from Hal Hoaglund's stutter to my recent ejection from Happy Valley. Winston Dane is that rare creature, a good listener—like Merv Griffin or Jack Paar in that regard. We had another round of drinks and two more bowls of potato chips before the story was finished. Winnie was silent for a few minutes afterward, nodding slightly, taking it all in.

"Television's become more exciting since my day," he said with a wry smile. "My advice to you, Steve— let the police handle this. Apparently you owe your life to a palm tree, however slender."

"But you see, I must be getting close," I said triumphantly. "The killer's worried about me. That's why he tried to do me in."

Dane's eyes suddenly brightened and he turned to face me more directly. "I've just gotten a sensational idea," he said. "I read that book of yours on China. What was it called . . . ?"

"Explaining China."

"Right. Nice piece of work, by the way—but if you care enough about the country to write a book about it and have done so many years of research, you really ought to go back there again, to see the incredible changes that have been worked under Deng Xiaoping in recent years. You and I would still prefer good old Beverly Hills, needless to say, but you've got to give the devil his due. The Chinese have definitely taken a few steps in the direction of freedom. They may, in fact, have given Gorbachev the idea for *glasnost* and I feel that—''

''Why are we talking about China?'' I asked.

''Because,'' he said, ''I'm going to Beijing after Honolulu. Why don't you come with me, just for the hell of it? We'd get a lot of media attention, that's for sure. Two old talk-show veterans traveling together and all that.''

''That's one good reason *not* to go.''

''I know,'' he said with a chuckle. ''Actually we could have it either way. But since you've asked my advice, I think the LAPD has a pretty good track record in cases of this sort. I think what *you* ought to do is get away from it all, not to coin a phrase, and what better place than the good old Middle Kingdom?''

''I'm tempted,'' I said. ''Jayne's made two trips back to the mainland, you know, but never did get to see Wu Chang, where she was born.''

''Well, my God,'' he said, ''then it's an even better idea.''

''In the abstract, yes,'' I conceded, ''but to tell you the truth, Winnie, my fur's really up over this. I'm going to nail this bastard and I'd like you to help me.''

''I don't see how I could.''

''I need information, Winnie. Tell me about Kathleen Cole, for instance. Why does she hate Terry so much? You must have known her way back, before she was even married.''

Winnie turned the stem of his sherry glass around slowly in his hand. ''She was Kathleen Donovan when I first met her. Eighteen years old, pale skin, smoky eyes. Absolutely lovely. She came from a nice family in Pasadena, but Hollywood was what she was after.''

"Now she worked for you, I always heard, back when you did the show?"

Winnie smiled. "She was a makeup girl. Thank God makeup was simpler back in the good old days of black and white, or Kathleen would never have lasted. Basically, she used her job to get a foot in the door. It was obvious the real reason she was there was to snag a star."

"She certainly did that," I agreed. "I don't imagine Terry was doing the show long before Kathleen got her hands on him."

"No, to do her justice, Steve, they became involved back when I was still on the show and no one outside of Iowa had ever heard of Terry Cole. This must have been about 1962. Terry had come west to do a network radio show—it was his first big break. He and Kathleen got together one night at the old Ciro's. At that point, he didn't have much to offer. Maybe it was lust at first sight. I always believed Kathleen helped Terry get my spot . . . after I was discharged," he told me with a rueful grin.

We had arrived at a painful subject: Winston Dane's fall from grace.

"Go ahead, ask me. It doesn't hurt anymore. The ax was swift and painless."

"Okay. Why were you fired? I've heard the usual stories."

"That I was seducing young boys? A wicked, nasty old fairy was Winston Dane?"

"Hey, I didn't make 'em up."

"Well, it's true. The network let me go on a morals clause. The age of sexual liberation had not arrived, you must remember, and we 'deviates' had to stay well back in the closet. Not only was I gay, I was politically left, almost a real Commie fag! I'm surprised I lasted in this town as long as I did." He laughed and sipped his drink.

"I'm sorry, Winnie. You were, and always will be, a first-rate talent."

"Thanks, but it was all for the best. I was simply at the wrong place at the wrong time. After I was ejected from television, my life actually improved. I was able to find myself."

"You have no regrets?"

"Not one."

"Let's get back to Kathleen," I suggested. "How could she have helped Terry's career? After all, she was just the makeup girl."

"Ah, yes—but what a makeup girl! She slept with the right people, using her considerable charms judiciously."

"She had influence with whom—network guys?"

"Oh, indeed. Kathleen was quite discreet, but she worked her way to the very top. Now I'm not saying that Terry would have gotten the show if he hadn't had his own kind of talent, but Kathleen certainly helped him get his chance."

"Was he grateful?"

Winston's laugh was an angry snort. "Terry Cole *grateful?* Don't be absurd! We're talking about very predatory people here, dear boy. Terry used Kathleen to climb up the ladder, just as Kathleen used her body to charm the head of programing."

"And yet Terry married her," I said.

"You know, that's always puzzled me. I would have thought he'd get what he wanted then dump her. I put it down to Kathleen's being more cunning than I thought.''

"She must have been just a little bit in love with Terry to take up with him when he was relatively unknown," I said.

Winston shrugged. "I think Terry was a long shot for her when she was feeling a little desperate. She'd been playing her hand for a few years by then, and still wasn't rich or famous, as we say.''

"Imagine that!" I said in mock horror. "But then why did such a well-suited pair ever get a divorce?''

"Oh, the years go by and I suppose you start looking for *real* love.''

"You think Kathleen and Terry ever found such a thing, separately or together?''

"I think what Kathleen has found is an endless succession of young studs. Really, I'm quite jealous! As for Terry, I always suspected that sex and love are not great motivating factors in his life. What he's after is power, straight and unadorned.''

"And yet the guy is funny," I said, coming to Terry's defense. To me, being funny covers a multitude of sins.

"Comedy!" Winston said with a sour look. "What better way to get someone in your power than to make him laugh? Don't you agree, Steve—the essence of comedy is to get the other guy's guard down. Then you move in for the kill.''

"Not necessarily," I told him. "Comedy is a way to explain the world. It's a philosophy. Maybe God created the universe so he could have a big laugh every few days.''

We joked around for a few more minutes. Then

Winnie said he had to leave to dress for dinner. We walked together along the corridor from the Polo Lounge back into the lobby.

"One thought," he said before heading toward his elevator. "You *are* determined not to leave this matter, as you should, in the capable hands of the police?"

"I'm determined," I told him determinedly.

"Then you might try to discover where Terry Cole was the night Bobby Dyer was killed."

"That's easy. Terry was busy being tranquil at Happy Valley."

"Are you sure? Is Happy Valley really a maximum security sort of place, or could someone like Terry come and go as he pleases?"

Winnie gave me a playful slap on the shoulder, one conspirator to another, and left me in the lobby of the Beverly Hills Hotel, all kinds of intriguing scenarios of murder running through my mind.

chapter 25

When I picked up my phone messages at the front desk, I saw that Detective Sergeant W.B. Walker had tried to reach me on three different occasions that day. Tessa Moore had also called in the morning, as well as three reporters, presumably hot on my trail for news.

Back in my bungalow, I said hello to my piano by playing a tune I'd been working on, more or less unconsciously. I didn't have any lyric yet, but the melody was haunting. I thought I might call it "The Happy Valley Waltz." We songwriters are always on the lookout for new material, wherever we find it.

Having convinced myself that, for all the murder and mayhem, there was still music in the world, I called the number Sergeant Walker had left for me. It turned out to be a non-emergency line to the Burbank police station.

"Hi, may I speak with Willie Buck Walker, please." Becoming a detective, you see, had made me cagey.

"Who?"

"You know, old Willie Buck—Detective Sergeant W.B. Walker. That's what the initials stand for, don't they?"

The lady chuckled but did not tell me the correct name. "Hold on, please," she said firmly, and she was gone.

"Good try, Mr. Allen," said the sergeant, "but Willie Buck is *not* the correct answer."

"Damn," I said. "Well, what's up, whoever you are?"

"That's what I'd like to ask you, sir. What do you know about someone shooting the hell out of a palm tree on Beverly Drive last Friday?"

"My goodness, not a palm tree!" I exclaimed. "Where will all this moral disintegration lead?"

"You may think this is funny," he said. "We do not. The BHPD pulled two nine-millimeter slugs out of a palm tree, and two more that were embedded in the lawn nearby."

"Oh?" I said noncommittally.

"And you know what else? The slugs were identical to the ones that killed Bobby Dyer. They came from the same gun."

That stopped my banter. Standing near my piano with the phone nestled up against my ear, I found I had to sit down.

"You can match the bullets that exactly?" I inquired.

"Indeed. No two gun barrels are exactly alike, and when the bullet travels through, it's left with striation marks that are as identifiable as fingerprints."

"Interesting."

"Yes, and it gets more so. The BHPD arrived at the scene in response to an anonymous phone call. When they started questioning the neighbors, they managed to locate a maid who had looked out an upstairs window when she heard the shots." He paused.

"So?"

"So when they asked her what—or whom—she saw, she said there was a guy in jogging clothes, and when they asked her what he looked like she said he looked a little like the TV comedian Steve Allen."

"A *little* like him?" I said weakly.

"Yep."

"You know, it's a funny thing," I said. "Ever since I got into TV, years ago, I've been hearing from people who look a lot like me. Some of them have sent me their pictures or they've come up to me on the street. In fact, one night, on the old *Tonight* show, four-hundred guys who looked remarkably like me showed up.''

''How did that happen?''

''Well, we'd announced for a week or so that on that night only men who looked like me could get in, and that's the way it turned out.''

''You don't say.''

I was beginning to wish I hadn't.

''Look,'' Walker said, ''can we just cut the crap here?''

''I suppose here would be as good a place as any,'' I said. ''But as long as it's crap-cutting time, it's probably also time to address each other on a first-name basis, don't you think? You can call me Steve.''

''And you can just call me Sergeant Walker,'' he said.

''I was expecting to hear maybe Wesley, or Wade.''

''Well, what I'm expecting to hear is a complete description of whatever the frig it was that happened in Beverly Hills. You realize, of course, that you're lucky to be alive.''

''Yes,'' I said.

''Why didn't you give me a call when this happened?'' he complained. ''I thought we agreed to be candid with each other.''

''I didn't think it was important,'' I told him weakly. ''Hell, the greenery took all the damage.''

''That's not the point. If you had called the police immediately we could have set up a perimeter around the area and maybe caught the bastard that was trying to kill you.''

This had not occurred to me. I felt it was time to be cooperative, so with no more prodding I described the shooting as clearly as I could remember. I realized I didn't have a lot of information to give W.B. about the person who had tried to deal me The Big Cancellation, as Raymond Chandler might have called it. After all, I had only a quick glimpse of a hand holding a pistol before I tripped and dropped my glasses.

"Let's talk about the car then. You say it was black."

"Yes, black—that I'm sure of."

"Was it a new car? Old?"

"New. At least it seemed shiny, sort of glossy. It looked expensive, I should say."

"If you had to guess a make, what's the first name that comes to mind?"

"A BMW," I told him, "maybe a Mercedes. Or a Jag."

"How about a Rolls Royce?" the sergeant asked sarcastically. I had listed the most common cars in Beverly Hills.

"I'm nearsighted without my glasses," I admitted. "Everything was a bit of a blur."

He wanted me to go over the whole story again, from start to finish. It was boring to repeat it, but I suppose this was a tried and true police MO.

"Now that we've covered the how, I think we can go on to the why, Mr. Allen."

"Why?"

"Exactly. Why would someone take shots at you?"

"I think that's obvious," I told him with a touch of pride. "The killer knows I'm hot on his trail and closing in fast. He's afraid of me, you see, and wants to get me before I get him."

"Him or her," the sergeant corrected.

"If you say so." Actually it was difficult enough for me to imagine an actual man as a murderer—to picture a woman was almost impossible. Chivalry, you see, is not completely dead.

"Of course, you could have been the target all the time. The shooting in Beverly Hills might have been an attempt to make up for missing you Monday night."

"You're just trying to burst my bubble."

"I'm trying to warn you, Mr. Allen. If the shooting Friday was the *second* attempt on your life, you know what they say about the third time."

"Yeah?" I said, treating W.B. to a version of my tough-guy, Edward G. Robinson imitation. "Listen, Sergeant, I've survived forty years in show business. After that, bullets are just a slight disturbance."

chapter 26

The other message was from Tessa Moore. I gave her a call after hanging up on W.B., and we agreed to have lunch the next day at the Bistro Gardens.

The Bistro, as you may know, is one of those posh dinner spots for the flamboyantly in-crowd. The Bistro Gardens, its sister restaurant, is only a few doors down the street on North Canon Drive, and does for lunch what big brother does for dinner. Generally, I prefer the more low-profile places. The Gardens is a place to see and be seen, for the famous to flaunt their fame and the gossips to lurk behind the shrubbery, pen or ear in hand.

I arrived at twelve-thirty sharp—I have a slight fixation about being on time. Tessa was twenty minutes late. Sitting at the table by myself, in the shade of the covered garden—dictating a few notes into my ever-present micro-tape recorder and munching on a breadstick—I realized I should have allowed for Tessa not to be on time. She arrived finally with a grand and chaotic entrance, making certain, I suppose, that all eyes would be upon her.

She was wearing clothes I hardly know how to describe: blue jeans set with sparkling rhinestones and a jacket that seemed to be made from multicolored feathers—a Brazilian rain forest may well have been raped so that Tessa Moore could make a spectacular lunchtime entrance into the Bistro Gardens.

Her hair, as usual, was sticking out in at least a few directions. It was the basic I've-just-put-my-finger-in-the-electric-socket look. She had done something to the color since I had last seen her. There was a kind of orange glow to the spikes, as though she had sprayed the ends with phosphorescent paint. Actually, her hair and multicolored jacket went together very nicely.

Tessa's entrance was complicated by the fact that she tried to enter the restaurant with a dog—a miniature terrier on a leash. It was the size of a large rat, with long hair covering its eyes. I can't imagine how the poor animal was able to see, and with Tessa leading him, I suppose it was a matter of the blind leading the blind.

Celebrity though she was, the *maitre d'* would not allow her little dog into the Bistro Gardens.

"But Wolfie is cleaner than half the people here, darling," she objected loudly. "He sleeps with me; we eat off the same plate."

The *maitre d'* had a very strained smile. "I'm so sorry, Miss Moore, but the health department, you understand, would have an absolute cow."

This went on longer than necessary. I noticed a columnist nearby taking notes. At last, Tessa agreed that a parking attendant might keep dear Wolfie in the lot next door if the kitchen would prepare, perhaps, a small steak *tartare* for his lunch. She gave the parking attendant a twenty-dollar bill for his trouble and then came slinking through the restaurant in my direction, stopping to kiss cheeks and accept hugs along the way. An entrance like this was fascinating to watch. Tessa elevated the restaurant experience to a work of art and a circus at the same time.

"Steve, darling. Have you been dreaming about me?"

"I've only been waiting for you," I told her.

Her laughter rattled wineglasses across the garden.

She ordered a double Johnny Walker Black Label while holding onto the waiter's hand, almost pulling him down into her lap. I ordered a Perrier. I had a feeling I was going to need all my faculties.

For Tessa, the theatrics could be turned on and off at will. As soon as our drinks came, she pulled her chair closer, lowered her voice, and tried to make herself invisible to her fans at the other tables.

"Say, Steverino," she said, "you've been having a time of it, haven't you? And poor Hal! How tacky of him to die like that your first night out!"

There was no suitable comment I could make. I merely shrugged.

"Hal was such a shy young man. So unusual and *so* sincere," she lamented. "I was always telling him he should go out and have more fun, poor darling, but he was worried about cholesterol and not getting his eight hours of sleep."

"You knew him?"

"I know *every*body, darling! Hal and I did a film together. Don't tell me you missed *Machine Man?*"

"Somehow I *did,* Tessa. Was that the picture where Hal played the android?"

"Mmm, a mechanical man where *everything* worked. I was the Queen from Outer Space. One of my better roles."

"When you say outer space, do you mean Pluto, by any chance?"

"What a strange question! Actually, it was always a little vague where I was from. But why do you ask?"

"Oh, I'm eternally curious," I told her. "Tell me more about Hal."

"What's there to tell? The girls were wild about his pectorals, but his ding-dong he kept to himself."

"Was Hal . . . you know."

"Gay? No. The idea would have shocked him. He was really abysmally straight. The milk-and-cookies type. Or in his case, it was carrot juice, sprouts, and handfuls of pills. As soon as he left the set, he'd head over to the health club to work out. Then it was home to beddy-bye, all by his lonesome."

"Which health club did he belong to, do you know?"

"The Beverly Hills, of course. I imagine his agent would insist, don't you think? There's no sense in looking like a million bucks if you aren't hanging out with the right crowd."

"Did Hal ever talk about friends," I asked. "Or perhaps enemies?"

"Oh, you're playing detective, you droll dear! How cute."

"A cute detective," I said glumly. "Well, I haven't learned a hell of a lot so far. But I *am* interested, you know. I feel responsible."

"Of course you do! What a terrible experience it must have been for you!"

"Worse for Hal, I'm afraid."

"Yes." She sighed. "Well, he didn't talk very much about friends. There was his mother, of course, and Marvin."

"Marvin?"

"His trainer at the health club. Marvin was always a great inspiration for Hal. A role model."

"What about his mother?" I asked. "Do you know where she lived?"

"Kansas, I think. Or was it Indiana? One of those Midwestern places whose names I can never remember."

We had ordered rather elaborate salads that came complete with edible flowers. When the waiter left us, I brought up a delicate subject.

"Tessa, my dear, I understand you had a short . . . relationship with Terry."

"Relationship?" she shrieked. "Oh, it was short, all right! About two and a half inches! I'm such a bad girl. I never should have done such a thing, but I was desperate."

"You desperate? I always thought you had your stable of admirers."

"How sweet of you to notice. But no, it wasn't sex I was desperate for—not with poor Terry, for God's sake! I was hoping I could be a regular on his show, do a five- or ten-minute spot every few nights. Like Joan Rivers on the Carson show. Poor Terry's so awfully lazy I thought it would appeal to him—he'd be able to do less work and more drinking."

"But he said no?"

"He wished to consider the proposition in his boudoir—actually, it was the back of his limousine, to be honest. Of course, I should have known it all along. He was afraid of the competition."

"You would have stolen the show," I told her gallantly.

"If only I *could* steal a show." She sighed, suddenly vulnerable. "It's been three years now since I was canceled."

Tessa looked suitably tragic. I told her it was a hard fate to be canceled. She ordered another Johnny Walker, letting the waiter know he had absolutely saved her life.

"I have so much to say. So many laughs to give. I just know that America will never forgive me if I take cancellation lying down."

"Tessa, my dear, why don't you come on *my* show this week?"

"Really? You lovely man! You're not just feeling sorry for me?"

"You'll be a hit," I assured her. "Our ratings will go through the roof."

"And those child-molesting morons who run the network will know how badly they need me, don't you think? If the Smothers Brothers and Perry Mason can return after all these years, why not me?''

"That's the attitude," I told her. Comedians have fragile egos that must be continually coached. I asked for the bill, realizing this was the reason Tessa had wanted to see me—to get herself on my show—and now our business was done.

She looked out dreamily over the gentle garden, not seeing the well-dressed, golden patrons or the quietly hovering waiters. Her mouth was set in an unattractive way, and I had a feeling I was getting a glimpse of the real Tessa Moore, if such a thing existed.

"I'd do anything to get my own show again," she said softly. "I think I'd even murder someone, darling. Wouldn't you?''

chapter 27

I went back to my bungalow and tried to take a nap after lunch but found myself staring at the ceiling instead. I was intrigued by the thought of the two dead men—Hal and Bobby—both so interested in bodybuilding. Would Sam Spade let such a coincidence stand unexamined?

I found my West Los Angeles phone directory and called the Beverly Hills Health Club, asked to speak with Marvin, and was put on hold for a few minutes, with Muzak piped over the phone into my ear. It isn't my favorite way to listen to music. We were halfway through a lovely Irving Berlin ballad when a hoarse voice broke in.

"Marvin here." It came across as a muscular whisper.

"This is Steve Allen," I told him. "Do you know who I am?"

"Yeah," came the whisper. "You're the man who killed a perfect machine."

"It was an accident," I assured him. I spent a few minutes trying to break through Marvin's initial hostility. It seems I had destroyed what he had created. I told him I certainly could understand why he was angry. Eventually, he agreed to see me for a few minutes later that afternoon, but he didn't seem thrilled by the prospect. I had a premonition he probably wouldn't ask for my autograph.

Cass was busy auditioning for the part of a senior citizen in a McDonald's commercial, and far be it from me to interfere with a budding show business career. So I took a taxi to the southern reaches of Beverly Hills where the Health Club had been in business a long time before the current exercise fad had taken hold. The Beverly Hills Health Club was a place with a long history. Big stars like William Holden had once tried to get in shape for pictures here after long alcoholic binges, sharing saunas with cigar-smoking producers and talking deals every step of the way. At one time you might have found Rock Hudson getting worked over on the massage table after a hard day on the set, swapping stories with John Frankenheimer or Cary Grant.

Today there was a new and younger crowd. Passing through the main exercise hall, I glimpsed some familiar faces from TV working on their various limbering routines to the various strains of loud garbage-rock—all rhythm, no melody. Marvin was the head instructor. I found him in a small, windowless office that smelled vaguely of sweat and massage oil. He was a trim man in his early forties with blond hair cut like a page boy and blue eyes that were looking at me in a none-too-friendly way. He was wearing a blue-and-white-striped tank-top shirt that revealed massive shoulders.

"I'm Steve Allen," I told him.

"I imagined you were," he said glumly.

"I'm really sorry about Hal, and I'm doing everything in my power to find out what happened."

"I don't know how I can help you," he said. "I told Sergeant Walker everything I know."

I was disappointed W.B. had managed to get here first. "Tell me about Hal," I asked. "I want to know what he was like."

"There's not much to tell. He was a serious young man, dedicated to a perfect physique. Frankly, it was a relief to instruct such a guy, after some of the dilettantes I get around here."

"What about his personal life?"

"He didn't have one. All he did was work."

"That's what everybody keeps telling me."

"It's true," came the hoarse whisper. "That guy could have gone on to become Mr. Universe."

"Wow. There was someone else killed last week, a fellow by the name of Bobby Dyer. He was into bodybuilding too. Do you remember his ever coming here?"

"The sergeant asked that question, too."

"Did he?" I was slightly miffed. "And what was the answer?"

Marvin treated me to an eloquent shrug. "Sure, Bobby Dyer came in here a lot. Why shouldn't he? He was a member."

That surprised me somehow. "Were Bobby and Hal friends?"

"Not that I could see particularly. As I told you, Hal didn't hang out."

"Well, did they talk at all when they exercised?"

"Mr. Allen, serious guys don't talk when they exercise."

"I'll remember that," I said. "So Bobby was pretty dedicated, too?"

"I didn't say that. Bobby Dyer was the kinda guy just in it for the short range. He didn't really care about his total health, you know—he just wanted to look good at the beach or in the sack. Some of the other members used to complain about him a little."

"In what way?"

"He was always trying to wheel and deal 'em in the sauna. He was trying to put together a film, or so he said. No one took him too seriously. Frankly, a guy like that shouldn't even have been allowed in this place. He didn't have the stature in the business. Hell, he couldn't even afford the dues."

"Someone else paid for him?" I was beginning to find this conversation more fascinating all the time.

"Yeah."

Marvin was getting on my nerves, but I played him gently. "Who?" I asked, soft as a song. "Who was paying Bobby Dyer's dues?"

"The same person who sponsored his membership."

I wanted to wring Marvin's neck, but it was too thick, murder wasn't nice, and I needed his information too badly. "Who?" I asked again. I was beginning to feel like an owl.

"Why, Mr. Cole, of course." I felt a small shiver.

"You sure? Terry Cole sponsored Bobby, paid his dues here?"

"That's what I told you, isn't it? Without a big shot like Mr. Cole behind him, a dude like Dyer would have been out of here a long time ago."

"Do you know why Mr. Cole took such an interest?"

"Haven't the slightest."

I was standing in front of Marvin's desk—he had never invited me to sit down—starting to feel good about my powers of detection.

"By the way, did you give this information to Sergeant Walker?"

"About Mr. Cole? No, the guy never asked."

I was feeling better all the time. I decided to go for broke. "Sergeant Walker . . . when he was here, I imagine he introduced himself to you, didn't he?"

"Of course. He showed me his ID too."

"He didn't by any chance tell you what his initials stood for, W.B. ?"

Marvin gave me as blank a look as I have ever gotten from a human being.

"What difference do his initials make, for Chrissake? We weren't here to shoot the breeze. Jeez, some guys!"

My lucky streak was over. Every gambler knows when it's time to stop.

chapter 28

Hollywood is a remarkably small town. Almost everybody's worked together, been represented by the same agencies, intermarried, bred, or gone to the same divorce lawyer. Or so it seems on bad days. The interconnections between my little group of suspects were beginning to be astonishing.

Tessa Moore had made a picture with Hal Hoaglund, who had gone to the same athletic club as Bobby Dyer, who in turn had been mysteriously patronized by Terry Cole, who generally didn't do favors for anyone. An interesting web. I wondered how many more connections I would find if I kept on digging.

I began my second week of shows with a TV cop, a Broadway playwright, a lady gossip columnist, and a man who trained animals for the movies and brought on stage this year's most recognizable mutt. The dog stole the show, but that's show biz. It wasn't the first time I was upstaged by some son of a bitch. (Okay, that's a lousy joke, but at least I didn't use it on the air.)

I was leading a double life, as usual. By night, urbane talk-show host, by day—and sometimes later— undercover detective. Steve Linder, our young assistant director, was turning into a friend as well as a source of information. I caught up with him in the wings during the long station break before the canine came out.

"Tell me about Bobby Dyer," I asked, having come to feel more and more that he was the key to this entire mystery. "What sort of guy was he?"

"Your basic pain in the ass," Linder said. "Loud, pushy, lazy. Most of us couldn't imagine how he scored the job of associate producer, much less hung on to it. As far as I could see, Bobby never did very much of anything except make a lot of noise."

"Did he have many friends here?"

"I wouldn't say friends. He liked to strut around, make loud, usually dirty jokes. Some of the guys responded, I guess. Personally, I always found him to be a jerk."

"Did he and Terry Cole seem to be close?"

The AD shrugged. "I don't think so. Mr. Cole didn't yell at Bobby, which I suppose was unusual now that I stop and think about it. He sure as hell yells at everybody else."

"Why do you suppose Bobby got this special treatment?"

"It wasn't his genius for hard work, I can tell you that."

"Then why?"

"I always figured Bobby was the sort of guy who knew where the bodies were buried."

"Blackmail?" It was amazing how easily such words came to my lips now. One innocent week ago I never would have thought of such a thing.

Steve Linder made a vaguely Italian gesture with his hands. "Bobby used to hint at all kinds of inside knowledge he couldn't divulge. I always thought he was trying to act important."

"But maybe he did know something?" I mused. I wondered what dark secrets he might have been privy to. "How long has Bobby been working on this show?"

"Forever. Way before my time, at least. I think he went back to the beginning."

"Fascinating. Do you know anything about his personal life away from here?"

"Only what he told us. He used to brag about the important people he knew, the fancy parties he went to, big-name actresses he screwed—you know the routine. Personally, I never believed a word of it."

"Did he ever mention the Beverly Hills Health Club?" I tried.

"Oh, yeah. All the time. That's supposedly where he hung out with all the big shots. Intimate talks in the sauna, all that jazz."

"Did he say anything about meeting Hal Hoaglund there?" It was a hopeful thought, but Linder shook his head.

"I can see what you're getting at, but no. Hal was

maybe the only celebrity in Hollywood he *didn't* claim to be buddies with."

It seemed I was barking up the wrong tree. Speaking of which, I then saw my next guest coming on stage, tongue lolling out of the side of his mouth, tail wagging.

Of course, I fell in love with him at once, being perhaps the world's biggest pushover for dogs. Big dogs, little dogs, classy dogs, dumb-looking dogs. Believe it or not, I've given a lot of thought to this, when perhaps I should have been giving thought to more weighty subject matter. Since childhood I've wondered why dogs love human beings more than they love other dogs. Dogs may have a sexual interest in each other, and mothers are moved by instinct to care about their pups, but that's about the extent of love relationships in a dog's world. As regards their human masters, by way of contrast, dogs seem to be as dippy about us as we are about them. In my own case the degree of attachment is perhaps odd because I'm a bit more wary about our furry little friends than are most people for the reason that during childhood I was bitten by them in several instances. The most serious incident happened when I was two years old and was standing on a curb in New York City next to my mother, who happened to be wearing a raccoon coat. She later conjectured that the police dog who was next to us, also waiting to cross the street, became confused when the animal fur rubbed against his own coat. The dog's response, in any event, was to turn and take my face in his mouth. To this day I have a small scar on the left side of my mouth and one on the right ear, caused by the same slashing bite.

Despite this horrifying experience, I have a special affection for dogs. My next guest and I were instantly the best of friends, and I returned to my desk to get on with the show.

chapter 29

Sonny Melnik came down to my dressing room after the show. He was wearing a bright yellow one-piece playsuit with white Italian loafers and no socks. Dressed for leisure, he seemed strangely ill at ease.

"Great show!" he said, his nervous little eyes darting about everywhere but my face.

"Come on and sit down," I offered, gesturing to the enormous entertaining area of my dressing room that I never used. "Have some smoked salmon, a glass of champagne, maybe an Oriental massage."

"A Scotch, I think."

"You know where it is, Sonny."

Melnik dealt himself a Scotch on the rocks from the wet bar and then made himself comfortable on the white leather sofa that was shaped like a crescent moon. He crossed one stubby leg over the other and tried to smile. It came out more a painful grimace.

"This is sure a swell dressing room, ain't it?"

"Better than swell," I told him. "You could build the next space shuttle here."

"I talked with Terry today. He's a little upset."

"Terry upset? The king of tranquility?"

"Steve, I wish you hadn't gone up to Santa Barbara like that. You don't realize how difficult Terry can be at times."

"I just wanted to see how he was getting on. What seems to be the problem?"

Sonny looked even more unhappy. "This isn't personal, man, but Terry doesn't want *anyone* to host his show while he's out."

"Doesn't that leave a rather large void on late-night television?"

"You're telling me." He sighed. Sonny had a mournful, martyred expression on his pudgy little face. "You don't know what it's like, dealing with Terry on one hand, the network on the other. And here's me—caught in the middle."

"What does the network have to say?"

"They want you to stay. Terry's been taking a hell of a lot of time off this season, if you want to know the truth. We've already used up our quotient of reruns. Any more and we'll be in violation of contract."

I made a small sympathetic noise with my tongue.

"You don't know how tough this is on me, Steve. A lot of people don't know this, but I'm a pretty sensitive guy."

"I can see that."

"What I am, Steve—I'm the kind of guy who stops to smell the flowers."

"I imagine you have to hide that side of you in this business, Sonny, or guys would take advantage of your good nature."

"I'm glad you can see that."

"So what are we going to do about this situation with Terry?" I asked. I actually didn't care that much. I could continue doing the show, or I could walk away. So far it hadn't exactly been the height of my career.

"I wish you hadn't gone to Santa Barbara," he said again, with a small nasal whine. "I was hoping to keep him in the dark."

"I guess that's the way to deal with a guy like Terry Cole, all right. Keep him in the dark, if you can. Like the way you passed on your bartender duties to Bobby Dyer."

Sonny grinned at me and gave a rebellious wink. "Terry would have killed me if he'd found out about that."

I shook my head. "Must be tough. But why such a big deal over who put the vodka in the fridge? Hell, as long as it got there each night, what difference did it make if Bobby, or the man in the moon, put it there?"

"It *doesn't* make a difference, that's the point—except Terry wanted it that way and he insists on getting his own way."

"You know, this doesn't sound too rational to me, Sonny. Are you certain Terry hasn't flipped out?"

"That would be a relief for us all," he said with a sigh, "but Terry's as sane as you or me, Steve."

"Hey, leave me out. The last time I saw him, he was talking about little guys from Pluto and feeding invisible ducks."

Sonny waved this aside as if of no major concern. "He's a comedian. Nothing personal, but you know how it is—guys like that live pretty close to the edge."

"Sonny, my impression of Terry Cole is that he's already fallen off the edge without a parachute."

"Oh, he'll be all right. Happy Valley will mellow him out and send him back to us, like they always do."

"He's been there before?"

"Several times—but don't tell anyone, okay? It wouldn't do any of us a lot of good. Fortunately, a big star like Terry, he doesn't have to function in the real world."

"Maybe not."

"Hey, it's not easy. The main thing is to get him in front of the cameras five days a week, at his desk with the Cajun vodka as his support system. He can be as crazy as he wants there and the public eats it up."

"But what about the rest of his life?"

"The last few years, I've been handling a lot of the practical details."

Sonny wanted me to know how misused and unappreciated he was. The millions who adored Terry Cole each week at eleven-thirty didn't even know there was a Sonny Melnik behind the scenes propping up their hero.

"So what are we going to do about the show?" I asked.

Sonny cracked his knuckles thoughtfully and told me it wasn't easy having the weight of such decisions upon his ungainly shoulders.

"He doesn't have a TV set up there at Happy Valley. Let's just go on for a couple of days and see if we

163

can sneak you by," he suggested. "If he finds out, hell . . . I guess I can blame the network."

A lovely man, Sonny Melnik, always willing to pass the buck.

"I wouldn't want to add to your problems, Sonny. Just let me know—I can retire from the late-night-host business any time."

Sonny looked alarmed. As I suspected, he needed me to fulfill his obligations with the network.

"Steve, you're no problem. What you are, you're a prince. And I mean that from the bottom of my heart."

I told him I was deeply touched, sentiments like this coming from a man of his profound sensitivity. He swallowed his drink, ice and all, stood up, and slapped me playfully on the shoulder.

"But you'll stay away from Happy Valley, won't you, kid? I mean, why rock the barge?"

"Okay. And by the way, how did Terry reach you about all this? I thought they kept everyone fairly incommunicado up there."

"Oh, you know Terry. Those people at Happy Valley are no match for him."

"Oh?"

"Sure. He had his limousine drive him down to my house in Beverly Hills last night. The doorbell rang, and there was Terry—at two o'clock in the morning. Does he care if I get any sleep, I ask you?"

"So Terry can come and go from Happy Valley whenever he likes?"

Sonny raised his shoulders. "He was back in his room by the morning. They probably never knew he was gone."

"How sneaky of him."

He put his glass down on the bar and was ready to leave, but I detained him with another question.

"I'm curious about Bobby Dyer," I said as casually as I could. "He seemed to get special treatment around here. I gather Terry even paid his dues at the Beverly Hills Health Club."

Sonny suddenly seemed very much on guard. "Yes?" he asked. "What of it?"

"Well, I'm just curious, that's all. It seems a little out of character for Terry to do anything nice for his crew."

Sonny gave me a slow, nasty smile. "Bobby goes way back," he said mysteriously.

"I've heard that. All the way back to the beginning, I was told."

"Before that, as a matter of fact. Bobby worked for Winston Dane. We kept him on."

I was surprised. "Oh? What did he do for Winston?"

"He was on the sound crew—a boom operator, if I remember right."

"Did you keep on many of the crew from Dane's time?"

"Not many."

"Then why Bobby?"

The venomous smile blossomed into a poisoned leer.

"You might ask Kathleen that question. I'd be curious what she'd tell you."

"Kathleen Cole? What does she have to do with Bobby Dyer?"

"A good question."

I tried to ask Sonny more, but he would give me

nothing but a nasty and knowing wink. He hissed good night, then oozed toward the door, padding off down the hallway in his yellow playsuit and soft Gucci loafers.

chapter 30

I had kept on digging and I'd found more connections, all right! Tessa had made a movie with Hal, who had gone to the same health club as Bobby, who had some as-yet-unknown connection to Kathleen, who both once upon a time had worked for Winston Dane. Not only that, but the man in the center of all this, Terry Cole, could come and go as he pleased from his Happy Valley retreat, and thus had no alibi after all for the murder of Bobby Dyer—or Hal Hoaglund, for that matter.

It was still confusing but neater. I was pleased with myself for finding out all these things. It wasn't until I awoke the next morning that I realized the obvious: the point of a murder investigation is to narrow down the field, not expand the list of suspects *ad infinitum*. Despite my cleverness, I was further from solving this case than when I started.

I wasn't certain how to proceed. In the back of my

mind, I knew I should call Detective Sergeant Walker and pass on the benefits of my expert detection. I'm not sure exactly what held me back. I suppose I wanted to wrap up the case and hand it over to W.B. on a silver tray.

"Well, my dear sergeant," I'd say in my best William Powell manner, "here it is, a stunning piece of detective work. Oh, don't bother to thank me! And please feel free to call again whenever you run into trouble."

I tried to phone Winston Dane at his room at the Beverly Hills Hotel, but there was no answer. I managed to get Kathleen instead, at her house in Trancas. She suggested I drive down to the beach for a late breakfast. I was slightly worried I might end up as the main course, but we sleuths have to take our chances in this jungle of wild women.

Cass was nearby and available. He hadn't gotten the job on the McDonald's commercial but was philosophical about it. It seems he spit out a wad of chewing tobacco into the casting director's wastepaper basket a few minutes into the interview. The casting director, alas, was a young woman recently arrived from Vassar, and she had no appreciation of Hollywood cowboys. The audition ended abruptly.

"At least I was myself this time," Cass told me as we were driving west on Sunset. "One of these days, the right part's gonna come my way."

"That's right, keep the faith," I said. In my mind, I was putting his last line to music.

Maybe I would start with a nice C-minor chord . . . *One of these days,* as Sophie Tucker had sung . . . go to C-minor/major seventh, which is to say, add the B-flat

167

to the chord . . . *One of these crazy days* . . . C-minor seventh . . . *The right part's* . . . C-minor sixth . . . *Gonna come my way!* And here I hit a luscious A-flat major seventh, a chord so beautiful they'll be throwing Grammys and weeping in the aisles . . .

"Steve, you got that faraway look."

"Thank you, thank you! I couldn't have written this song without the help of my friend and driver, Jimmy Cassidy."

"Huh?"

Cass gave me a sideways look and kept driving.

"I think that *Guinness Book of World Records* entry has gone to your head," he said.

It's true, there is such an entry. The Guinness people had found out that I'd written more songs than anybody else alive so they duly noted the fact. I wish I could take credit for it all, but I'd be lying if I did. The thing is that the songs just come to me, while I'm in the shower, onstage, sometimes even asleep. "This Could Be The Start of Something Big," in fact, came to me in a dream. Thank God I was able to remember the melody and the first few lines of the lyric when I awakened that morning.

A few numbers over the years have come to mind while I was on the right-hand seat of Cass's burgundy Cadillac limousine.

I had several lines completed by the time we hit the Pacific Coast Highway, and was into the bridge by the time we passed Malibu. The final section was missing one last rhyme by the time we pulled up in front of Kathleen's futuristic beehive.

I stepped up to the door, absorbed with the task of

finding something that would rhyme with *tries*. Skies? Lies?

"Hello, Steve," came Kathleen's elegant voice over the speaker by the door.

"Thighs," I said experimentally.

"Steve, how provocative!"

"Oh, not yours," I told her hastily. Unfortunately, when you wear as many hats as I do, your realities tend to overlap. I was blushing already and hadn't even managed to get inside her front door. There was a small electronic buzz and I did just that. Kathleen met me on the landing. She was dressed, thank goodness, looking very Grecian in white muslin pants and a loose peasant blouse to match. Her long blond hair was pulled back to emphasize her classic features and golden tan. When she kissed me on the cheek, she smelled faintly of jasmine.

We went downstairs to a sunny breakfast room where a glass door opened to the beach. She offered me a Bellini, which is fresh peach juice and champagne. There were croissants on the table and a bowl of fresh fruit and a vase of freshly picked red and lavender flowers. A young Mexican girl with a shy smile carried in a bowl of cracked Dungeness crab on ice. Kathleen was not one to stint on her personal pleasures. Outside the half-opened glass door, I could hear the hypnotic sound of the surf breaking and receding on the sand.

"Crab always reminds me of an insect," she said, breaking off a leg, "a great spider of the sea."

I sipped my champagne slowly, wanting to keep my head clear. Kathleen was smiling at me as inscrutably as any Mona Lisa. "Well, darling, how's your little mystery? Are you finding all kinds of nasty evil lurking in dark passages?''

"What I've found," I told her, "are a lot of interconnecting people. How they fit together *is* still a mystery."

"But this is a small town," she reminded me. "All the people who count know each other, and may even have been lovers at one time."

How incestuous, I thought, glad that this was not my Hollywood. "Like you and Bobby Dyer," I suggested, making a wild guess.

Did Kathleen's eyes open just a bit wider before she regained her poise? She took a thoughtful sip on her Bellini and gazed out the sparkling clean window at the Pacific Ocean.

"Bobby Dyer," she said, "now there's a name that takes me back."

"He was—what?—a boom operator for Winston, when you did the makeup?''

"Yes, and I shared a house with three other girls in North Hollywood. We were all determined to be filthy rich and famous one day. Ah, those were the good old days, Steve."

"Were they, really?"

"Sure. It was a ball to be young and on the make— for life, I mean. God, when I think about all the funny times! You know, being rich and living among the famous didn't turn out to be nearly as much fun as I used to imagine."

"You were ambitious?" I prodded gently.

"Of course. I had no real talents, I realized—I couldn't sing or dance or act. I wasn't even terribly good with makeup. So I put my hopes into finding a rich man. It's a rather tedious and commonplace story, I suppose."

"So where did Bobby fit into this?"

"He didn't. That's the point. But he was lots of fun then and . . . well, rather good in bed if that's what you're hinting at. It was one of the few times I threw caution to the winds."

"You were in love with Bobby then?"

"Oh, I wouldn't say that. It was just a youthful fling, I guess. Bobby became a bit ridiculous toward the end, but when I first knew him, he had an infectious energy—we used to go dancing all night long, and then drive to the beach and drink champagne until the sun came up. It was all reckless and young—but it didn't mean a thing. I finally realized Bobby would always be a loser. When it got right down to it, he was your basic Hollywood hustler, and as he grew older, his boyish charm began to fade."

"How long did you . . . er . . . date?"

"Oh, it was a very on and off sort of thing that lasted a couple of years."

"Before you met Terry?"

"Mostly. I knew Terry was going to be very big so I decided he was the man for me. But he was always such a bore."

"Even, uh, romantically?"

"Especially. He was the sort to roll over and go to sleep the second *he* was satisfied."

"So you went to Bobby for consolation?"

"Sometimes. I'm a woman with deep appetites," she confessed, giving me a look that could burn a forest to ash.

"Did Terry know?"

She shrugged. "Not in the beginning. Later in our marriage, it didn't matter much to either of us what the other did."

"That's sad," I said. "I'm trying to keep the chronology straight. So you were seeing Bobby back in the Winston Dane days. And when did you meet Terry?"

"It must have been 1962. You were just starting your own crazy series for Westinghouse, down on Vine Street. Terry was in town to see about some radio deal. Actually, Bobby and I were together at Ciro's with a couple of friends, and Terry was at the next table. Some of our group knew the people Terry was with, we all got drunk together, and the rest is history."

"So Terry must have known you had something going with Bobby?"

"He never said anything. I always assumed he didn't care, or that a man like Bobby would be so reduced in importance in contrast to him that it just wouldn't matter."

"Terry wasn't jealous?"

"He was too self-absorbed to care about anything I might do, as long as I was there for him."

I chewed on a warm, moist piece of croissant and tried to think of a polite way to phrase my next question. There was none, so I went ahead and asked it anyway. "I had a drink with Winnie the other day—he seems to think you were instrumental in giving him the boot and getting the job for Terry. Is that true?"

She laughed. "Oh, my! Did Winnie actually say that? Poor old thing. It's not really true, you know. At least about giving Winnie the boot. I never had that much power, and I was always fond of the poor dear. No, Winnie has no one to blame but himself. He let his ratings slip, and you know what that's like—instant death.''

"But he was let go on a morals clause," I objected. "Fired in the middle of the season, if I remember."

"That was just a convenient way to get rid of him. The network couldn't care less, my dear, if Winnie was screwing giraffes or young boys. The real problem was his dwindling audience."

"So that left Terry with an opening. I imagine you were able to advance his cause."

Kathleen smiled. "How could I do that? Li'l ol' me, the makeup girl?"

"Somehow I think you'd be able to find a way."

She laughed, not her elegant, silvery laugh of a Hollywood wife, but something more earthy and dangerous. "All right," she said, "you got me, Doctor. I see I'll have to tell you my deep, dark secrets."

"Think of me as a kindly old grandfather," I suggested. "You'll feel so much better."

"Yes? Well then, I had a gentleman friend back in those days whose name I won't mention. He was on the board of directors for the network. He was also married. For a time there I thought I could get him to leave his wife and become my knight in shining armor—rescue me from sharing a house with three other girls. But it was not meant to be. Poor, dumb, virginal me! I was seduced and abandoned. However, I was able to prevail upon the dirty old goat's sense of guilt to get my Terry a chance in the big time."

"Terry must have been grateful."

"Wasn't he, though! So grateful, he asked my fair hand in marriage. That was our deal."

"Your *deal?*" I exclaimed.

"Certainly. You don't think I would do all that work for nothing! I made Terry promise he'd marry me if I got him on the show."

"Weren't you afraid he'd back out after he got what he wanted?"

She gave me a smile that would have done credit to Lady Macbeth. "Oh, Terry knew better than to try to double-cross me."

My croissant stuck in my throat and I was suddenly not at all hungry.

"How long did you keep seeing Bobby?"

"Oh, that was all over ten years ago, at least. Bobby got a little too old for me, you know, and rather abrasive. I lent him money one time too many for it to be at all romantic—but I was sorry to hear he died."

"Were you? But why did Terry keep him around all these years?"

"That I can't imagine. Trying to figure out Terry Cole's reasons for doing things is a rather uphill struggle. I gave up years ago."

"Then you don't have any idea why Terry was paying Bobby's dues at the Beverly Hills Health Club?"

"Not the foggiest, dear Steve. And you know what? This may sound terrible . . ."

"Go ahead, say it."

"I really don't give a damn."

chapter 31

It was a dismal-looking afternoon at the beach. A ceiling of low clouds from the ocean mixed with our local smog to form something some Californians call "smaze." Unlike good old-fashioned haze or smog, smaze has an unhealthy yellow-brownish tinge that makes you consider moving to the outback of Australia.

Today the sky and ocean merged into a snarl of depressing gray, and the air was close and dense and still. Cass brought us out of Broad Beach Road onto the Pacific Coast Highway. The Caddy's big V-8 engine purred softly, pulling us up the long hill after Zuma and past the turnoff to Paradise Cove.

"Steve, I can't swear to it, but I think we're being followed."

"Really?"

"Look behind us—see that black Buick fifty yards or so back in the right lane? I have the damnedest feeling he was with us on the way out here from Beverly Hills. I first noticed him when he followed us through a yellow light going through Bel Air, but I didn't pay any—"

I looked out the rear window to see the kind of anonymous black American car I'd have had trouble telling from a million others. At least it wasn't a *fuzzy* black car, but of course, now I had my glasses on.

"You think it's the same one?"

"I don't know, man. That's what I'm telling you. But it could be."

I watched the car through the rear window for a while. It seemed to be matching pace with us, but since we were both doing about five miles over the speed limit, this wasn't a remarkable coincidence.

"Slow down, Cass. See if he passes us."

Cass slowed down from near sixty to forty-five. The black Buick gained on us, then slowed himself so that the distance didn't change.

"Pretty suspicious," I said.

"It could be nothing."

We drove in silence in our two-car formation until we came down the grade toward the Malibu Colony. Both of us now knew this was not nothing. There wasn't much traffic on the road on an overcast weekday like this and it was too unlikely for the black car to be matching our pace so exactly. The light in the intersection was about to turn red.

"Pull off here," I told Cass, *"fast!"*

We left a little rubber going around the corner, made a fast right turn toward the gas station, and feinted a move in the direction of a nearby supermarket. I couldn't see the Buick behind us anymore. We drove through the supermarket parking lot and then pulled around toward the rear of the Malibu Colony Coffee Shop. We sat at a booth and drank some coffee and felt fairly pleased with ourselves. But when we got on the road again ten minutes later, the black Buick was there again, fifty yards back, trailing us with a deadly patience.

My heart was beating slightly faster than usual. Too many people had been dying recently for me to be nonchalant. I saw Cass's mouth tighten as he looked up into the rearview mirror.

"She-it," he said.

We passed the Malibu pier and were coming up to the turnoff to Topanga Canyon on the left.

"Cass, I think it's time to take evasive action."

"I think *you* should tighten your seat belt," he told me with a wink.

I took his advice, strapping myself in, and that's the last sane thing I remember for some time. Cass made a wildly illegal left turn on the red light against the oncoming traffic into Topanga Canyon. I saw the Buick had been taken by surprise, moving to the left to make the turn, but then stopped by the flow of traffic. Cass accelerated sharply, but I managed to get a fleeting glimpse of the Buick turning against the red and roaring after us in hot pursuit.

"Whoopee!" Cass cried, and I knew I was in trouble. The look on his face was as close to sheer radiance as I had ever seen it. I dared myself to glance down at the speedometer to see we were traveling just a hair over 95, which was far from reassuring on this narrow, two-lane highway up into the hills.

"Cass. . . ."

"Relax, man, they'll never get us, not in this baby!"

You've never lived until you've almost died. We went into a sideways skid around a curve and regained control just inches from a telephone pole.

"That was a *controlled* skid, Steve. It just looked reckless, like the TV commercials."

I tore my eyes away from the dangers of the onrushing highway and turned around to see how we were doing against the competition. Fast as we were going, the Buick—a newer car—had managed to catch up. There was another small matter I thought I should mention.

"Uh, listen, I think we'd better pull over."

"Jeez, Steve, this is just getting to the good part! Son of a bitch, we'll race this sucker through the canyon clear to the freeway, and then there's no way he'll be able to match the horsepower of *this* pony!"

"But, Cass, they have a red light flashing in their windshield."

"Ride 'em, cowboy!" he cried. I think I mentioned before that neither Cass nor I have ever completely grown up. "Whoopee!" he sang again.

I had to shout to get his attention: *"Cass, they're the police!"*

I hated to see the look of dejection on his face when he took his foot off the accelerator and looked up into the rearview mirror. He pulled over onto the gravel pullout. The Buick came up behind us and screeched to a halt. Out of the passenger side emerged the familiar shape of my round little Napoleon in a wrinkled brown suit. From the driver's side, a cop I'd never seen before came out in a crouch with his pistol drawn. I was glad to be taken seriously, but Napoleon gestured for him to put his pistol away.

I settled back in my seat with a sigh and pushed the button to lower the electric window as the brown suit came up alongside.

"Mr. Allen, for a comedian, you're a positive menace, you really are!"

I tried on my most hopeful smile. "Well, hello there, W.B. You're just in time for lunch."

When he said he wasn't hungry, I knew I was in trouble.

chapter 32

We were taken without ceremony to the Malibu Sheriff's Department, a long, shedlike building on the Pacific Coast Highway. There Cass and I were separated. He went with the cop I had never seen before and I was taken into a small cubicle with Sergeant Walker.

"I must say, W.B., I'm a little disappointed to see you wasting your time following me when you could be out there solving a murder."

"Oh, but it's fun to follow you, Mr. Allen. And very entertaining! The way bodies keep turning up around you, I thought it was the wisest thing to do."

I made a grumpy sound in my throat. I was sitting in an uncomfortable wooden chair with a straight back. W.B. had perched his plumpness on the edge of a tired, wooden desk and somehow managed to cross one short leg over the other with neither touching the floor. He was studying me with a kind of good-natured malice.

"I hardly know how you have time to do all the things you do, Mr. Allen, and still manage a TV show five nights a week—Sunday in Santa Barbara with Terry Cole, drinks in the Polo Lounge with Winston Dane, lunch with Tessa Moore at the Bistro Gardens, a trip to the Beverly Hills Health Club, a private chat with Sonny Melnik in your dressing room, and now a romantic rendezvous with Kathleen Cole. My, my. Such a busy beaver."

"Okay, you've made your point. You probably have someone sleeping under my bed as well. Be sure to tell me what I say in my sleep—I've always wanted to know."

"You sleep very quietly," he said deadpan. "You hardly even snore. You're just miffed because you thought you were so clever, sneaking around pulling the wool over my eyes."

"You're a real bloodhound."

He leaned closer. "What I am, actually—I'm a professional, Mr. Allen. I've had two teams on your tail ever since the attempt on your life Friday morning. I've been rather hoping they'd try again."

"You've been using me as bait," I sputtered. "Dangling me out on a line, hoping some big fish would come along and take a bite!"

The sergeant shrugged modestly. "It was an idea. Of course, we hoped we could act fast enough to keep you from actually getting stiffed."

"How thoughtful!"

"Well, you got yourself into this situation, and speaking of risking your life, I don't think stretch limos were designed for the thrill of the high-speed chase. I hope your driver has another way to make a living. Somehow I don't think he'll be allowed to work as a chauffeur for a while.''

This made me feel really rotten. ''Look, Sergeant, we thought you were the bad guys in the fuzzy black car coming to kill us—we didn't know you were the cops. We were running for our lives.''

''Why didn't you think of calling 911 on that fancy cellular phone of yours? We would have come to your rescue.''

''Sure. And arrived to find two bloody corpses on the side of the road. No thanks. I'm taking care of myself. And as for Cass—he was just doing what I told him. He doesn't have any part of this, so if you're going to arrest somebody, arrest me. Okay?''

W.B. raised his right eyebrow at me. ''That's an idea, isn't it?'' He went through an elaborate process of recrossing his legs in the opposite direction, balancing himself rather precariously on the edge of the desk, like Humpty-Dumpty about to take a fall.

''Yes, I might just book you, but perhaps not quite yet.''

''And Cass?''

''I suppose it was reasonable to make a run for it, under the circumstances. I could probably persuade my colleagues not to press charges.''

''I have a feeling you're not giving me this for nothing.''

''Oh, there's a price, all right. No more playing hotshot, Mr. Allen. I don't mind your asking questions, but from now on you come directly to me with all the answers. You understand me?''

I told him I understood. I was feeling quite humbled; all in all, not exactly the world's cleverest detective. I began my penance with a recount of all my meetings, lunches, and conversations since seeing Terry Cole on Sunday. The sergeant was interested in my impressions as well as the facts, so this took some time. With all the things that were happening to me—high-speed chases and nearly getting arrested, and all—I nearly forgot about doing the show that night. Walker was asking me something about Winston Dane when I happened to catch sight of the big, round electric clock on the wall behind him.

"Oh, no!" I cried, "I've gotta be in Burbank in half an hour!"

"Relax. God forbid a TV show shouldn't start on time. I'll arrange a police escort."

And this he did. It was my second high-speed drive of the day. A sheriff's car took the lead—siren screaming, lights flashing, to clear the way. The burgundy-colored Cadillac stretch limousine came next in formation, and holding up the rear was the black Buick driven by the plainsclothes cop who had questioned Cass. W.B. and I were ensconced comfortably in the backseat of the Cadillac watching the scenery whiz by. We took the coast highway to the Santa Monica freeway, and then Interstate 405 toward Burbank. The cars that pulled over to let us by must have thought I was the president of some new African state. Sergeant Walker appeared even more Napoleonic than usual as he gazed out the tinted window. He had to try out the TV set in the back to make sure it really worked, and he helped himself to a soda water from the bar and a kosher dill pickle that someone had left in the small refrigerator.

"A guy could get to like traveling like this," he said. I smiled, but his next statement reminded me we still weren't exactly friends: "I imagine some people would commit murder to live this good."

"Don't look at me," I objected.

"I wonder," he said thoughtfully, casting a speculative eye in my direction. "You know, it's funny; everybody seems to have known everybody else in this damn case, except Winston Dane. He didn't recall Bobby Dyer, even though the guy worked for him once."

"He didn't tell me that," I interrupted.

"Well, he told *me*. You see, I had a little chat with Mr. Dane right after you left him in the lobby in your hotel."

"Boy, are you sneaky."

"I had to know what you two had talked about. Anyway, I was surprised Bobby didn't leave more of an impression on him."

"Come on, W.B.—Winston hadn't seen the man since 1963. You don't remember someone who just worked the sound boom, after all that time."

"No? Would it surprise you to learn that Bobby swung both ways? He went with guys as well as gals— a real equal-opportunity seducer."

"Oh, come on! Just because Bobby might have been AC/DC doesn't mean he had anything going with Winston. That's utter nonsense. Besides, Bobby Dyer was macho man, great in the sack. That's the reason Kathleen went out with him."

"Yes? Well, in recent years he had been flexing his muscles for people his own sex, though he continued to use women as well."

"Use?" I asked, intrigued by W.B.'s choice of words.

"My impression is that Mr. Dyer was not exactly a nice man. He was willing to have sex with man, woman, or baboon, if it would help his career."

"To become associate producer? Give me a break. That's one job you don't try out for on a casting couch."

"Maybe our dead friend had higher aspirations."

"Like what?" I challenged.

"Now, now, I can't tell you everything I know, Mr. Allen. God forbid you end up solving this case before I do."

Detective Sergeant W.B. Walker gave me something that was probably as close to a friendly smile as he was capable of mustering. There was only a small hint of sneer in it.

Our motorcade arrived at the main network gate, with the sirens fading. The uniformed guard jumped out of his booth to see what big shot was arriving with a police escort. He must have expected to see the head of the network, or Bob Hope, at the very least.

"Oh, Mr. Allen," he said with some surprise. I tried to look as nonchalant as I could. I gave Cass an imperious wave to proceed inside the gate, and the guard—so help me—actually saluted as we went past.

This had been quite a day. I wasn't sure exactly what to make of it. But at least my status in Burbank had gotten a shot in the arm.

chapter 33

After the show, I called Jayne in Hawaii just to remind myself I still had a normal life somewhere that was waiting for me to rejoin it. We talked for almost an hour about Hal Hoaglund's death, and I began to feel human again. But bad dreams were waiting in the middle of the night.

I dreamed I was running down a narrow street lined with towering palm trees, and as I ran from tree to tree I was followed by a black car that meant death—I knew this in my dream—if I allowed it to get too close. The scene changed. Now I was in the limo with Cass, with the black car still in hot pursuit. Only our Cadillac didn't have an engine—it was one of those pedal toys built for children, and Cass and I were pumping like crazy, trying to get away.

I don't know about you, but I hate dreams where I have to work. I pedaled that kiddie car seemingly for hours trying to get away from some lurking danger that was always a few feet behind. It was exhausting. I half awakened twice to fall asleep again, only to find myself in the same predicament. Finally I gave up. I sat up in bed and read a nice escapist mystery all about people being murdered. It was a way to leave my own troubles behind. I read until Dawn spread her rosy fingers above Beverly Hills, and then there was a knock on my front door.

I had my robe on and was halfway to the door when I realized it was a little early for room service. I'm a trusting soul, however, and my forward motion took me to the door to see who it could be at this hour.

"Why, hello there, snookums! Don't *you* look cute in a bathrobe!"

Lord help me, it was Tessa Moore. I wasn't sure if I wanted to weep or slam the door in her face. I glanced over to the travel clock on my piano to see it was six-thirty.

"Do you know what time it is?" I complained.

"Oh, Stevey-poo, you're not mad at wittle Tessa-pie, are you? I was out jogging and thought it would be fun to drop in on you."

"Jogging?" I repeated dubiously. "It looks as if you could fly in that outfit."

Tessa Moore, in fact, was in a Supergirl costume: blue tights, red running shoes with stars on the toes, a glossy blue sweatshirt with a big yellow S on the front, and a short red satin cape. It was too early in the morning for such a blazing sight. I wanted to flee back to my bed and hide my head beneath the pillow.

"You'll buy me breakfast, won't you, darling? I absolutely ran all the way from Bedford Drive—I'm so famished I could eat an entire football team."

"Super," I told her. "You didn't cause any accidents along the way, I trust—drivers turning to look at you?"

"Li'l ol' inconspicuous me?" she cooed. "Why, I'm almost invisible without my jewelry, darling."

I was still blocking her entrance to my bungalow. After all, I'm hospitable to one and all, but this six-thirty visit was going too far. I might have succeeded in taking a firm stand, but just at this moment, the incognito lovers in the bungalow next door emerged with their floppy hats and enormous dark glasses. They glanced over at Supergirl and probably wished they could fly away.

"Bill!" Tessa shrieked. "Why, I thought you were in Wyoming!"

The incognito couple gasped and fled back into the safety of their bower. I took Tessa firmly by the arm and led her inside my bungalow before she could do any more damage.

"I'm shocked," she said.

"That's good to hear," I said. "I didn't think you could be shocked by anything."

"That's not nice," she said, pretending to be offended. "But I really had thought Bill was one of the good guys in town and that he didn't do this sort of thing."

"That's interesting," I said. "We both know that sort of thing goes on, and certainly not only in show business, but it's at least a bit refreshing that everybody disapproves of it, even the most depraved people we know."

"Well, enough about that," she said. And before I could say no, she was giving me her breakfast order: blueberry waffles, a side of ham, two eggs over easy, coffee, and a bottle of Moet et Chandon. The way my friends were eating around here, I was relieved Sonny had agreed to pay my hotel bill.

"I'll just take a shower while we wait for breakfast," she informed me.

"You will do no such thing."

"Darling, after all that exercise, I smell like a horse." She began to strip out of her Supergirl outfit. I didn't think I'd find Clark Kent underneath.

"All right, go take a shower, but please close the door!"

She giggled. I certainly can make people laugh when I'm not trying. I called room service and then sat down wearily on the living room couch. My nightmares were turning out to be preferable to the mares of the dawn. I listened to the shower running in the next room and could hear Tessa singing a tune I thought was from *Phantom of The Opera,* if there is one.

My favorite waiter, Sergio, arrived with the breakfast cart just as Tessa was coming out of the bathroom wrapped in nothing but a towel. Sergio would like to be a movie star—like most of the waiters in this town—and we sometimes spend a few moments discussing new films we've seen. This morning, Sergio used all his powers of polite waiterhood not to stare at the blond alien from planet Krypton who was standing nearly naked in my living room. I signed the bill without meeting his eye. I had given up any illusions as to what people must think of me by now. At this rate, I was probably going to end up in jail anyway, with a lot of thieves, murderers and drug addicts. A little more shame shouldn't bother me.

"Well, what is this all about?" I asked with a sigh

when Sergio had opened the Moet et Chandon and departed.

"Darling, you're so suspicious. I thought we were friends."

"Friends, Tessa, do not barge in unannounced at six-thirty in the morning."

She pouted a bit. Said I was being awfully bourgeois, and that she always imagined a man of my sophistication would be above the triteness of mere social convention.

"Anyway, sweetheart," she said, starting on her eggs, "I wanted to be the first to inform you of great and wonderful tidings."

"Yes?" I asked guardedly.

"You're going to be *so* glad I stopped by, when you hear what lovely news I bring."

"Then tell me," I suggested, my patience at a low ebb. "And please put some clothes on."

Tessa was still wrapped in one of the hotel's towels, her Supergirl attire on the floor of the bathroom.

"Well, what do you want first? Clothes on, or the good news?"

"Tessa. . . ."

"I'll tell you the good news," she decided brightly. "There's word that Terry's *not* coming back to the show. Apparently, one of the biggies at the network went up to Happy Valley yesterday and divined that sweet Terry isn't exactly in his right mind. The decision's not quite final, but aren't you glad now you're having breakfast with me?"

I muttered a few dark thoughts beneath my breath.

"And the good news goes on and on," she bubbled, undaunted by my scowl. "The network has a list of

189

three names for a permanent replacement, should Terry really be unable to continue. So go ahead, ask me who."

"Okay . . . who?"

"Isn't this fun? Just like twenty questions! Well, the first nominee wears glasses, plays the piano, and is awfully sweet, even if he is a bit square at times."

"Me?"

"Exactly, snookums. And the second nominee is a beautiful, sexy blonde, known for her fabulous wardrobe and keen wit."

"You?" I asked, more dubiously.

"Oh, you're so clever, Steve! But nominee number three, you're not going to guess."

"Try me."

"Well, he's even older than you, darling."

"Thanks!"

"He's very bright, though a bit cutting, and hasn't been on television for a long, long time."

"Winston Dane!" I cried. "That's preposterous!"

"Is it, darling? This is the age of nostalgia, you know—*Beaver,* the *Honeymooners,* all those *Perry Mason* reruns you see on the odd channels. With Winston Dane, America could return to the Fifties all the way."

"But Winnie would never do it," I said. "He's only in town on his way to China. He doesn't want any part of show business anymore."

"You don't believe *that* nonsense, do you? Don't be naive! Winnie would love a chance to get a show again."

" You think so?" I was surprised by the idea. Tessa reached over the breakfast cart and took my hand.

"What about you, Steve?"

"What about me?"

"Do you want the show?"

"I don't know," I lied, although I *did* know: no way did I want a regular nightly TV show again. But there was no harm in keeping my options open—or in keeping Tessa guessing.

She seemed disappointed with my answer. "But when would you have time to write all those books and songs, darling? Doing all those symphony concerts? TV is such a rat race."

"I'm touched by your concern."

"Honestly, I *am* concerned. What if Beethoven had a TV show to do five nights a week and he hadn't been able to finish the Ninth Symphony?"

"I see what you mean," I admitted, "though I didn't have in mind anything quite as elaborate as the Ninth."

"I have the answer," she announced. *"I'll* do the show, and you can come on anytime you want. That way, you'll have lots of exposure on television, without the horrid responsibility."

"You would do this for me?"

"And you can write your great symphony, darling. And perhaps name it after me." Her eyes were glistening with emotion. "We'll have the debut at Lincoln Center. What a party I'll throw afterward! With Jayne's help, of course."

I was thinking about how I might get rid of her, when there was a knock on the door. I thought perhaps it was Sergio come to fetch the roll-away table, but it was my old buddy, Detective Sergeant W.B. Walker.

W.B. looked at Tessa Moore in her skimpy towel, and then over at me. He shook his head in disbelief.

I was blushing again. Here I'd been thinking I had sunk beneath the possibility of further shame, only to find I was still capable of being embarrassed. I suppose, all things considered, it was a hopeful sign.

"We were just having breakfast," I said weakly. "Care to join us?"

"Oh, dear me, I'd better get something on," Tessa said coyly, slithering off toward the bathroom and closing the door.

"You must have been mighty hard up," the sergeant told me softly.

"W.B., it's not the way it looks. I'm a married man."

"So you keep telling me."

"I can't take this anymore," I muttered. "I wish someone would arrest me, or murder me, or something—just get it over with."

"Now, now, Mr. Allen, no need for such dire thoughts, a big stud like you."

Tessa came out of the bathroom in tights, sweatshirt, sneakers, and shiny red cape. W.B.'s eyes opened just a bit wider than usual.

"Well, boys," she said, "it's been swell. But I gotta fly."

chapter 34

"**M**r. Allen," said W.B., "I used to think that celebrities didn't really lead more interesting lives than the rest of us—but after watching you the last few days, I've changed my mind."

"Would you care for breakfast?" I asked with only a slight tinge of sarcasm. "The lady never touched the waffles or the ham."

"Well. . . ."

I persuaded him that the still-warm remains were too good to pass up. I could see it was dangerous being a cop; if the bad guys didn't get him, his eating habits eventually would.

We didn't talk about anything too serious until after he had dipped the last forkful of waffle in the remnants of the maple syrup and brought it to his lips.

"Ah, breakfast," he said with a near mystical sigh. "It's good to have a full stomach when about to make an arrest."

My own stomach tightened. W.B. looked at my expression and laughed. "Not *you,* though a few days in the slammer might be just the vacation you need."

"Who, then?"

He kept smiling at me, stretching out the suspense. "Do you think Kathleen Cole would adjust to prison life?" he asked.

"Kathleen! Hold on a moment. She might dislike her ex-husband, but I can't see that she has a motive for murder."

"Can't you, now? Perhaps you don't have all the information I do."

W.B. was being intolerably smug, which I thought was a lousy way to repay me for a nice breakfast.

"Okay, so tell me what you've got. You're dying to lord it over me, so go ahead."

"Mr. Allen, frankly you never had a chance to solve this crime. Nine-tenths of being a detective is having the right kind of resources and connections—like the police do."

"I'm still waiting for the stunning revelation about Kathleen Cole."

"Okay. Mrs. C. is the major beneficiary of Terry C.'s estate, in the case of his death. She has about thirty-million-dollars-worth of motive to see her ex-husband dead."

"How did you get a peek at Terry's will? The poor guy isn't even dead yet."

W.B. fluttered his eyebrows. "That's what I mean about having the right resources. Don't blame yourself—you never would have gotten near that will."

"Okay," I admitted, "Kathleen obviously had a motive, but that doesn't mean she did it."

"She was playing hide the sausage with Bobby Dyer."

"A long time ago," I objected.

"Not so long ago. Bobby spent the night at the Trancas beach house just two weeks ago."

"Were you hiding under the bed?"

"The maid told me, of course. Bobby was a frequent visitor to Kathleen's house. The number of visits had actually increased in the past few months."

"I still don't see it," I complained. I wasn't sure I could say I *liked* Kathleen Cole—she was a proud, cold beauty—but I still couldn't quite cast her in the role of murderess.

Suddenly I laughed to myself but did not bother to explain to Walker that what had caused my chuckle was a recollection of one of the stand-up routines that Don Adams used to do on my show, the one where he did an impression of William Powell in one of his *Thin Man* films, summing up a case. "Ladies and gentlemen of the jury," he would say, "are these the legs of a murderess?"

"She had the motive; she had the opportunity. Not only that . . . Hey, you know, you *are* pretty good at getting me to tell you things I hadn't intended."

"It's my TV host training," I said. "Well?"

"Okay. Dyer bought the rat poison. We took his photograph around to all the hardware and garden shops in West L.A., and a salesman at a small nursery on Santa Monica Boulevard remembered him. Bobby bought a bottle of *Drop Dead* rat poison two and a half weeks ago. Like an idiot he paid with a credit card, so we were able to verify the transaction."

"And was *Drop Dead* . . ."

"Yes, the forensic lab confirmed. *Drop Dead* was the brand of poison that killed Hal Hoaglund."

I sat digesting this information for a moment. I must admit, I was impressed at the efficient way professional policemen accumulated bits of information, and I could see it was a more scientific approach than my own bumbling attempts, driving hither and thither about town. But there was still something that disturbed me.

"Listen, I get all my information about courtroom procedures from *Perry Mason* and *Jake and The Fatman,* but isn't your case pretty circumstantial?"

"Very good. But why?"

"Well, Bobby Dyer might have purchased that particular brand of poison but you can't prove he put it in the bottle that killed Hal Hoaglund. Maybe there were rats in his building. You may be able to show that Kathleen could benefit from her ex-hubby's death—she might even have had a relationship with Bobby Dyer—but that doesn't mean either one of them plotted a murder."

"Good, now you see the problem," W.B. told me, pushing back the table and standing up. "I won't detain you any further, Mr. Allen—you have your work cut out for you."

"Now hold on one damn minute," I cried. "I'm not on your payroll!"

"But you can dig around. Discreetly. Cultivate Mrs. Cole's friendship, get the proof we need. I can't do that."

"Whoa! I have other responsibilities, like doing a TV show—and I'm not so damned sure my wife would like me associating with a woman like that on a regular basis."

Detective Sergeant W.B. Walker's sleepy face lit up in a pudgy, knowing radiance. "Oh, you'll do it, Mr. Allen. Being a detective is not so much a vocation as an addiction. And you, my friend, are hooked."

chapter 35

When I stuck my head out of my bungalow, there was a gorgeous spring morning at my disposal. There was a fragrant dampness in the air, smelling of moist earth, lawns, and flowers. Normally I might take a walk on a morning like this, but my appetite for that kind of exercise had fallen off sharply since Friday afternoon. I decided to take a swim instead.

The pool at the Beverly Hills Hotel is more decorative than functional, a place to pose, act Hollywood, and look at everybody else. Generally, the only people who actually swim there are young beauties in skimpy bikinis determined to show off their forms, or innocent children happily oblivious to the social subtleties. I fall somewhere between these two categories.

It was still early enough for the pool area to be uncrowded. The early morning gawkers were most likely still eating breakfast at the Polo Lounge, keeping a sharp lookout for the entrance of a film star, or people who might at least *look* like one. At this moment a lovely young woman was stepping out of the pool, breathing hard from doing laps, looking very much like Venus emerging from her bath.

The sight of her was energizing. I waded into the shallow waters and cast off when I was waist deep into the turquoise coolness. I had the pool to myself now and began to swim slow, rhythmic laps from one end to the other. It was really quite blissful, an embryonic feeling of being suspended in the primal waters.

Water has always had a profound effect on me. For one thing, I find being thirsty a terrible torment. On the other hand, when my thirst is finally slaked, the enjoyment I feel from that cold trickle across my tongue, down the back of my throat, and into my gullet is exquisite. Fortunately I rarely have to go thirsty for any length of time these days. This was not always true. When I was going through basic infantry training at Camp Roberts, California, during World War II, our company was being trained for duty in North Africa, so we were often placed on "water discipline" during ten-mile hikes in the midsummer sun. All of us in Company B must have looked like ants crawling up a lion's flank as we trudged through the dust and heat of the tawny central-California hills. Once thirst became acute, we impersonally hated our lieutenants, dreamed of sloshing steins of beer, of oceans, rivers, washbasins, glasses of ice-cold tea, of taking cool showers. Eventually I was near hallucinating. I talked to the guys near me, saying, "You know what I see? I see a swimming pool, with gorgeous women swimming in thousands of gallons of ginger ale and ice. I mean a whole damned pool with glasses of lemonade, and blondes and redheads serving it to you while sitting with cold hips on big blue cubes of ice, their bathing suits all juicy and sloshing. Can you imagine falling in, shivering and gulping it all down?" Somebody would finally yell, "Shut up, Allen, you crazy bastard."

Once that summer I was so maddened by thirst that I deserted my post. Well, actually, I had no post; my company was simply lined up for inspection after one of those desert training hikes. We had deliberately not yet been permitted to drink anything and were standing there sweating and faint. Since I was the tallest man in my company, I was in first position to the left this particular afternoon when I noticed that the officers were down at the other end, seemingly engaged in idle banter.

"I'll be right back," I said to the man next to me and slipped away, behind the barracks, before he could say anything. A few feet away, on the grounds of Company C's barracks, there was a canteen and in it, I knew, an enormous cooler that held scores of bottles of pop and beer, nestled in icy water. I walked in as if I had a right to be there, gave the uniformed attendant two quarters, took a cold beer from the icy depths of the cooler, snapped off the top, and drank it all in just a few greedy mouthfuls, without taking my lips from the bottle. Before sixty seconds had passed, I was outside again, walking quickly in the shade of our barracks. When I peered around the corner where our company was still standing at attention, nothing had changed. Nobody had noticed my absence. I stepped into line with the sweetest smile in the world on my face.

The sun was warm on my face now, my eyes were closed—I was smiling—when I collided with another swimmer and got a mouthful of chlorinated water.

We had bumped heads. I turned around groping and disoriented and sank underwater before coming up coughing for air. I reached out and was able to grab hold of the side of the pool. The person with whom I had collided was hanging on to the ladder, sputtering mad.

"Damn it! Can't you look where you're going!" he cried, and then he peered at me more closely. "Oh, my God, it's Steve. I didn't recognize you without your glasses."

"I don't recognize anybody without my glasses," I said, "but I can certainly pick out a voice like yours."

It was Winston Dane. We both had a laugh about the way we kept running into each other.

We drifted off toward the shallow end and sat on the steps there, submerged to our necks. A palm tree by the side of the pool flickered in the soft breeze and sent a movement of shadows across the rippled surface.

"Southern California," Winston said dreamily. "When you're away, you tend to think of smog, the architectural hodgepodge and the freeways, how very ugly it is. But there really is a beauty to this place, isn't there?"

"I understand you may be staying, Winnie."

He laughed. "Incredible! Rumors fly in this town faster than a speeding bullet. So what exactly have you heard?"

"That you've been offered Terry's show. That is, if he doesn't return."

Winston shook his head and chuckled. "No, no, that's not quite true," he said quietly, because a middle-aged couple were just pulling up deck chairs to the side of the pool. "I *was* approached, on a very hypothetical basis, to see if I was interested. I must say, I was surprised. I'd expected to be completely forgotten after all these years."

"Not you, Winnie. But I'm curious—who approached you?"

He mentioned the name Al Considine, a vice president at the network, whom I had met a few times. Winnie stressed that the overture was very speculative.

The overtures usually are. I remember when an executive from NBC called me and said, "I'll deny on my mother's honor that this conversation ever took place, but I must ask you, in the strictest confidence, if you would be available to host the *Tonight* show again."

"That's not the kind of question to which I can give a simple yes or no answer," I replied. "I'm happy in my present situation and I'd have to give very careful thought to the matter of ever again incurring an obligation to turn out five ninety-minute shows a week, but I'm not totally ruling out the possibility, assuming assorted demands could be met."

"Fair enough," he said. "I'll get back to you if there turns out to be any more on this."

There didn't.

It occurred to me a few months later that I had been an unwitting participant in one of the many negotiating ploys for which our industry is infamous. If a performer begins to believe his own publicity and starts making exorbitant demands, or causing trouble of any other sort, you make a few casual calls around town to possible replacements or their agents. Given that there are damned few true secrets in our industry, the network actually hopes that the rumors will get back to the ear of their prima donna of the moment. Sometimes it works.

"Well," I said to Winnie, "are you interested?"

"Not on your life," he said, which I thought not a very appropriate expression, under the circumstances. "But I didn't completely say no."

"Why not?"

"Well, I was flattered, I have to admit, and I was curious how serious they were—if there would be a follow-up or if the offer would fizzle out. But listen, if you're trying to get the show for yourself, old man, I'll call the network this morning and let them know I'm out."

"No, no—I've decided I'm not interested either, Winnie. I don't want all my time tied up like that. I've paid my dues with twelve years of talk-show duty. There are too many other things I'm involved with now."

"I guess that leaves Tessa Moore," he said. We both cracked up at the idea, in a silly, spontaneous kind of laughter. The idea of Tessa taking over *The Terry Cole Show* seemed the funniest thing either of us could imagine. We couldn't stop laughing. Finally, Winston splashed me with both hands, and I splashed back. The couple by the pool were looking in some alarm at two grown men having a water fight. I had a feeling they were tourists. Winston and I horsed around for a while, and then we got out and warmed ourselves on chairs in the sun.

By now others had decided this was a splendid morning for the pool, and a number of prosperous-looking men and women had arranged themselves in comfortable groupings. Waiters trooped back and forth with coffee, sandwiches, drinks, and cordless telephones. Two chairs to the left, a large man with an unfortunate stomach and a loud Hawaiian shirt was talking locations and casting requirements into his plastic mouthpiece, while to the right, a young woman was talking to her agent. Not far away, I could hear the soft sounds of a tennis game in progress: *thunk . . . thunk . . . thunk.*

Morning in Beverly Hills. Winston and I sat in a companionable silence, eyes closed, soaking up the local ambience.

"I don't know how you manage to live here," he said after a time. "I could never take it seriously, as a real place, you know—like New York or Chicago or London."

"You shouldn't. The thing is simply to relax and enjoy it," I told him. "And to change the subject, how do you think Tessa learned you were being considered for Terry's job? The network wouldn't have blabbed."

"Kathleen told her. I'm afraid the lady can't keep a secret."

I absorbed this briefly. The moment reminded me of one of those drawings in the Sunday comics where you have to discover what is wrong with this picture.

"But how did Kathleen find out?"

"Sonny told her."

"Sonny!" I exclaimed. "Doesn't anybody shut up in this town? And why would he tell Kathleen, I wonder?"

"Probably to impress her with his insider knowledge. Sonny's been working to impress Kathleen for years now—without much success, I'm afraid."

"He has a thing for her, does he?"

"Well, some years ago they had a brief affair. *Very*

203

brief. Of course, Kathleen was only using Sonny to try to make Terry jealous."

"He strikes me as very poor casting for that role," I said.

Winston laughed. "Terry couldn't have cared less, of course, so Kathleen cut poor Sonny adrift. He's always been a bit like the crocodile in *Peter Pan* who got one bite of Captain Hook and has been lurking around ever since for more."

"But Sonny's a married man," I objected, thinking briefly of Sergeant Walker.

"Poor old Sonny," Winston said mournfully. "He's been Terry's flunky for so many years now! I guess he just wants a bigger share of the prize. Maybe a piece of the show."

It's quite a common disease in this town, and industry. The creative people, obviously, originate everything, but it takes the salesmen—the agents, the managers, the hypesters—to convert the dreams and ideas into reality. Naturally they want to profit from this, as they should. But the old days when they were satisfied with ten percent are long gone.

"So Sonny would like more of the fame and fortune?" I asked.

"Oh, yes! And fair Kathleen by his side. He feels he's done all the work, while Terry reaps all the rewards."

"I should think that would make him a bitter man."

"Sonny's a tragic figure, I've always thought. A few years ago, he tried to get a bigger credit at the end of the show. He wanted a neat logo that would say, 'A Sonny Melnik Production.' Just a few seconds of recognition."

"I bet Terry didn't go for it," I said.

Winston laughed sharply. "No way! Sonny's credit rolls by so fast you'd have to be on speed to catch it."

I folded my hands in my lap. "How do you hear all these little tidbits?" I asked.

"Mostly from Kathleen."

"You've remained close all these years?"

"Oh, God, yes! Kathleen spent two months with me at my villa outside of Rome last summer. She tells me I'm better than a girlfriend. She's kept me up on all the juicy gossip while I've been away."

I looked at Winston's handsome, aristocratic face and realized it made a very good mask to hide whatever he might truly be feeling.

"And yet when Sergeant Walker asked you about Bobby Dyer, you told him you couldn't recall the man. Surely Kathleen would have told you all the details of her many affairs?"

Winston looked blank, then smiled indulgently. "There were rather *too* many affairs, I'm afraid. I could never keep all the Bobbys straight from the Tommys and Billys and Mels. After a while, I stopped trying. One would need a computer, dear boy, to keep abreast of Kathleen's love life."

"And yet Bobby Dyer worked for you. He was on the sound crew, wasn't he?"

"Yes, when Sergeant Walker mentioned that, I did vaguely remember such a person—but I may have been confusing him with someone else. Memory becomes a bit blurry at my stage of the game. I was sorry not to be more helpful."

It was hot in the sun. We ordered two glasses of fresh orange juice. I was feeling pleasantly drowsy.

"So, Winston, are you still leaving for China to-morrow?" I asked. Somehow I knew the answer would be no. He laughed a little sheepishly.

"I guess I'm going to stick around for a while, Steve. You're going to think this is terrible, but I'm simply too curious to see if they're *really* going to offer me Terry's show."

"I don't think that's terrible at all," I told him.

"Oh, it is, because it would be a cold day in hell before I'd ever take that show. But I still want them to come to me, maybe beg me to do it—and then I'll smile and tell them no."

chapter 36

I stood in my shower under the hot spray, letting the water massage my neck. A shower is a great place to think deep thoughts, write songs, and/or solve murders. I closed my eyes and tried to make my mind blank so that I'd be open for inspiration.

Not much inspiration came, however. What a tangled web this was turning out to be! Now I could add to all the other interconnections the fact that Sonny had had a fling with the boss's wife and had lusted for her thereafter. This was getting out of hand. There were too many facts, too many motives, and far too many suspects.

Think, man! I chided myself. I felt I should know the answer by now. I could almost sense the truth waiting coyly off to one side of my brain behind a gossamer curtain. If only I could just concentrate a little harder, I might understand.

I stepped out of the shower and enveloped myself in one of the large white hotel towels. The only thing I had managed to come up with in my brainstorming was the obvious: the series of crimes beginning with Hal Hoaglund's death had its roots in the distant past. The incestuous relations between Winston Dane, Terry Cole, Kathleen, Sonny, and Bobby Dyer went all the way back to the Sixties—with Tessa Moore a recent addition, a wild card thrown into the deck for laughs. If I was going to solve this crime, I needed to know more about that crucial period when Winston was fired and Terry took over his show.

One of my friends, Charles Eastman, writes for the *Los Angeles Times*. Since Charlie knows everything about this town, I decided to try him at the City Desk. He had stepped off down the hall, but I left a message. He called back in a few minutes.

"Hey, Steverino, you seem to be in the news lately. What gives?"

"I wish I knew, Charlie. Having people drop dead on my show is not exactly my idea of good publicity."

"There are rumors abounding that Hal did not exactly die of natural causes."

I could hear Charlie Eastman's newspaperman's heart beating a bit more loudly. He was the last of a dying breed: a cocky, chain-smoking, coffee-drinking, hard-living reporter—who still wrote first drafts on an ancient typewriter that might have been used by Tolstoy. He was a friend, but if he could get a scoop from me, he would. I had to do some bargaining to get his full cooperation.

"I wish I could tell this whole story to someone," I said with a sigh.

"Why not me, pardner? I'm all ears."

"You can't use it," I told him. "Not yet. But when the case is wrapped up, you'll be the first to know all the gory details. Okay?"

"And what do you want from me, good buddy?"

"Information."

"Ah! Hard currency. Okay, it's a deal. What do you want to know?"

"I want to go back to nineteen sixty-three," I told him, "back to the days when Cadillacs got five miles a gallon and crewcuts were still the rage, and an unknown comic from a small-town radio station in Iowa managed to score a big-time network TV show."

"Are we talking about the low-life joker, Terry Cole?"

"We are indeed. This may seem an off-the-wall question after all these years, but do you have any dirt on how Terry managed that little feat?"

I could hear Charlie Eastman lighting up a cigarette with a snap of his gold Zippo and taking a long drag.

"I heard his wife went to bat for him, slept in the right bed."

"I've heard that too," I told him. "But surely there's more."

"You don't think a network TV show is a fair exchange for a night of love with Kathleen Cole?" he asked with a chuckle.

"I don't think a chairman of the board would be so sentimental, or so foolish. Sex is one thing, ratings another."

"Well, they had to find someone pretty quick," he reminded me. "If I remember, Winston Dane had to leave town in a hurry."

"Oh? Why?"

"There were rumors. I don't know for sure."

"Tell me rumors then."

"*Confidential* was about to do a big exposé on Winston. Supposedly there were photographs showing him with young boys."

"Swell," I said. *Confidential,* you may remember, was *The National Enquirer* of its time, though much worse, actually malicious. Of course, back then scandal had more power to do damage than it does today. This was before the so-called sexual revolution, and there were moral codes, and hypocrisy, to uphold—the transgression of which could get you into serious hot water. And in the old pre-*Confidential* days, of course, a really bad scandal could end a career in mid-flight. The case of Fatty Arbuckle and the actual or alleged death-by-Coke-bottle incident comes to mind in this connection. In today's depraved society if that had happened, Arbuckle probably would have ended up doing a TV commercial for Pepsi.

"I don't remember *Confidential*'s ever doing anything on Winnie," I objected. "If they had photographs, why did they hold back?"

"They made a deal with the network, arranged by a lawyer with Mafia connections. That's what I heard—large amounts of cash changed hands to keep the whole thing quiet. The story got buried, but Winston decided to leave town fast."

"Sad."

"Well, in a sense the early sixties were still part of the fifties, you know. Time of the great witch-hunt. If you were different, look out! Winnie was actually lucky to survive McCarthy. His political leanings, too, were slightly left of apple pie."

I could hear Charlie lighting up yet another cigarette and sucking in the smoke. I knew he had changed to a low-tar brand and had to work harder now to ruin his lungs and shorten his life.

"I guess that explains Winston's sudden exit, but I still don't see the network's gambling on a complete unknown like Terry Cole, even if his future ex-wife did make it with the big boss."

"This may sound crazy," he said, "but I think Terry was simply lucky—at the right place at the right time. After Winston's sophisticated humor and ornate life-style, they probably thought a fresh-faced kid from Iowa would be just the thing."

"I'm surprised they didn't hire Shirley Temple."

He laughed. "So what else can I tell you?"

"What about Sonny Melnik? Did he have any part in these Machiavellian maneuverings?"

"Nah, Sonny was just part of Terry's baggage, then and now. From what I hear, no one at the network takes him too seriously. They originally wanted to get a real professional in that producer spot, but they put up with him because of Terry. And, after all, what the hell is there to producing a talk show once the thing is on the air and running?"

"Since you've asked the question, you're entitled to an answer, Charlie," I said. "The answer is: nothing."

Just part of Terry's baggage, I considered. What a fate. I was certain there were more questions I should be asking Charlie Eastman—he's a walking encyclopedia of knowledge about this town. But for the moment, I didn't think my fragile ears could handle any more dirt.

"Oh, one more thing," I said. "You ever hear of a cop, a Detective Sergeant W.B. Walker?"

"Homicide, right? Burbank?"

"That's him. Well, you don't happen to know what his initials stand for, do you?"

"Whatcha doing? Sending him a monogrammed tie?"

"Charlie, this is just a simple question."

"Hmm, W.B. Walker? No, I don't know offhand, but I'll take a look at our files. Maybe we got something."

"I would owe you, Charlie. Like maybe a very upscale dinner one of these nights."

"Promises, promises," he said, sighing.

chapter 37

The only good thing about being awakened by someone like Tessa Moore at six-thirty in the morning is that your day is a lot longer than usual. I decided I had time to call up Jimmy Cassidy and have him drive me over to Bobby Dyer's final residence on Dixon Way.

I told you that Tessa was the wild card in my deck of characters, but thinking about it, I saw this was not so. Tessa, Terry, Sonny, Kathleen, and Winston all belonged to the same group—they were show-biz types, successful in their field, available to be pointlessly shouted at by Robin Leach, more or less at the top of the Hollywood heap. If they'd had dealings over the years—both lust and business—it was not that surprising, because the insiders in this town form a fairly small and well-guarded clique.

No, Bobby Dyer was the joker in my pack. He was the one who didn't fit, and if I was going to solve this crime, I had to figure out what he'd been doing here.

Cass met me by the side entrance to the bungalows and I slipped in next to him in the front seat.

"Where to, chief?" I could see Cass was ready for

anything. He was enjoying this cops-and-robbers stuff a little too much. I told him our destination, and he seemed uncommonly pleased.

"Damn, do I remember that night! Rain pourin' down. Dark as a night in hell. The dead man shot full of holes, lying against the bed in a pool of his own blood."

"You've been reading too many paperbacks, Cass. We were lucky not to get arrested that night. *That* would not have been too much fun."

"There ain't no jail built that could hold guys like us, Steve."

"We're real macho maniacs, all right."

"Jimmy Cassidy and the Talk Show Kid," he mused. "I like the way that sounds."

I was getting worried about the way Cass was carrying on. It occurred to me I'd better solve this thing fast and get us both back to normal living before I did irreparable damage to our characters.

"I brought a long steel pick in case we need to break into anyone's house," he told me happily.

"Cass, we're not going to break into anyone's house. I only want to talk to Bobby Dyer's neighbors—see if they can tell me anything about him and the kinds of people he hung out with."

Dixon Drive looked very different today than last week in the pouring rain. Smallish, old-fashioned houses stood in the bright afternoon sunshine, each with a small patch of front lawn and a flower bed or two. The styles ranged from Spanish stucco to California arabesque, with a little gingerbread thrown in. These had originally been middle-income dwellings built forty or fifty years ago, before Hollywood Boulevard had fallen into shabby disrepute. The mock medieval castle where Bobby had lived looked more false—downright silly, in fact—in the light of day.

We parked on the street and walked up the short driveway to the front door. There were no knights in shining armor anywhere to be seen, but loud rock music was coming from one of the upper apartments.

I rang the buzzer for apartment A, being inclined toward alphabetical order, but, receiving no answer, moved on quickly to letter B. A detective, I had learned, is nothing if not methodical. There was an electric buzz and the front door swung open. Cass and I walked up a winding staircase with a wrought-iron railing. Apartment B seemed to be the source of the earsplitting music. A barefoot youth in a dirty T-shirt answered the door. He looked at us both like we were utter creeps to be beyond the age of twenty-five.

"Yeah?" he snarled. Not a very charming young barbarian. Somehow I didn't think he would remember me from the Golden Age of television, so I took out my wallet and gave him a very fast look at the most official-looking piece of plastic I had handy. It happened to be my Screen Actors' Guild card. It seemed to do the trick.

"We have just a few questions to ask you, son. Nothing to get upset about."

"I already told the other cop everything I know," he whined.

"The short, fat one in the brown suit? He doesn't know diddly, son. We're from another department."

"What's you name, kid?" Cass asked him, getting in the mood.

"Bones."

"Bones who?" It sounded like part of a knock-knock joke.

"Just Bones," the young man told us. "Take it or leave it."

"We'll take it," I said. "Where were you Tuesday night?"

"The night Bobby was skagged? Like I told fatty in the brown suit, I was out smashing cars in the Valley."

"What?"

"Yeah, we go out to a junkyard I know and smash windows and fenders, break up things. It's a blast. If you don't believe me, you can ask Corky or Twister or Spit—the whole gang was there."

I pretended to write down the names for verification. "Let's get back to Mr. Dyer," I suggested. "What did you know about him?"

Bones seemed reluctant to talk. I hinted that if he was not forthcoming, we would be forced to take him downtown to the *special room* we had for people like him.

I repeated my question.

Bones shrugged. "I don't know. Bobby was a big-shot TV producer. He was the guy who produced . . . what's the name of that show?"

"The Terry Cole Show?"

"Yeah."

"Didn't it strike you as odd that a big-shot producer would live in a place like this?"

"He said it was a tax dodge."

Young Bones didn't seem terribly bright. "How often did you see him?"

"Now and then. You know. I'd be working on my Harley in the driveway and he'd bring out a six-pack."

"A wheel like that, I'm surprised it wasn't champagne."

Bones squinted at me. "You're kinda weird," he said, "for a cop."

"It's the company I keep," I told him, trying not to sound too much like Joe Friday. "Now what else did you and Bobby talk about?"

"Things."

I exhaled wearily and gave him my I-might-have-to-hurt-you look. "What *kinds* of things, son?"

"Nothing special. Insider stories about show business, that sort of thing. For an old jerk, the guy was pretty interesting."

"He talk about the stars?"

"Sure. Like I said, Bobby was a real insider."

"What stars did he talk about?"

"Well, like Marilyn Monroe, for instance. I bet you don't know that Bobby Dyer was the love of her life?"

"Hell, everybody knows that," I said.

"Yeah, right before she bought the farm she called him up on the telephone and said that if he hadn't left her, things would have turned out a lot better."

"Did Dyer ever use the expression, 'Yeah, that's the ticket' or do Isuzu commercials?" Cass stifled a guffaw, but I was beginning to despair. A dead witness was bad enough. A dead witness who happened to be a pathological liar made things pretty tough, even for a hardworking detective like me. Without waiting for an answer, I went on. "Did Bobby ever talk about Terry Cole?"

"Yeah. He sort of discovered Terry Cole—gave him his first break on TV."

"That's what he told you?" I asked in disbelief.

"Sure. Bobby was the one who got Terry his show. That's why Terry was always so grateful. He was always giving Bobby all sorts of presents, you know."

I couldn't help but wonder if, within this fabric of lies, boasts, and adolescent fantasies, there were any truths to Bobby's claims.

"What kinds of presents? Did he say?"

"Sometimes it was money. Once it was a membership to the Beverly Hills Health Club. I don't know exactly. Bobby used to go on and on. To tell ya the truth, sometimes I didn't listen that close."

"Bones, I want you to think back very carefully, okay?"

"I'm thinkin'," he told me, frowning very hard. It seemed to cost him a great deal of effort, and since I didn't want to leave him in this agonized state for too long, I fired the question at him fast.

"Did Bobby ever tell you *how* he managed to get Terry Cole his TV show?"

Bones shrugged. "He never really said. I always thought it was because he was such a terrific talker and all."

"Tell me something. The last few days before he was killed, what was his mood like? Did he talk about anything special?"

"He seemed pretty excited. He said he was about to come into a big wad of money."

"Where was this money coming from?"

"He said it was his bonus."

"Bonus? Did Bobby tell you what he did to earn this bonus?"

"Not really. Just that he was taking care of some trouble for someone. With me, he only talked about

217

how he was going to spend the dough. He was planning to buy a new BMW, one of those convertibles they've got now. I told him, 'No way, man! Buy yourself a nice 'Vette, why doncha?' That's what I'd do if I had the bread. Buy American."

"I'm glad to see you're patriotic, son." I said. "Let's get back to the trouble Bobby was taking care of for someone. Did he mention what kind of trouble it was?"

"Naw," said Bones. He didn't seem greatly interested. I tried a few more questions, but I saw I had lost him to the more important issue of which particular Corvette he should go out and buy if he had oodles of money. Unfortunately, Cass became involved in this pressing issue, and they debated sharply whether to go for a classic '57 Stingray convertible—fire-engine red— or one of the new luxury models.

I wanted to know what other friends Bobby Dyer might have mentioned in his fantasy ramblings, but in Southern California you soon come to realize there is no way you can compete with a car.

In this fair city, Fame is our official goddess, with Fortune sitting at Her right-hand side, and Wheels on the left—Her golden chariot in which She travels these sun-washed and increasingly blood-spattered streets.

chapter 38

An odd thing happened on the show that night. I was talking to one of the cameramen during a station break, standing off to the side of the stage. In the past week and a half, the crew had become more talkative and less fearful as they discovered I didn't actually tear apart cameramen and assistant directors with my bare hands. They were getting used to my asking questions, just as my celebrity guests had become accustomed to my occasionally jumping up during a commercial and walking over to chat with one of the crew.

The cameraman I was talking to was a clean-cut, blond California kid in his mid-twenties who wore tennis shoes, a Hawaiian shirt, and a sunny smile. His name was Butch Calhoun, and according to Steve Linder—my assistant director friend—Butch was one of the people with whom Bobby Dyer had been friends.

"I won't say actual friends," Butch told me. "We never went out drinking after work, or anything. But yeah, we used to shoot the breeze. Basically, I'd just listen. Bobby was a guy with a lot of stories. He used to exaggerate a little."

"Like how he made it with Marilyn Monroe?"

Butch grinned. "Yeah, total bull, of course. The guy was a con artist, but I got a kick out of him."

"Bobby got special treatment around here, I gather. He and Terry were close?"

"That's what he told everyone, but personally I never saw it. Mr. Cole treated Bobby like he treated everyone else—like he was some piece of slime he didn't want anything to do with."

"Odd. But Bobby didn't seem to be as afraid of Terry as everyone else was?"

"No, I guess not."

"This may sound ridiculous, but did Bobby ever claim he had something to do with Terry's getting this show, way back when it first started?"

"Well, not directly. But he hinted around, you know. How Terry Cole really *owed* him."

"Owed him what?"

"He never said. It was just a . . . a manner Bobby had, like he really knew where the bodies were buried, and so Terry had better watch his step."

I was struck by the fact that Dyer had made a lot more concrete claims to his neighbor than to his colleagues on the TV show. Probably he knew the other crew members were not as gullible as the not-so-bright Mr. Bones. I had met people like Dyer before in Hollywood. This town attracts more than its share of dreamers and schemers who couldn't survive very well in the "normal" world and arrive here to live on the fringes of imagined glory. It was possible Bobby truly believed Marilyn Monroe had tried to call him the night she died.

The line between fantasy and reality can become

blurred in a place like this, and I don't mean only on the part of the losers and third-raters. Even the stars, the successful executives, too, convince themselves that possibilities—or, for that matter, patent impossibilities—are realities. Thus, Bobby Dyer was not so different from most others in this town.

I was trying to decide if he really had any dirt on Terry Cole, or if it was as removed from reality as his affair with poor, sweet Marilyn. Probably it was a little of both. After all, there had to be *some* reason Cole had paid Bobby's membership dues for the Beverly Hills Health Club.

The simplest thing would be to ask Terry himself about this—if I could get into Happy Valley again, which wouldn't be easy, and if I could tear him away from his invisible ducks.

"There sure are a lot of flakes around here," I remarked grumpily.

This was when someone shouted: *"Look out!"* and a woman in the audience screamed.

The cameraman reacted first, pushing us both against a wall so hard I felt as if I'd been tackled by a Chicago Bear. It took me a moment to see what had almost happened. A medium-sized but heavy light on the rail above my head had come loose so that it was hanging precariously upside down by one wire.

I had almost been killed. Again.

"How the hell did that light get loose?" Lawrence Washington was screaming.

Somebody else shouted, "Stop the tape!"

An electrician was scrambling up a ladder to examine the situation. "Jeez," he said, "the screws got loose. It just rolled over."

"There are too goddamn many loose screws around here," Lawrence lamented, rushing to my aid. "Are you all right, Mr. Allen? That thing almost came down on your head."

"I live a charmed life," I told him, gazing up at the rafters. "Was anyone up there just now working in that area, or earlier?" I asked the electrician as casually as I could.

"Jeez, I don't think so," he called down.

I took the director by the arm. "No, it's all right— no harm done. I wouldn't want to see any heads roll just because mine nearly did. Maybe it was just metal fatigue, or a careless piece of work a week or so back."

Who could tell?

Probably I wouldn't know for sure if someone was trying to kill me until I was dead.

chapter 39

After the show, I telephoned Kathleen Cole from my dressing room. Her machine told me she could not come to the phone right now and that I should leave a message. I'm not terribly keen about conversations with machines, but I was leaving a message anyway when her real voice came over the receiver.

"Steve, so sorry about the nasty machine—don't you hate them?" she sang. "But I'm avoiding one or two people right now."

"Kathleen, I need to talk to you. A few things have come up."

"Let's make it tomorrow, shall we? My brain is reduced to absolute putty, and I was about to go to bed."

"It's urgent, I'm afraid."

"How boring."

There's a certain way that sophisticated people—thank God not all of them—use the word *boring*. They don't mean by it what you and I mean, and certainly not what the dictionary means. They use the word when something about the subject matter makes them uncomfortable, perhaps even angry, but they mask their discomfort with that world-weary word. Oddly enough they almost invariably apply it to a dramatically important thing. "Oh God—isn't it boring—he had AIDS."

Thus Kathleen was bored with the subject of murder. I decided to lean on her.

"The police have been after me to tell them what I know about your relations with Bobby Dyer. I've been holding out because I wanted to speak with you first, but I'll probably have to talk with them in the morning."

"More and more boring," she lamented. "Well, hold on, darling. I'll see what I can do."

The line went dead as she put me on hold. I had a suspicion Kathleen was not alone. I wondered what kind of activity I had interrupted.

"Where are you now?" she asked, coming back on the line.

"At the studio in Burbank."

"Poor you. I'll tell you what, my dear—there's a bar I sometimes go to in Malibu. The Captain's Quarters, a fun little place right by the end of the pier. Do you know it?"

"I've passed it," I told her.

"Good. Meet me there in forty-five minutes."

I stared at the telephone after she hung up, feeling a vague unease. Cass was sprawled across from me on one of the circular white couches, reading through a racing form.

"Do you own a gun, Cass?"

In all the years I had known him, I'd never had occasion to ask him that. His watery blue eyes looked up at me sharply across the paper in his hand.

"I have my old twelve-gauge back at my place. Want me to bring it along for the ride?"

"I guess not," I told him, feeling absurd. Cass rented an apartment in Glendale and we'd never make it to Malibu on time if we stopped there to pick up his shotgun.

"You think Mrs. Cole is dangerous?"

"I *know* Mrs. Cole is dangerous. But what can she do to me in a public bar?"

I had already wiped off my TV makeup, showered, and changed, so we were ready to leave. Outside it was a cool, starry night, with a crescent moon sitting on the horizon just above the man-made monoliths of downtown Burbank, which of course has no downtown. We took the Hollywood Freeway to the San Diego Freeway, and it to the Santa Monica Freeway, and as we approached the ocean ran into a fog bank that was slowly meandering inland—a giant, slow-motion wave swallowing up the land. You drive into a fog and everything changes. The temperature dropped and suddenly we could hardly see twenty feet beyond the windshield. By the time we reached the Pacific Coast Highway, we were traveling through an atmosphere as dense and wet as clam chowder. Cass slowed down to twenty miles per hour, his eyes straining to see the road.

"Turn back if you think it's too dangerous," I told him.

"Naw, we've come this far," he said. "Not much sense in turning around now."

We didn't talk as we inched up the highway toward Malibu. Occasionally I could hear waves breaking on the beach not far away, an invisible, brooding presence. After half an hour or so, we arrived at the stoplight at the intersection to the Malibu Colony, and realized we had passed the pier in the fog. We did a careful U-turn and pulled around south for a quarter mile until I got a glimpse of the orange neon light of a beer sign, writing and erasing itself in the fog. Beyond that was the vague outline of the entrance to the pier. Cass pulled up to the front door of the bar.

"Want me to come in with you?"

"No. The lady might talk more freely if we're alone. Will you be all right?"

"Sure," he said. "I'll just climb into the backseat and watch *Jake and The Fatman*. It's *you* I'm worried about, good buddy."

I gave him my Dashiell Hammett smile, full of wise irony. "Ain't a dame I met I couldn't handle," I told him, doing Bogart.

"Yeah? How about Tessa Moore? How about—"

225

"Hold on, you gotta leave a guy some illusions."

I walked into the bar, which was decorated with all sorts of nautical knickknacks—a ship's wheel, brass barometers, netting, and a lot of polished wood. Ten-thirty on a Wednesday night and the place was dead. The eyes of all four customers turned as I came through the door, looking to see what stranger might be coming in from the fog.

"Good evening," I muttered to no one in particular.

It was a dissolute-looking group. A man in a Forty-niners sweatshirt and baseball cap was nursing a bottle of Budweiser at the bar. Three stools down, a skinny guy in a Hawaiian shirt and a brassy woman sat breathing cigarette smoke into their martinis. Further down the bar was a screenwriter I had met once or twice. I was relieved when his alcohol-blurred eyes gazed at me without recognition. They all looked as if they had been sitting there a long, long time.

Kathleen Cole was nowhere to be seen. I sat down in one of the booths and the bartender came over to see what I'd like. He was middle-aged and had once been good-looking—maybe he had been a surfer or an actor—but now his features were wide and boozy, and his belly hung over his pants.

"Whad'ya want?"

"Tea," I said.

He considered this for a moment. "What kind?"

"Lipton, if possible."

He gave me a dirty look. "Peppermint, Earl Grey, English Breakfast, or Jasmine?"

Yuppies had obviously been here and revived the place. "Jasmine," I told him.

He moved off heavily to fulfill my order. "Hey,

aren't you . . . wh . . . what's-his-name?'' he asked when he came back with my tea.

"I hear that all the time," I said. "He's a much shorter fellow." I gave him a ten-dollar bill and said he should keep the change. He left me alone after that. The heavy drinkers at the bar likewise paid no further attention. I was one of the fixtures now, a part of the still-life tableau.

The place was lonely, depressing. Such joints sometimes look interesting if you see them on a TV show or in a film, but in reality there's no glamour at all, only a kind of quiet sadness. The man in the Hawaiian shirt ambled over to the jukebox and played an ancient Nat Cole recording called "An Old Piano Plays The Blues," which surprised the hell out of me because I had written the song, which Nat had recorded back in 1950 on the Capitol label. Maybe it was one of those places where the clientele was mostly over forty and preferred the older records. I drank my tea and waited, watching the door. I was about to ask for another pot of hot water when she came in.

She was wearing a tight black dress with a slit up the side clear to her thigh. She was also wearing black stiletto heels and a mink coat that was probably worth half the price of the Malibu pier. The collar, raised in back, framed her stunning face. All eyes turned her way.

"Evening, Mrs. Cole," said the bartender.

Answering him with only a nod, she glided my way, looking like the answer to every sailor's prayer.

chapter 40

When Kathleen brought a Dunhill cigarette to her lips, the bartender nearly leapt over the bar to arrive with match in hand.

"Thank you, John," she said, blowing smoke in his eyes.

"The usual, Mrs. Cole?"

"I'm bored with the usual," she said. "Let's try something new."

I had a feeling John the bartender would have jumped off the end of the pier if she had asked him.

"Cute little neighborhood place," I told her.

"People from the Colony sometimes drop in during the week." She shrugged. "On the weekends, it's full of tourists."

"So is the planet Earth," I suggested.

Her cool blue eyes were studying me. John arrived with a drink that had a piece of pineapple in it and an orange paper umbrella. She took a sip without looking at him.

"This tastes like battery acid, John. Throw it away and bring me the usual."

"Right away, Mrs. Cole. Sorry."

The usual turned out to be a Scotch and water. When it came, Kathleen turned the glass absently in her hand.

"So, what are the police saying about me?" she asked.

"That maybe you had your friend Bobby put the poison in your ex-husband's Cajun vodka," I replied as casually as one can say such a thing.

She smiled. "But why would I do that, darling? Terry takes such good care of me. I wouldn't kill the goose that lays such nice golden eggs, would I?"

I leaned closer across the table that was separating us. "In this case, maybe the goose was worth more dead than alive."

"Stop! You're making me hungry," she cried mockingly, "and it's such a long way to Christmas!"

"I'm referring to Terry's last will and testament, Kathleen. The police know you're the major beneficiary of his estate."

Her smile flickered. "Am I? How sentimental of dear Terry."

"Come on, you can't pretend you don't know about Terry's leaving you all his millions."

"Can't I? Oh, well then, I won't. It was part of our divorce settlement that those lovely millions would come my way if he died before me."

"That seems like a highly unusual provision."

"Well, Terry and I are not your run-of-the-mill couple. However, if you read the will carefully, you'll find I inherit only if Terry dies an *accidental* death, or of natural causes, darling. This was Terry's insurance that I wouldn't murder him."

"Sounds like true love," I muttered. "Well, I suppose that lets you off the hook."

"Of course it does. If those silly policemen break into Terry's safe-deposit box, at least they should learn to read more carefully. I'm the one person in the world who has a vested interest in Terry's *not* meeting with foul play."

Kathleen stubbed out her half-finished cigarette and fished a new one from her purse. John hurried out from behind the bar and materialized at her side with a match.

"I'll have another drink, John. Try to put some Scotch in it this time, there's a good boy."

I mentioned I was game for another pot of tea, but I doubted that he heard me. Kathleen Cole took up all of John's attention.

The man with the Hawaiian shirt was playing something by Ella Fitzgerald on the jukebox and dancing in front of the bar with the brassy blond lady. Everybody was having a gay old time. The screenwriter had his head on the bar and seemed to be asleep. I figured if I was ever to get anywhere with Kathleen Cole, I'd better start pressing.

"You lied to me," I told her, boring in like Ted Koppel after an evasive guest.

"Did I, darling?"

"Looks like it. You told me you hadn't been seeing Bobby for years, when actually he spent the night at your house just two weeks ago."

"Jealous?" she asked with a smirk.

"Kathleen, this is serious."

"Well, all right. I fibbed just a bit. Maybe I wanted you to think I was pure and innocent instead of a woman desperate for love." As a put-on artist, she was one of the most charming.

Our drinks came, including—to my surprise—a new pot of jasmine tea.

"Let's talk about the past," I suggested. "The thrilling days of yesteryear."

"Must we? It always makes me feel so old."

"Tell me about the story *Confidential* was going to do on Winston Dane."

"What's there to tell? It was not an enlightened era for homosexuals."

"I don't think enlightenment was exactly the point, was it? I mean we're not just talking about gaysville here. Some major stars, even in the early days of Hollywood, were gay and never got arrested for it. The problem with Winnie was that he was chiefly attracted to very young teenagers. I've even heard reports that some of them were younger than that. In any event, whatever the age arithmetic, that *is* against the law, whether you're gay or straight."

"Of course," she said. "Whether *Confidential* ever found out about that part of it I don't really know, but they certainly were going to make Winnie pansy of the year."

"The network was able to pay them off. How did they learn Winston was gay?"

Kathleen shrugged. "How did *Confidential* learn anything? Perhaps they had people hiding in the bushes with little cameras."

"They had photographs?"

"I don't know, darling. I'm just making small talk."

"Tell me then, who did know about Winston's big secret? People on the show, I mean."

"Darling, back then everything was very hush-hush. I knew, of course, and maybe one or two others, but it wasn't common knowledge."

"How did you find out?"

"Simple. Winnie took me out a few times in order to appear in public with an attractive woman. At the end of one of our evenings—to explain why nothing further was going to happen—he discussed his true inclinations."

"Did Bobby know?"

"I doubt it. Winnie was never an obvious gay—with that deep voice of his—and I can't imagine he would tell someone on his crew."

"And *you* never told Bobby?"

Kathleen had a faraway look in her eyes. "I don't think so. Normally I don't gossip about things like that, especially since I was very fond of Winnie."

"But you don't remember?"

"Not really. Bobby and I were spending a lot of time together in those days, and it may have come out, I suppose. Why do you want to know?"

"Because I'm wondering if Bobby tipped off *Confidential* and helped Winston get fired. It would explain why Terry felt he had to be grateful to an unimportant audio man for all these years, making him an associate producer and all."

"That seems a fairly wild guess."

"Do you think so? Bobby used to brag to his next-door neighbor that he got Terry his start. Maybe there was some truth in that claim."

Kathleen laughed. "Bobby had quite an imagination. Anyway, as I told you, *I* was the one who helped

Terry get started, by putting in a little work with my gentlemen friend on the board of directors."

I took Kathleen's hand across the table. Her fingers were as cool and delicate as marble.

"Maybe you and Bobby did it together," I suggested. "He went to *Confidential* and got Winston fired. Then you went to the powers at the network and used some heavy body language to sell them on Terry. All so you could become a rich and famous Hollywood wife."

Her blue eyes gazed back at me without emotion; her cool hand in mine never flinched. Yet somehow I felt she was forcing herself to remain calm.

"This is what the cops think?"

"Maybe this is what *I* think," I told her, "and I'm way ahead of the cops."

Quite carefully, she took her captive hand out of my grasp and put it around her drink. "They say a little knowledge can be a dangerous thing, Steve."

"Then tell me more, Kathleen, so I'll know a lot. Why did Bobby put rat poison in Terry's Cajun vodka?"

She downed the rest of her Scotch and gave me a lopsided grin. "You know, you're cute," she told me. "Jayne's a fool to leave you in this town all by your lonesome."

I tried to bring her back to the subject of murder, but she had reverted to what I took to be her mock-flirtation mode. Or, I don't know, maybe it was legit at that moment. If this had been a scene in a movie, you would have thought it all very romantic—the old Gordon Jenkins ballad now emanating from the jukebox, with a million violins and Gordon's sensitive, one-finger solo technique, the flickering glow from the fireplace, dim lighting, the fishnet decor, the soft, hypnotic whish of the sea outside, and a strikingly handsome woman smiling at me. Somehow I couldn't bring myself to work on the question of whether she found me attractive or was just flashing her charm around as a way of closing the door on any further discussion of murder. So, at the moment, I felt two kinds of frustration: one sexual, if low-key, the other more acute—a sense that I had been close to the truth but had allowed it to slip through my fingers.

"Let's get out of here, Steve," she said. "This place has become boring."

I asked for the bill, but the bartender said it was on the house.

"How sweet of you, John," Kathleen told him, hardly giving him so much as a glance. I helped her on with her mink coat, which she had thrown carelessly over a chair. A hundred little creatures had given their lives so that Kathleen Cole could be so stunningly elegant in a sleazy waterfront bar. She was a lady who expected great sacrifice to her beauty and did not give a lot in return. I was glad we were about to part company.

All the eyes that were still able to focus watched us make our departure. The man in the Hawaiian shirt gave me a broad wink. I felt like punching him in the nose.

chapter 41

Kathleen and I walked out of the bar into a fog so thick I could barely see more than a few feet in any direction. A flashing orange light on the highway cast a diffuse, fun-house glow. I put up the collar of my sports coat against the rawness of the air, and Kathleen put her hand through my arm. I wondered where Cass was. I couldn't see the limousine anywhere.

"Walk me to my car," she asked. "I'm parked across the street."

I wasn't too thrilled, but I couldn't leave the lady on the side of the highway on a night like this. She seemed to know her way here better than I did, pointing us toward the crosswalk that led to the other side of the coast highway. At least there was no traffic moving anywhere on the road near us. The fog made everything unnaturally still and quiet, with only the ocean pounding softly against the sand like some primeval heartbeat of the planet itself.

"Why did you park all the way over here?"

She laughed. "Oh, only a habit. When I leave a bar, I like my car waiting on the right side of the road, pointing home. I'm in that little lot in front of the coffee shop."

I knew where she meant, having passed this complex of small stores and fast-food restaurants countless times over the years. But the fog so late at night had transformed everything into an eerie and unknown landscape. We guided ourselves across the highway by pointing to a neon blur of light in some unseen window. I was glad when I looked over my shoulder to discover I could still make out the half shape of the bar we had just left, though it was like seeing through a curtain of gauze. Kathleen had a yellow Rolls Royce convertible, the top of which was securely fastened down against the weather. There was a street light nearby that cast a glow strong enough for her to find the key in her purse. I held the door open as she slipped into the leather interior.

"Do you want to come home with me?" she purred.

"I don't think that would be a very good idea, Kathleen."

"It sounds good to me," she said, "but suit yourself." She put her key in the ignition and the expensive engine came discreetly to life. She let down the window when I closed the door.

"You know, Steve . . . maybe you're looking into things that might best be left alone."

"Are you trying to warn me off, Kathleen?"

"Lord, no. I'm trying to give you some friendly advice. Why not let the police do what they're paid for? You wouldn't want Jayne to find herself an unexpected widow."

Kathleen flashed me a Sphinx-like smile, and before I could ask her any more questions, she and her yellow

Rolls were floating up the highway toward Trancas. I watched the red taillights until they were swallowed in the fog. When she was gone and I couldn't hear the engine anymore, I felt like the last human being on Earth. It wasn't the best feeling I've ever had. We comedians generally require more of an audience.

A breeze came up, lifting the fog for a second. I could see the Malibu pier across the road, the bar, and several parked cars. Was one of them Cass's Cadillac? I wasn't quite sure and I didn't have time to find out, because a new wave of cloud blew in from the ocean and engulfed me so totally that I could see almost nothing at all—not the bar, not even my feet.

I whistled a few bars of an Ellington jump tune, always a good way to cheer up. But I still felt fear. Standing lost in the density of this fog was like being buried alive.

"Cass!" I called. "You there?"

There was no answer.

"Oh, Ca-a-ss!" I tried again, louder and more desperate. Finally I gave it the full power of my lungs: *"Cass! Where the hell are you?"*

The breeze from the ocean began swirling the fog about more rapidly. To my relief, the air suddenly cleared and I could see somewhat better. I began walking into the crosswalk, determined to cross the road while the visibility was still good, but I wasn't fast enough. A new cloud rolled in and covered me even more completely than before. Now I was totally lost. I kept going, my hands pointlessly in front of me to feel the way, hoping to get off the highway at least, though I was no longer even certain in which direction I was going.

That was when I heard a car engine nearby. It seemed to come up from nowhere. I could see the headlights now, dim, but coming my way.

Was I still in the middle of the road?

The sky cleared, and yes, I was—smack dab in the middle of the Pacific Coast Highway with a big black car bearing down on me. I waved my arms wildly above my head.

"Hey!" I shouted. But the car, instead of slowing down, was actually speeding up, rushing my way with the obvious intent of cutting me down.

I staggered backward toward the curb, but the car veered my way. This all seemed to be happening in slow motion, a great mistake, a most undignified way to die. At the last second, I half fell, half leapt backward, foolishly doing a backstroke through the empty air—as if in a nightmare—trying to get away.

I hit something, or something hit me—I was too confused to say exactly which. Then a darkness more profound than fog settled over my brain, and time itself seemed to stop.

chapter 42

Dreamless sleep.

I don't know how long I was out. It seemed like eternity, give or take a few hours—but it couldn't have been that long because when I came to, I was in the back-seat of Cass's limousine, and it was still the same damnably foggy night in Malibu.

Cass was trying to pour brandy down my throat from his silver flask. I believe that back in Wyoming this is considered the proper cure for just about anything. I sputtered and sat up and became aware of a giant headache that made me wish I had stayed asleep a little longer.

"How you feeling?" Cass was asking me. His voice sounded worried and far away. He lightly slapped my face and spilled brandy down the front of my shirt. None of this made me feel any better.

"Will you stop pouring brandy all over me, for God's sake! If someone comes by with a match, I'll be funnyman *flambé.*"

"Sorry."

I tried out the various parts of my body to make

certain everything still worked. Except for the giant headache, I seemed to be all in one piece.

I heard a siren coming down the highway. "That should be the ambulance," Cass said. "I called 911 as soon as I got you in the car."

"What the hell happened?" I asked, massaging the back of my neck. "I couldn't see you when I came out of the bar."

"I was parked by the pier. I guess you couldn't find me in the fog. I saw you crossing the highway with Mrs. Cole, and then it got real thick and I couldn't see you anymore. A little later, I saw a car coming down the highway real fast, and I heard you calling for help. Thank God the fog lifted a bit or you'd still be lying in the middle of the road."

A sheriff's car and an ambulance were pulling up alongside.

"That's all of it?" I asked.

"Yep. I picked you up—which ain't easy—carried you into the backseat, telephoned for help, and tried to bring you around."

"The car that tried to run me down—where'd he come from?"

"Jeez, I don't know. He seemed to come out of nowhere."

"Then you didn't hear him coming down the highway?"

"No. I'd say he must have parked just a little ways up the road—like he was waiting for you."

"That's a sobering thought," I muttered. Had Kathleen set me up to be killed? A young sheriff's deputy was opening up the door to the backseat, with an ambulance attendant standing behind him.

"You the people who called for help?" The sheriff stuck his nose inside and winced at the alcoholic fumes. His eyes narrowed in grave suspicion.

"Someone tried to run me over," I explained. "I was knocked unconscious, but my friend here managed to pick me up out of the middle of the highway and carry me back to the car."

I had the definite impression this young sheriff was not fond of people in burgundy-colored stretch limousines who reeked of brandy.

"You were just wandering around in the middle of the highway on a night like this?"

"I wasn't *wandering,* Officer. I had been in the bar over there earlier . . ."

"Bar? Would you step out of the car, please?"

"Officer, someone just tried to kill me."

"Sure. Now step out of the car, please. You, too," he said to Cass.

"Does anyone here require medical attention?" asked the ambulance attendant, who didn't seem pleased by this late-night trip.

"I'm all right," I said. "My head feels like the day after New Year's Eve, but other than that, I'm fine."

"Steve, you might have a concussion," Cass objected. "Officer, I think Mr. Allen should be taken to the hospital."

"Will everyone just shut up?" the sheriff requested patiently. "Now, let's see which of you gentlemen can walk a straight line."

"Officer, you've got this all wrong!" I objected.

"Or you can take the breath analyzer," he said. "It's up to you."

"Damn it, you're going too far," I shouted. "Here

I've been led astray by a woman, abandoned in the fog, nearly mowed down by a killer automobile—and you think I'm drunk!"

"Just turn around," the sheriff ordered. "Hands against the car. Spread your legs. You too, mister," he said to Cass.

He began to pat me down for concealed weapons. Then he pulled my hands behind my back and snapped cuffs around my wrists.

"You have the right to remain silent; you have the right. . . ."

Cass and I were put in the backseat of the sheriff's cruiser. There was wire mesh separating him from us, so we wouldn't be able to bite him or anything. The sheriff whistled as he drove the short distance to the Malibu station up the road.

"Well, I guess we're outlaws now," Cass drawled. I began to laugh and then couldn't stop. Probably this was unwise in light of my suspected insobriety, but this entire evening was beginning to seem like a bad joke. When we arrived at the station, my chuckling stopped. The duty officer behind the front desk was a sergeant I recognized from our previous Malibu fiasco. I tried to avert my face, but it was no use.

"Hey, I remember you guys," he said in that jolly tone cops use when they have you totally at their mercy. "You two are the fellows we brought in the other day after that high-speed chase, trying to resist arrest. My, my, aren't you something."

I had an inkling Cass and I were in the kind of trouble it wouldn't be easy to talk our way out of.

"Officer, I know this must look bad, but there's really a very simple explanation."

I tried to tell him my simple explanation: about the multiple murder case I was trying to solve, and the fuzzy black car from which somebody had tried to shoot at me, and how a beautiful but deadly woman had possibly tried to have me run down.

The sheriff looked at me sadly and pursed his lips with grim satisfaction. I guess it wasn't every day a peace officer had the pleasure of booking the likes of Jimmy Cassidy and The Talk Show Kid.

"You're guests of the county now, gentlemen. And I have a feeling you might be with us for a while."

chapter 43

I was allowed to make one phone call to my lawyer, but I learned he wouldn't be able to get Cass and me out of the Malibu jail until the following morning, at which time hopefully a judge would set bail.

Our clothes, wallets, belts, and shoelaces were taken away, and we were given orange jumpsuits with *L.A. County Jail* written across the back. Then we were shown to a cell with a concrete floor, four bunk beds and unsightly metal bars. We had a roommate who was snoring loudly on one of the lower bunks. I sat down glumly on the opposite bed, surveying my new surroundings. It wasn't exactly the Beverly Hills Hotel.

Cass was more philosophical. He climbed up into the bunk over my head and suggested we both just go to sleep. Morning would come a lot faster that way, he said.

Cass took his own advice, and I sat for a long time listening to stereophonic snoring. Just when I thought I couldn't take it anymore, one of the snorers woke up. It was our roommate, a man in his late thirties, unshaven with wild brown hair and two small pink eyes.

At first he looked at me without interest, stared back at the wall for a few seconds, and then—I swear—did an actual doubletake. He looked at me intently for a moment and then said, "If I didn't know I was in the can, I'd swear you look like that guy on TV."

"Who's that?" I asked.

"You know," he said, "the guy with the glasses."

"Steve Allen," I said resignedly.

"No," he said. "Wait a minute—yeah, that's it. You look like him, but he's younger lookin'."

"That is right," I said. "Of course those characters on television use a lot of makeup. They have people to do their hair, that kind of stuff."

"You sound like him, too," the man said.

"Yeah," I said, "I hear that all the time."

He looked away, then back at me again.

"Hey," he said, "you puttin' me on?"

"No," I said, "I'm just sitting here minding my own business."

He didn't take the hint.

"You *are* Steve Allen."

"I used to be," I answered, giving up.

"Don't feel so bad," he said. "I never used to be anybody."

"Aw, everybody's somebody," I said.

"Not me, man."

"Don't be so hard on yourself," I said.

"How's your brother-in-law gettin' along?" he asked. The question stumped me. I had one living brother-in-law, Jayne's brother, Edward, an attorney, but he did corporate work for Continental Airlines and I couldn't see how my cell mate could have met him.

"You know my brother-in-law?" I said.

"Yeah," he said, "Ralph Kramden." It took me about ten seconds to figure that one out.

"Mr. Gleason is dead," I said.

"Oh," he said. "That's too bad."

His name was Earl and I soon learned he was right: the poor guy was nobody. I discovered why no woman would put up with him (he was crude and unreliable), no employer would hire him (he was lazy), and why he had never even made good as a crook (he was stupid). About the only thing Earl could do well was drink, though this generally ended up with Earl in jail.

His story was so depressing it finally put me to sleep. I awoke the next morning, stiff and sore, to find my situation had not dramatically improved. I wanted to close my eyes and hibernate until this nightmare was over, but a deputy I had not seen before was poking his nose through the bars.

"Someone's here to see you," he said.

The deputy unlocked the cell and led me down a bleak corridor to a small interrogation room. Sergeant Walker was sitting behind a small desk waiting for me. He handed me a bag with coffee and doughnuts in it, and I was so grateful to see his pudgy face I nearly wept.

"You need somebody to look after you, Mr. Allen."

"It's just a streak of bad luck," I told him. "At least I'm still alive."

"Tell me about it."

So I told him about my late-night meeting with Kathleen Cole and the car that tried to run me down. I was not in a holding-back mood. I even recounted some of the juicier details I had previously been keeping to myself, such as the *Confidential* story that was never printed and my suspicions that Bobby Dyer had some part in getting Winston Dane fired from his show.

"That's why Terry promoted him from boom operator to associate producer and kept him around all these years," I said. "The way I see it, Bobby was a blackmailer. His neighbor said he was expecting a big wad of money—that would be the payoff, you see—but whoever he was blackmailing decided to deal him out for good."

"So who was he blackmailing? Terry Cole?"

"Probably. If Terry got his show in some unethical way, and Bobby knew about it, he'd have a meal ticket for life."

W.B. was smiling at me. "So you think Terry killed Bobby Dyer?"

"It's possible," I insisted. "Listen, Terry can come and go from that place in Santa Barbara anytime he likes."

"All right, but why did Bobby leave the rat poison in the Cajun vodka?"

I didn't have an answer for that. If Bobby was blackmailing Terry, he would not have tried to kill his source of income.

"I guess it's still a mystery," I said with a sigh.

"Don't fret, Mr. Allen. We simply don't have all the facts yet. Let's get back to last night and the car that tried to run you down. Did you see the driver's face?"

"No," I admitted. "The car came out of the fog and the headlights were shining in my eyes."

"What about the car? Can you describe it?"

"Well, it was black . . . and sort of fuzzy," I had to say, "what with the fog and all."

"Another fuzzy black car?" W.B. inquired gently.

"I realize it's a big coincidence."

"Could it have been the same car from which somebody took a shot at you on Beverly Drive?"

"Who knows?" I lamented.

"You say the car actually veered toward you when you tried to get out of the way?"

"That's right."

"Of course, you were lost in the fog and you don't really know in which direction you were going. Maybe you were walking the wrong way, into the traffic rather than away."

"What are you getting at?"

He shrugged. "Maybe it was just a car coming down the coast highway that didn't see you in the fog. You *were* in the middle of the road. Maybe no one was trying to murder you at all."

I was getting mad. "Look, Sergeant, you were bugged when I didn't tell you about the shots taken at me in Beverly Hills. Now someone tries to run me down and I tell you everything—and you don't believe me."

"I'm not saying I don't believe you; I'm just looking at all the possibilities. For instance, if someone *was* out there waiting for you, he or she probably would have had to have been tipped off by Mrs. Cole."

"That's right."

"In other words, Mrs. Cole deliberately parked on the far side of the road to set you up? But why would she do that? You just got through presenting a convincing theory that Terry Cole is the killer, not Kathleen."

"I don't know," I said. My head still hurt and I'd had enough. I stood up and began to pace around the small interrogation room like a caged animal. "Furthermore, I don't even *want* to know. From now on, I'm leaving police work to the professionals. Detective Allen has just retired from the case."

"What a pity. It'll be dull without you."

"You can watch me on television," I told him grumpily. "If they ever let me out of this damned jail, and someone doesn't murder me first."

"Oh, the jail part's been taken care of," Walker told me with a sly smile. "Your driver has been fetching your limousine while we've been having our little chat. You see, John the bartender confirmed you were only drinking jasmine tea and left his bar cold sober. And believe it or not, people aren't arrested for walking a lady to her car, not even in Malibu."

I was fuming mad. "Why didn't you tell me that right away? Here I've been a free man for the last forty-five minutes and I didn't even know."

"I like to save a surprise for the end."

The sergeant walked me back down the hall to the main desk and helped me get connected with my wallet and clothes.

"Congratulations, you're a free man," he told me with a wink. "Now we'll see what we can do about keeping you alive."

chapter 44

I was glad to return my attention to my show. Comedy and television were subjects I knew something about, and the last twelve hours had considerably dampened my enthusiasm for detection work as an alternative career.

There were now only two nights left in my two-week tenure as guest host for *The Terry Cole Show,* and I wanted to go out with a bang. (Though not too literal a bang, if I could help it.) Then I'd take a short vacation in Hawaii with Jayne, and get on with the other various projects up my sleeve—books and songs, TV specials, a film I'd been asked to direct—leaving Terry Cole and his bloodthirsty, blackmailing cohorts behind me.

In short, I was ready to be myself once more, forget

all this nonsense, and never see the inside of a jail cell or Detective Sergeant W.B. Walker again.

Thursday afternoon I took a nap in my comfortable bed, soaked in the bathtub, and when I looked in the mirror, was pleased to see my usual self peering back. Late-night America would probably not even guess they were looking at a jailbird who was hoping to work his way back into the good graces of society.

It's not that I'd never been behind bars before. In fact, I once did three days in the tiny city jail of Del Rio, Texas, when I was sixteen years old. I'd been on the road for a couple of weeks, had run out of money, had no food, and therefore was so desperate that I had, for the preceding few days, been trying to talk my way into various jails as I passed through a succession of side-of-the-road communities. It was patiently explained to me, of course, that I could not possibly enjoy such accommodations without committing some formal offense. Anyway, in Del Rio I was finally desperate enough to go into the Bluebird Cafe (I wonder if it still exists), order a hot roast-beef sandwich with gobs of mashed potatoes and gravy, apple pie *à la mode,* and three cups of coffee, even though I didn't have a penny in my pocket. When the counterman said, "Will there be anything else?" I actually said, "Yeah, I'll have the same thing all over again," and did.

Then came the tough part. At the cash register I said to the owner, "I'm sorry to have to tell you this, but I don't have any money to pay for the food I just ate. But I'll be happy to wash dishes, mop up the joint, or do any other work you might want me to do." Well, my offer wasn't received too favorably. The local fuzz were called and a tall, lean Texas Ranger-type, with a kindly air, took me to the local bastille and signed me in. Jails haven't improved much in the intervening years.

The show Thursday night went well, but Friday was the best of all, the culmination of the two weeks. My principal guest was Tessa Moore and we got away from the talk-show format by doing a sketch we'd worked out in advance. The art of the TV sketch is something I pioneered on my shows back in the fifties and sixties—along with people like Sid Caesar and Jackie Gleason—and it's a form I still have fun with.

Tessa and I appeared as Jim and Tammy Bakker, having a vicious but sanctimonious argument about finances and infidelity. The sketch ended with Jim's being exiled to the infamous air-conditioned doghouse.

You might wonder if this kind of playacting is proper employment for two adults. I can't say, but it was fun—and eventually we returned to being Steve and Tessa, with me behind the desk and Tessa in the hot spot on the couch.

"Tell me, Tessa—this is a question I often ask comedians—when did you first discover you were funny?"

"I must have been seven or eight, Steve. I found out I didn't get into trouble when I screwed up if I could make people laugh."

"Recall any examples?"

"Well, I once broke the proverbial cookie jar—I really did—trying to get it down from the top of the refrigerator at a time my mother told me I wasn't supposed to snack. I mean, we're talking major crime here! The whole thing came down, *boom*, all over the floor, chocolate chips and broken pottery everywhere.

My mother came in and boy, was she mad! I knew that unless I could make her *smile* I was in for a major spanking. It was definitely all-hail-the Emperor-Gluteus-Maximus time.

"So what did you do?"

"Well, first I just stood there and made my eyes very big." Tessa did that now, giving us a sublimely innocent big-eyed look, which transformed hatchet-nosed Tessa Moore into the sweetest little girl since Shirley Temple. With Tessa, the transformation was so absurd the audience broke up.

"And what did your mother do?"

"She stood over me, about twenty-five feet tall—you know how parents can get when they're mad—shaking her finger at me. And she said, 'Tessa, you bad girl, tell me how this happened?' And I said, 'Mother, I cannot tell a lie. I was climbing up on top of the refrigerator to get the whiskey bottle you've got hidden up there were Daddy won't find it.'

" 'That does it,' she said. 'Now I'm gonna beat you within an inch of your life.' I started to run away and she said, 'Where do you think you're going?' I said, 'I'm gonna get a tape measure.' 'Why?' she said. 'Well, you said within an inch of my life and I wouldn't want you to slip and make it an inch and a half.'

" 'And another thing,' she said, 'that isn't whiskey up there. That's my medicine.'

" 'Oh, yeah?' I said. 'Then how come the only time you're any laughs is when you're sick?' "

We had gone from the broken cookie jar to broad comic exaggeration.

"Seriously, Tessa, when did you first decide you wanted to be a comedian?"

"What time is it now?" she said, pretending to look at her wristwatch.

"Believe it or not," I said, laughing at her, "I'm serious. There are a lot of young people out there right now who think they'd like to get into the comedy field. It might be instructive for them to learn how you did it."

At that she turned at least partially serious and quickly reviewed some biographical data.

Tessa had grown up in the San Fernando Valley but went to New York after high school to hit the early comedy clubs in the Village and absorb the heady satire being created at the time by people like Mort Sahl and Lenny Bruce. Most professional comics begin at something else. Woody Allen and Mel Brooks, for instance, were writers. Sid Caesar played the saxophone. But Tessa had never done anything but comedy. She'd worked her way up the ladder slowly, tooth and nail, playing the resorts in the Catskills and Atlantic City, and the small clubs from coast to coast. It's not an easy life, particularly for a woman. There's little glamour and few rewards on the lower rungs of show business.

Tessa's first break in working her way up out of the cellars and dives, was getting a few bookings on the old Playboy Club circuit back in the mid-sixties when Bunny Power was at its height.

From the Playboy circuit she and her agent were able to parlay a few favorable reviews into a last-minute booking at The Sands in Las Vegas when, as I recall, Phyllis Diller had to cancel because she got sick. Because the Vegas critics and bosses had never seen her before, she was the new, fresh face in town, and when she scored well the opening night, that led to even more important local bookings during the next few years, and that in turn—at incredibly long last—had led to television.

The only comedian who took even longer to have any good fortune was Joan Rivers. Both women had put up with years of literally being told to get out of show business. But here was Tessa, still struggling for her life. A few years back, she had had her own weekly summer television show, had *almost* become very big—but two years from now she could be broke and forgotten.

Looking at it this way, being a comedian is sometimes not very funny. As I listened to Tessa tell her story on my final night of hosting *The Terry Cole Show*, I empathized with her.

Hearing stories like Tessa's sometimes makes me feel a twinge of guilt that my own adventures in the funny business have totally lacked struggle and rejection. There was, quite literally, only one period of three weeks, in 1944, when I walked the streets looking for work. Since that time employment has been steady, as a result of which I can get quite depressed thinking of extremely talented people who have had to do it all the hard way, and without any guarantees of continued success at the end of the line either.

"Seriously, life, for most comics, is tough. Have you ever been tempted to give it up and become anything else?" I asked her.

She threw back her head and laughed, quite heartily. "Never," she said. "Like most people in show business I wouldn't know how to make an honest living in any other field. You know, that reminds me, my father—who was very conservative politically—used to do that cliché number about public figures who never met a payroll. That's the way he used to put down politicians, mostly Democrats. He'd say they never met a payroll. Well, Ronnie Reagan never met a payroll either. It's a funny thing, nobody ever would have dreamed of hiring him to run General Motors, run a university, run a department store, run any business at all, really. So what job do they give him? Running the whole goddamned country. Go figga.''

It was my turn to laugh. "So all right," I said. "You're obviously going to stay in comedy. Are you one of these comics who would do almost anything to get the right part?"

She gave me a sly look. "Oh, yeah, anything," she said.

I felt a shiver. Millions might be watching, I knew, but I felt as if we were alone. We both knew we weren't talking in the abstract anymore, but about something closer to home.

"To get your own show again would you cheat?" I asked, with a smile.

"Oh, all the time."

"Lie?"

"Like a rug."

I had to ask it. I'd come this far. With a warm smile I said, "How about murder, Tessa? Would you do that?"

The visitors, who had been laughing themselves silly only a moment earlier, now suddenly were strangely quiet. This was not the kind of dialogue they had come to hear. I didn't care. I had the crazy feeling Tessa might confess to me, right there on network TV.

But she only smiled. "Kill people?" she asked innocently. "No. In this business, that's something only the critics do."

chapter 45

Sonny Melnik was smoking the biggest cigar I'd ever seen as he sat behind the gargantuan desk in his office looking like emperor of the dwarfs. He had suggested I stop by after the last show, so here I was.

"That was a damned peculiar interview," he told me.

"This has been a damned peculiar two weeks."

He shrugged and gave me a tired little smile.

"I suppose you're glad it's over?"

"Doing the show was fun," I said, "but I could have done without the extracurricular activities."

He sighed briefly and conducted a meaningless examination of the wristwatch and fingernails on his left hand. "Well, anyway," he said, "I've gotta thank you for doing a hell of a job."

I must explain that he would have said that had I turned in the worst performance in the history of talk shows. "Thank you, Sonny," I said. I'm always ill at ease in the presence of compliments, however insincere.

"So now," he said, "you can go floating off into the night, but I'm still stuck here trying to keep this goddamn ship from sinking."

"Hey," I said, "it's not as bad as all that."

"The hell it ain't," he said. "You wouldn't believe all the crap I've had to take over the years. Terry screws up and the network crawls all over *me* as if it was my fault. Sometimes I swear to God I'm really tempted to tell 'em what they can do with their goddamn show."

"Sonny," I said, "did you ever try driving a truck between Cincinnati and Louisville for a living? Did you ever try working as a policeman in the Bronx? Did you ever try working as a coal miner in Pennsylvania? Personally I think practically everybody who works in show business ought to look around every morning to make sure nobody's listening and then whisper a little prayer, just in case God's tuned in. 'Thank you, O Mighty Spirit, for letting me get away with murder and get paid goddamn good money for it.' "

I could sense at this point that Sonny had stopped listening to me.

"Be that as it may," I continued using one of my favorite tongue-in-check conversational jumper cables, "when is Terry coming back?"

"Another week or so. Who knows? He has all the fun, I do all the work." Obviously my little speech had made little impression on him.

"That's tough. What about the show next week?"

"Reruns. We're going to have a *Best of Terry Cole Festival.*"

I knew what I should do now was get up, shake

257

hands, and wish Sonny lots of luck. Yet there was something holding me back.

"Sonny, I hate to mention this, but you know, don't you, that Terry might never come back."

"You think so?"

"The little guys from Pluto might finally carry him away," I suggested.

"Naw, Terry's not that crazy. He's just putting everyone on. Anyway, I guess if worse comes to worst, *I* could do the show. Hell, I do everything else around here! Whad'ya think, Steve? I've always had this deep feeling inside I'd be dynamite on television."

"You'd be a blast, all right."

"I'd blow them away," he said, sucking belligerently on his cigar. "Terry thinks he's the only one with talent around here."

I had taken about as much of Sonny Melnik as it's possible to take in one sitting. I stood up and we shook hands and lied to each other about what a tremendous pleasure it had been the last two weeks.

Why couldn't I leave well enough alone? Sonny walked me toward the door, but I turned to him before leaving.

"I'm curious, Sonny—what did Bobby Dyer actually do as associate producer, besides stocking the refrigerator with the vodka?"

"Not much. Sometimes he'd pick up guests at the airport, or arrange their hotel reservations. That sort of thing. I used to tell Terry it wasn't worth the money we were paying him."

"Then why did Terry keep him on?"

Sonny gave me one of his martyred shrugs. "Who knows what Terry's thinking? Not me."

"You were never curious why there was this extra person on the payroll all these years who didn't really do anything?"

"Curiosity killed the cat," he said, looking at me in an odd way.

It was my turn to sigh. "Yeah, I guess so," I said. I had a brief image of myself standing in the middle of the Pacific Coast Highway staring into the headlights of a big black car that was about to run me down.

I said good-bye without a question more.

chapter 46

Cass helped me clean my belongings out of the dressing room, which didn't take long. In two weeks I had never moved much of myself into the place, nor had I ever felt completely comfortable with the glitzy decor or the size.

"You're going to take some of the booze, Steve?"

"No. You go ahead if you want, Cass."

"What about the smoked salmon?"

"The fish is all yours, man," I told him.

This delayed our departure as we had to carry all the booty to the limousine. At the end of our labors, Cass would be able to open up a small delicatessen. I was glad when it was done. The giant network complex had begun to depress me and I was anxious to get on our way.

Outside, there was a dull overcast upon the city, turning the night sky milky white from the reflection of all the lights. I was feeling weary and out of sorts, which is not like me at all.

"You don't look glad," Cass remarked.

Sometimes it is a pain to have someone around who knows you too well. I decided to ride in the back of the limousine for a change, since I didn't want Cass to see me, or tell me what I looked like, or give me any advice. I just wanted to be alone.

We pulled out onto the Hollywood Freeway and the posh, overstuffed feeling of the back of the limo made me feel like I was riding in a very grand casket. I wasn't certain why I was feeling depressed. I asked myself if it was because I was going to miss being on TV every night, and my answer was yes and no. There was a certain letdown returning to low-profile existence, but it was a relief to have it over with as well.

So why was I blue?

I decided I just didn't feel finished somehow. There were too many questions I didn't have answers for, including who had been trying to kill me. Also I could still see Hal Hoaglund's accusing eyes whenever I closed my own, looking at me in endless reproach.

Trust me, kid.

Would I ever be able to live with his death?

Down the hatch, kid!

I didn't think so. Restlessly, I turned on the TV and scanned the channels. I watched the local news for a while as Cass piloted us off the freeway onto Highland and started driving toward Beverly Hills. On the local news, I learned about a rape and a murder and drugs in the public schools, as well as tomorrow's weather and all the latest sports.

I tried, Hal, I told his ghost. *It's not my fault I wasn't able to figure out why you had to die. I'm a comedian, you know, not Dick Tracy.*

Hey, don't worry about it, he told me. *What the hell. My mamma warned me about guys with glasses offering strong drink—I should have listened.*

I even almost got killed myself a few times, I assured him. *That's how hard I've been trying to figure this out.*

I appreciate it, Steve. It's not your fault you make a lousy detective. Go back to writing songs.

I wasn't feeling very musical though. I'm not used to failure. The problem was, I still had ideas. There were people I could put some fairly serious questions to now, like Terry Cole, for example, who might have a hard time explaining why he put up with a hopeless braggart like Bobby Dyer all these years.

Forget it, buddy. Jayne wouldn't like it if you got killed too, said the ghost of Hal Hoaglund.

That's true, Hal.

Sometimes you have to accept failure. It's called maturity, Steve.

We argued back and forth. The reasonable side of me did battle with the impulsive side. It was a close race, running neck and neck, and I still didn't know who was going to win.

Give me a sign, Hal. I can't figure this out!

The TV was on to a commercial. An elegant young woman was sitting by an open window, looking me in the eye.

"Bored? Depressed?" she asked.

261

You said it, baby.

"Has your boyfriend left you?"

Hey, who do you think I am?

"Lost your job?"

You're warm.

". . . then escape to *Santa Barbara!*" she extolled, telling me about a popular, daytime soap.

I ask you now, was this or was this not a sign?

I pressed the button to lower the glass divider between Cass and me.

"Turn around," I told him. "We're heading back to the freeway."

"Where we goin'?"

"North," I said.

"Now?" He turned to look at me like I was crazy.

"Don't worry about it," I said. "I'm operating on instructions from a higher source."

chapter 47

We stopped for gas and I moved around from the back to the front seat of the limousine. I was feeling pretty good about myself, all in all. With me, depression disappears the moment I have a plan of action. We were headed toward Santa Barbara.

"So what's the plan, boss—you going to climb over the stone wall maybe?"

"Maybe," I told Cass, irritated because I had not quite thought this far ahead. "We'll see how I feel."

"I hope you're feeling strong," he remarked.

"What's a slight stone wall?" I muttered.

"A six-foot-high stone wall," he reminded me, "with spikes and barbed wire on top."

We rode another ten minutes in silence. "Listen, I got an idea," I told him. "We'll walk around the perimeter of the property until we find a tree growing alongside the wall. Then we'll just climb the tree and jump over to the other side."

"I can see why you're the boss, all right."

"There's no need to be sarcastic, Cass."

"I was just hoping we could swing over the wall with a hanging vine, Tarzan-style. We'll carry flashlights with our teeth."

"Okay, okay, I get the point."

Cass and I had arrived at an age beyond which it was advisable to climb trees and/or scale stone walls with nasty spikes on top. If we were going to break into the Happy Valley Center to see Terry Cole, it was going to have to be done with brains, not brawn.

"So what are we going to do?"

"It's a good thing they call me the king of ad-lib," I told him, and left it at that. Cass looked at me from time to time as we drove, but I offered no further comment. When we left the freeway in Santa Barbara, I told him to pull over at a supermarket we were passing that was open twenty-four hours.

"You want me to come in with you?"

"If you want to, Cass."

Cass was not about to let me out of his sight. He locked up the Cadillac and followed me through the hiss of the electronic door into the brightly lit market. It was nearly midnight, but a fair number of Californians were doing their weekly shopping, grazing up and down the long aisles. The store was enormous. You could buy everything here from a lawn chair to a T-bone steak, with a change of oil for your car and twenty different brands of aspirin for your headache.

Cass followed me to aisle 12B, where I was able to pick out a large manila envelope. Then we walked past a freezer section that was so long and cold I wished I had my overcoat, past baby food and breakfast cereal to the paperback books and the vast array of magazines. After some consideration, I picked out an issue of *Soldier of Fortune* magazine, *Modern Muscles,* and *Motorcycle Mania.*

"You *are* going to try to scale the wall," Cass mused.

Without answering, I led our way to the checkout stand where we had to wait behind a lady whose cart was filled with potato chips, Wonder bread, Oreos, and diet soda. I hated to imagine what her family looked like, if they were still alive.

"I know! You're going to hire a mercenary—is that it?—to take care of this little problem for us."

"Don't you want to be surprised, Cass?"

"That's just it, man—I don't."

He followed me out of the store and opened up the car. I sat in the front and turned on the overhead light. I put the three magazines I had bought into the manila envelope, and then wrote with a pen on the front: "MR. TERRY COLE, c/o The Happy Valley Center, Santa Barbara, CA." Underneath that, in the lower left-hand corner, I printed neatly: "BY HAND." In the upper left-hand corner, I indicated—falsely—that this package was being sent courtesy of "Sylvester Stallone, Bloodthirsty Productions, Inc.," whose address in Beverly Hills I cheerfully created.

When this was done, I used the front-seat telephone to call Happy Valley. A man answered the phone.

"Hello, this is Bloodthirsty Productions," I told him. "I have a package for Mr. Terry Cole from Mr. Sylvester Stallone that will be delivered by special messenger in approximately fifteen minutes."

"What's that?" The man on the other end didn't sound too quick on the uptake. Maybe he had been playing water polo too long. I gave him the message again, word for word.

"Whoa! Hold on! You can't deliver a package this time of night."

"Why not?" I asked.

"First of all, the guests aren't supposed to have any contact with folks from the outside, and second, there's no one here right now to receive a package even if it *were* all right."

"And who exactly are you?"

"Just the night watchman, bub."

"And your name, please?" I asked briskly.

"Norm," he told me reluctantly. "Norm Williamson."

I leaned on him a little. "Mr. Williamson, a special messenger has been dispatched all the way from Beverly Hills so that Mr. Cole can receive this package on a priority A-1 Urgent basis. Which means *right now,* mister, and I can tell you, Mr. Sylvester Stallone is *not* accustomed to failure."

"Uh, this is *the* Rambo we're talking about?"

"Himself," I assured him. "Look, all you have to do, Norm, is sign for the package when the special limousine reaches you. You can give it to your supervisor tomorrow and let him deal with it, okay? That way we're both off the hook."

"Well, I don't know." He hesitated. "I'm not supposed to open the gate for nobody this time of night. Can't you come by and deliver this package tomorrow?"

"That's negative, Norm. The big N-O. The messenger is almost there, and quite honestly, if he has to come back all the way to Beverly Hills, heads are going to roll." I lowered my voice. "Look, I'm not supposed to tell anyone this, but I want to do you a favor. The package contains a script for *Rambo V.* Mr. Stallone is interested in Terry Cole for one of the big parts. I hope you realize how serious this could be if Mr. Cole doesn't receive his script on time."

"Jeez, Terry Cole in a *Rambo* movie? You sure you got this right? Terry Cole's sort of a skinny little guy."

"That's right, Mr. Terry Cole, Room 124. That's what the envelope says."

"Wait a sec, Terry Cole's not in room 124. I knew there must be some mistake here. He's in the redwood unit out back, Suite C."

"You're sure of that? Well, I still think with something this important, you'd better sign for the script and give it to your supervisor first thing in the morning. That way you're covered, Norm. No one will be able to say it's your fault."

"Jeez," he said with a sigh, "this is really something."

Norm wasn't used to such a load of responsibility. I made it easier for him by hinting that powerful people and major film studios and at least one foreign government would make the rest of his life hardly worth living if he stood in the way of this important package's reaching its proper destination.

Norm wisely agreed not to be the one to interfere with *Rambo V.* If the messenger rang the buzzer by the main gate, he would be duly admitted to Happy Valley.

We drove along the country highway into the hills outside of Santa Barbara toward health and rejuvenation. The landscape looked very different at night. The thick foliage blotted out the stars and made it seem like driving through a tunnel.

"You're sure this is a good idea, Steve?"

"What have we got to lose?"

Cass flashed me a quick look and I knew what he was thinking we could lose, but I quickly shut off the thought. We reached the high, wrought-iron gate to Happy Valley and found there was a light by the buzzer and speaker.

Cass rang. "The messenger here from Mr. Stallone," he sang.

"Drive toward the main house and I'll meet you there," came Norm's disembodied voice.

The gate slowly swung open and we passed inside, up a small rise, down along a creek bed, and wound our way through a small forest before the road came out onto the wide meadow where the main house sat in dark splendor, with only a few lights on downstairs.

"This place looks mighty gloomy. I'd watch out for vampires if I were you, Steve."

I told Cass not to let his imagination get the better of him. He slowed down to let me out when we were still a hundred yards from the house.

"How are you going to get out of here?" he asked. "Have you thought about that?"

"Listen, from my experience it's easier to get ejected from Happy Valley than gain entrance. Just wait for me outside the main gate."

Cass didn't seem pleased. I had a glimpse of him shaking his head as I stepped out of the limousine onto the wet grass. It had been a long time since I had stood beneath an open sky in a country night. When the limousine pulled away and the headlights moved toward the house, I felt an unfamiliar darkness all around. Crickets were performing their nightly serenade. Somewhere in the distance I heard the hoot of an owl followed by the cry of a small animal. The immensity of planet Earth struck me as a palpable thing. And here I was in my Italian loafers with my socks already damp!

I moved away from the driveway and started crossing the meadow toward the main house. Up ahead, I could see Cass handing the manila envelope to a small figure in the light of the front door. Cass returned to the Cadillac and drove back along the driveway. I hurried out of the way of his headlights and tripped over an uneven patch of ground. The grass was soft but wet, and the knee of my trousers was now splattered with mud. Daniel Boone I'm not. I was beginning to hope there weren't any packs of wild dogs in the neighborhood. A city boy's imagination can do big things in a country night. I wondered if there were any mountain lions left in this part of California. Or maybe a lonely grizzly bear hungry for Big Time Comic.

I walked a little faster. This resulted in my losing an Italian loafer and being flung face forward into the long grass. My Neiman-Marcus sports coat took the brunt of the injury, but I could not find my lost loafer anywhere. I hobbled on with one shoe, humbled and wet and covered with mud. I was glad no one could see me in the dark.

I made a wide circle around the old main house to the newer living quarters in the rear. I remembered the setup from my earlier tour here. I hoped Doreen wasn't around this time of night, or any of the boys in the white uniforms.

The building where I hoped I'd find Terry was a rambling, modern redwood structure with lots of dramatic angles and plenty of glass. There was a hot tub built into the deck and I could hear a man and a woman having a late-night soak. From their direction, I could smell a faint wisp of marijuana carried on the evening breeze. I walked as quietly as I could along the side of a gravel path, up the redwood steps to the front door.

I found myself in a large common room with a stone fireplace, which reminded me of a ski lodge. Doreen had given me only the briefest tour of this area so I had no idea where I might find Suite C. At least no one was around to ask me what I was doing. I had a feeling I looked like something you'd find at the bottom of a swamp.

There were two hallways, one off each side of the common room. I went off to investigate, limping on one wet loafer and one muddy sock, making a soft, squishy sound followed by a dull thump as I moved over the wooden floor. Each of the rooms in this part of the building had a name. I passed Nirvana, Inner Peace, Enlightenment, and Material Reward before coming to Broom Closet. At the end of the hallway, I discovered redwood stairs, which took me down to a lower level. Here there were four suites marked simply A,B,C, and D.

I had arrived.

I knocked softly on the door to C. Terry appeared almost immediately.

He was wearing a silk robe. "Come in, come in!" he invited. It was strange, but Terry Cole didn't seem at all surprised to see me.

chapter 48

"**Y**ou look like a man with one black shoe," Terry Cole said thoughtfully. I couldn't think of a snappy answer.

"It's dark outside."

"It usually is at night. You know, I'm positive I had a joke somewhere about a man with only one shoe, but I can't remember."

"You're probably thinking of a line Dick Cavett used to do," I said, "although it was in the public domain long before that. You know, the one about the guy who was wearing one brown shoe and one black?''

"Right," Terry said. "He waits until somebody mentions them and then says, ''You think that's funny? I have another pair just like 'em at home.''

"That's the line," I said. After a while your brain's like one big gag file.

Terry scratched his head. He seemed wistful. "I've been remembering a lot of things, sitting here."

"Good! I'm glad I've caught you in such a pensive mood."

"The old days. The new days. The salad days with blue cheese dressing. We are tossed like croutons, my friend, in the Great Wooden Bowl of Life."

"You're probably right," I told him. As usual, it was hard to know if Terry was completely sideways or just putting me on. I sat down in a rocking chair in front of a blazing fire that had thick glass across the front to keep the heat from getting into the room. I suppose this is useful if you like fires but live in a warm climate like Southern California. Terry's suite was redwood rustic with woven scatter rugs on the polished wooden floors and comfortable furniture. I noticed Terry had a number of old photo albums spread out on a coffee table in front of a green leather sofa.

"You've certainly had a long and fascinating career," I told him encouragingly.

"Would you like to see my baby pictures?"

"That would really be something," I said. I moved over to the sofa so I could be next to him as we started our journey through the significant events of Terry Cole's career.

We began at day one, literally, with tiny Terry naked on a blanket, and a woman—his mother, I presume—making eyes at him from above.

"Wouldn't *Penthouse* like to get their hands on this!" I joked.

Strangely, Baby Terry had an amazing resemblance to Terry as he was today: not much hair, and a wizened, elfish face. His parents must have thought the world of him, since they had photographed him from every possible angle, asleep, awake, learning to crawl, taking his first step. I had come here to speak about the past, though this was quite a bit further in the past than I had intended to go.

I tried to speed up the page turning, rushing through kindergarten to the first grade. Terry was not pleased.

"Hey, if you're not interested, we can do something else!"

"I'm interested," I lied. And so we worked our way through elementary school, summer vacations, the Cub Scouts, Little League, and finally high school, where black and white gave way to early faded color. It was in college that I saw the first semiprofessional photograph of Terry behind the microphone at his school radio station. At this point, press clippings were taped in the scrapbook alongside the pictures.

After college came a three-year stint in a Cedar Rapids, Iowa, radio station. Terry was a staff announcer at first, but he used to encourage his listeners to call in until there was gradually more talk than music on his record show. This was when his talent began to emerge.

At last we arrived in Hollywood and the exact period of time I was most curious about. A brand new photo album began with a black-and-white 8x10 of Terry sitting at a table in a nightclub, wearing a dark suit, a thick tie, and a buck-toothed, newly-arrived-in-the-big-city grin on his face. In the photographs, Terry still wore his hair in a highly brushed flattop, and you could see freckles on his cheeks. He looked exactly what he was: a painfully innocent, corn-fed boy from Iowa.

"This was taken at Ciro's," he told me. "I don't think I'd been in Hollywood more than three days."

"Imagine that."

In the photograph, Terry was in the middle of a group of three. Kathleen was on his right—a dazzling, younger version of herself, who must have looked better than Lana Turner to a boy from the sticks. On the other side was a young man in a checkered sports jacket and a bow tie. He was a smooth-looking fellow with a slightly feral expression. Both Kathleen and the young man were leaning in toward Terry so they all could get into the photograph. They looked like two big city hustlers moving in on their prey.

"I bet that's Bobby," I said.

Terry looked up at me. "How did you know?"

"Just a guess. Kathleen told me you all met at Ciro's. You look like you're having a great time."

Terry shrugged. "We look young," he said flatly, moving on to the next page. Kathleen, Bobby Dyer, and Terry were on the beach in Santa Monica, all in swimsuits. Kathleen was the eye-stealer in the group, posing seductively in the smallest bikini you could get away with in 1963. Bobby looked like he spent a lot of time at the beach. He was tan, fit, and California healthy, with muscles and massive shoulders. Once again, Terry was standing between them looking very much the odd man out—skinny and pale, wearing a swimsuit shaped like boxer shorts, which seemed a few sizes too large.

Once again, I had the feeling that Terry, fresh from Iowa, was getting the big-city hustle from real pros.

"Who took this?"

"Bobby's girlfriend at the time. I think her name was Lynda."

I studied Terry closely. "Weren't Bobby and Kathleen having a bit of a fling when you first met?"

"I didn't know that then," he told me. "Who cares?"

"Do you think they wanted to conceal it from you?"

Terry looked at me with amusement. "Maybe. Kathleen was trying to land me, you know. She had her heart set on marrying a star, and I was her candidate."

We had come to a rather pivotal point. "But you weren't a star yet," I reminded him.

Terry grinned. "I guess she recognized potential," he told me.

"Of course, Kathleen helped you get your TV show, didn't she?"

"Hey, what's all this stuff about Kathleen, for Chrissake? I thought we were looking at photographs, not playing twenty questions."

"Sure, let's look at pictures," I said soothingly. I had touched a nerve and would have to proceed carefully. All in all, I had a lot to think about. I felt I was getting close to the truth, and two pages later there it was: a photograph that explained nearly every twisted thing that had happened to Terry and his group since 1963. I was so excited I didn't trust myself to speak, but let the picture pass by without comment.

With a terrible logic I now understood, the next group of photographs went on to document Terry Cole's rise from a skinny kid with a flattop and freckles to one of television's more successful personalities. It was a fascinating story, but I was hardly listening. I had gotten what I had come for and now I was just biding my time until I could leave.

Two albums later, we had arrived wearisomely at 1976. Terry, thank God, got up to go to the bathroom. As soon as I heard the door close, I picked up the correct album, thumbed through the pages quickly until I came to the picture I wanted, and removed it from its plastic sheath. I had the picture folded gently into my inside coat pocket when Terry returned.

"Where were we? Oh, yeah, that *fabulous* skit with Bob Hope where we both dressed up in drag!"

I helped him relive those glorious moments. Terry was so self-absorbed in his glorious career I hardly felt he'd miss me if I slipped away.

"Well, it's been a long day," I said with a stretch and a yawn. "I think I'd better go get myself some sleep."

"Don't you want to see me at the White House with Nixon?" Terry seemed hurt that I might be able to drag myself away from the contemplation of his career. "And after that there's my triumph in England where I played before the Queen."

"Wow," I told him. "We'll have to save this for another time. Being with you is like going to the Louvre."

"Going to the loo?" he said, aghast.

"The museum. You know, the big place in Paris.

You can't take in so much greatness in one visit—you have to do it in small doses."

"Ah!" he agreed. "Well, if you ever sneak into this joint again, be sure to drop by, okay?"

I wasn't sure I liked the way Terry was looking at me. The moment I stepped out of his front dor, I realized he must have used the telephone when he went to the bathroom.

There were two hefty-looking young men waiting for me in the hallway, dressed in their official white pajamas.

"Oh, dear," I said with the most innocent smile I could muster, "I bet I'm in trouble now."

I don't know how they could resist me, but they did not smile back.

chapter 49

I was hustled out fast. The young men were pure California youth: blond, tan, with sunny faces and a certain lack of respect. Under the right circumstances, they might be swell guys—around a campfire, for instance, or if you met them on the crest of a Pacific wave about to break off Malibu. But this was not one of those occasions.

Blond Kid #1 took my right arm and Blond Kid #2 my left. I was hurried out of the redwood building and along the path to the main house. The night air was cool and sweet.

We traveled in a most undignified manner to the main house, where I was rushed down a hallway to an oak-paneled study that was lined with books. Doreen Hanson, whom I'd met on my last visit, was sitting behind a desk, dressed in a terry-cloth robe that was belted tightly around her waist. Doreen had curlers in her hair. She wasn't glad to see me.

"Mr. Allen," she chided, "whatever are you doing here?"

"I couldn't stay away, Doreen."

"Cut the crap," she said. "I'm going to have you arrested for trespassing."

The two young men had remained in the room, watching to make sure I didn't try anything funny, or even serious.

"Look, let's be reasonable. What harm has been done? I had an urgent need to speak with Terry Cole— a life-or-death situation, if you want to know the truth. So in I came, and we had our little conversation, and I was about to leave when these sterling examples of Hitler Youth accosted me."

Doreen was opening a familiar-looking manila envelope on her desk, pulling out *Soldier of Fortune* magazine, *Modern Muscles* and *Motorcycle Mania*.

"Is this supposed to be some kind of joke?" she asked.

"No," I said, "just a random sampling of a magazine rack in Santa Barbara."

Doreen wouldn't even look at me as she picked up

the phone to call the cops. She left the room after that, with Blond Kids #1 and #2 standing watch. Fifteen minutes later, two sheriffs came into the room. They looked bigger and meaner than the sheriffs in Malibu, but otherwise had the same cowboy hats, six-shooters on their belts, and silver stars on their chests. I was becoming an old hand by now at getting arrested, and I tried to make it as painless as possible. Cass got in on the act as well. They picked him up outside the gate and charged him with illegal parking, vagrancy, and aiding and abetting an act of criminal trespass. I could see I was going to have to start giving him hazardous-duty pay.

Cass and I were handcuffed and taken from Happy Valley in the backseat of the sheriff's cruiser. I had a sense of *déjà vu*. We were driven to a substation close to Santa Barbara, our clothes and belongings were taken away—with my prize photograph still folded carefully into the inner pocket of my sports coat—and we were given orange overalls with "SANTA BARBARA COUNTY JAIL" written on the back. I was wondering if they would let me keep them as a souvenir, since it would certainly give my grandchildren a chuckle.

I think we even had the same drunk in our cell, though I never saw his face. In the morning he was gone, and shortly after breakfast—a meal I will not describe—I was told there was someone outside to see me.

I knew who it was. I put on my cheeriest expression and went out to meet Detective Sergeant W.B. Walker.

chapter 50

"Hi," I said, not very creatively.

"You've become a menace to society."

Sergeant Walker did not look his usual self. Not that he wasn't dressed in one of his brown suits—but he didn't look well. He seemed exhausted and on the verge of coming down with the flu.

"Sergeant," I said, "don't look so glum! I've figured this whole thing out." He looked at me suspiciously. I have to admit, I didn't blame him for not trusting me.

"Sure," he said. "Tell me about it."

"Well, that's just it. I can't. Not quite yet."

"Why not?"

"There are a few things I still don't know, details mostly. And of course, I can't prove anything yet."

"Sure," he said grimly. The man was in a down mood. "Why don't you tell me what was so important that you had to break in to see Terry Cole in the middle of the night?"

"Oh, just a few more details," I said.

Walker was not happy with the answer. "You know what? I think this time I'm going to leave you in jail here, let you rest a while. Maybe it'll make you more cooperative."

"Damn it, I've solved this thing for you. All I need is one more day and I'll hand you your murderer, confession and all, on a silver platter."

He gave a bitter little laugh. "Sure," he said dejectedly.

"Stop saying that! I'll tell you what, W.B. Make a reservation tomorrow night at Chasen's restaurant for. . . ." I had to stop and count quickly in my head. "Eight people. I'll produce your murderer after coffee but before dessert. Really."

"Dinner for eight, Mr. Allen? And who would that include?"

I named them: "Kathleen Cole, Tessa Moore, Winston Dane, Sonny Melnik, and Terry Cole."

"That's five."

"And you and me and Cass make eight."

W.B. narrowed his eyes at me in his most coplike manner. "Is your driver a suspect, too?"

"Cass comes along because he's been in on this from the beginning, and he enjoys a good meal, same as you."

The detective was looking more interested at the mention of food. "Chasen's, you say?"

"The food's great and you'll see all sorts of celebrities, besides witnessing the pyrotechnics of my superb detective skill."

"And who'll pay the bill?" he added, ever practical. "Feeding seven murder suspects at a place like Chasen's won't be cheap."

"Please, there'll be *five* murder suspects and dinner will be on me."

"And you propose to solve this mystery after coffee and before dessert?"

"Absolutely," I said.

"All right, let's say I'm on. Let's say I'm curious about what kind of interaction we'll see between that crowd around a dinner table. But how do we get them there? Maybe Tessa Moore has a club date or something."

"That's *your* job. That's why I'm giving you twenty-four hours to get this together."

"You kidding?"

"Not at all. I'm going to be busy taking care of a few loose ends—I won't have time to play social secretary. You can make our guests feel that perhaps they really shouldn't miss this. Compared to you, I'm a lightweight at coercion."

The sergeant stretched out thoughtfully in his chair. "Terry Cole might present a problem. He's hidden himself away pretty thoroughly at that place."

"I have faith in you, Sergeant. Get a court order if the gift of gab fails you."

"Okay. This is daffy, but I'll give it a try. What time do you want them at the restaurant?"

"Let's keep it simple. Dinner at eight, for eight. Use my name to make the reservation."

chapter 51

After getting out of jail, the best thing I can think of is taking a long soak in one's bathtub at the Beverly Hills Hotel. I was becoming an expert in these matters. A few more trips to the slammer and I felt I might be able to write a book: *The Compleat Jailbird*. I wondered what Jayne would think of it.

When I arrived back in the hills of Beverly from Santa Barbara, there had been a stack of pink message slips waiting in my box in the lobby. About half of them, I'm glad to say, had nothing to do with this case. There were job offers, business propositions, and calls from friends, all of which I put aside to wait till I was a normal human being again—I hoped in about twenty-four hours. The rest of the stack was pertinent to my investigation; in fact, the entire damnable lot seemed determined to reach me.

I soaked in the hot bath with the pink slips arranged carefully on a chair by the side of the tub. In descending numerical order, there had been five calls from Sonny, four from Kathleen, three from Winston, two from Tessa, and one—most intriguing—from Terry Cole himself, which had been logged by the hotel operator at ten-fifty this morning, shortly before I arrived back.

Terry's message read: "You have something of mine I want back. I'm serious." There was no return phone number. I stared at the pink message slip for some time, trying to gauge its danger.

The other messages were less exciting. Sonny's first call had come last night, with a mere "Please call back" and a phone number. By this morning, the word *urgent* had been used as a prefix to the rest of the message, and the last call—an hour ago—had *very urgent* on it. Kathleen, Winston, and Tessa had left no messages— they had simply wanted me to know they had called.

I certainly was feeling popular.

The phone rang while I was in the bath. There is a high-powered Hollywood type who can't sit in the bathroom without making a million-dollar deal on the telephone, but I'm not like that. A good soak in the tub is one of the more relaxing things I can imagine, and I would not have answered the ringing telephone under normal circumstances. These, I figured, were not normal circumstances. There was a phone within reach on the wall and I picked it up with a soapy hand.

"Steve, thank God I got you!"

It was Melnik. He sounded out of breath. "How's the boy?" I greeted.

"Damn it, did you go up to Happy Valley last night? Sneak in or something? Do you realize what you've done?"

"Now hold on, Sonny. It wasn't that major an occurrence. We had a little chat in front of Terry's fireplace and we looked through old photo albums."

"Did you take something?"

"What do you mean?" I responded pleasantly.

"*Something!*" he cried. "How the hell do I know?"

"But how the hell do *I* know, if you don't the hell know? I think we're in communication breakdown here."

"Don't joke, please. I can't take it anymore!" He truly sounded beside himself. "Steve, he *fired* me."

"Terry? Where did you see him?"

"He came down to Beverly Hills, woke me up at five this morning. He said you'd stolen something important from him and it was all my fault, and I'd better start looking for another job."

"With your credentials, I'm sure you'll find all kinds of opportunities. You know, Sonny, getting fired might be a blessing in disguise."

But he was weeping now. A show of emotions doesn't bother me, but Sonny sounded like a giant, fat, abandoned baby.

"You don't understand. Too many people hate my guts. They only put up with me all these years because I was Terry's right-hand man and they needed the show. Now everybody will treat me like slime."

It's a terrible thing to witness the disintegration of a once-powerful man. I had never been fond of Sonny—who had?—but I offered to make a few phone calls on his behalf.

"I tell you what, Sonny. Meet me at Chasen's tomorrow night at eight, and I'll see what I can do for you."

"Tomorrow night?"

He seemed to be losing his grip on things. "That's right," I said patiently. "Don't be surprised if Sergeant Walker gives you an invitation as well. He's acting as my social secretary.''

"You'll really help me get a job?''

"Sure.''

Failing that, the state of California might find something useful for him to do, like making license plates for the next thirty years.

chapter 52

My hotel bathroom phone had two lines. The second was ringing before I even managed to hang up on Sonny Melnik. Perhaps it was someone wishing to confess to murder.

"Steve, I'm glad you're in. I need to see you, like immediately.''

It was Winston Dane, and he too seemed frantic.

"At this exact moment, Winnie, you *wouldn't* want to see me. I'm in the bath.''

"Steve, listen—I think maybe it's not such a good idea what you're doing.''

"What am I doing?'' I asked innocently.

"Stirring up old ghosts. Maybe there are things that should best be left back in 1963.''

"The Twist would be a good instance,'' I told him.

"The *what?*"

"The Twist. *It* should be left back in 1963."

"Steve, this isn't a joking matter."

"Isn't it?"

"You don't understand. . . ."

Unfortunately, I never learned what I didn't understand, since at that moment someone started making a ruckus at my front door. From the way a fist was beating on the wooden panel, I knew it wasn't room service.

"You son of a bitch!" someone was shouting through the door. "Let me in!"

"Ah, Winnie, I must go now," I said calmly into the phone. "I have an admirer outside who probably wants my autograph."

"*Steve.* . . ."

"I'll tell you what, Winnie. Meet me at eight o'clock tomorrow night at Chasen's. We'll have a good long chat then."

Winston was still speaking as I hung up on him. It's nice to be in demand, but this was getting ridiculous. My admirer was still outside, trying to gain entrance.

"I know you're in there, you bastard! And, if you know what's good for you, you'll let me in and give me back my photograph."

It was, of course, Terry Cole. I wrapped a towel around my waist and cautiously approached the door.

"Calm yourself, Terry. There are spies for the *National Enquirer* behind every palm tree."

"Then let me in," he said more quietly, "or I'll tell everyone you're a big snitch."

"Terry, I just got out of the tub. Give me a moment and I'll get something on."

"Don't try anything funny," he muttered.

"God forbid," I told him. I was rushing about looking for my clothes. Somehow I couldn't find anything. I jumped into a pair of gabardine slacks and threw on the sports coat that had the important photograph inside.

"Steve?" came Terry's voice through the door.

"Coming!" I sang sweetly. I had no socks, shirt, or underwear, but it was definitely time to take a powder. I walked out the back way to my bungalow's private garden. There was a table near the far wall and I dragged it closer so I could get a leg up. The wall was covered with ivy and not much higher than the height of a man. I was able to swing a leg over and step down onto a chair in the garden that belonged to the bungalow next door.

I was feeling pleased with myself until I remembered about the clandestine lovers. To my horror, there they were—in bathrobes, thank goodness—sitting on the edge of a double bed.

I saw them before they saw me, through a half-opened glass door from the garden. The man was a Very Famous Actor, whose name I won't mention. The woman was a Not-So-Famous Actress, but famous enough so that you might recognize her too. They were both married, but—more's the pity—not to each other.

The Not-So-Famous Actress saw me first, and quite properly screamed: "Eeek! There's a man in our garden and he doesn't have all his clothes on!"

The Very Famous Actor turned to see. "Oh, don't worry, it's only Steve Allen," he said, waving to me.

I walked inside their bungalow and shut the glass door behind me. "Look, this is awkward," I said, "but

I'm in a bit of a fix. I've been staying next door, you see, and I had to leave quite suddenly. There was someone I . . . uh . . . very much wished to avoid.''

The Very Famous Actor nodded his understanding. "The husband," he said grimly.

I nodded back. "You know the bit."

The Not-So-Famous Actress let out a nervous laugh. Probably she was not yet completely hardened to the basic sadness and danger of romantic intrigue.

"Can you help me get away?" I asked. "People in our situation should stick together."

The Actor nodded gravely. "We won't tell anyone we saw you," he suggested. "And you won't . . . er . . ."

"Of course not." I used their telephone to call Cass. He was free and said he'd meet me at the side entrance in about ten minutes.

"So far so good," I told the unfortunate pair. "Now I just need some sort of disguise."

As it so happened, my new friends were quite experienced at disguise.

"You must be new at this," giggled the Not-So-Famous Actress as she helped me into her wide, floppy hat and wraparound dark glasses.

"And at your age!" said the Very Famous Actor with a grin, helping me into his ankle-length raincoat, with high collar and belt.

"Hey, remember to return this stuff, okay?"

"Sure."

I'm certain I was totally beyond suspicion as I stepped out of the lovers' bungalow in the trench coat, floppy hat, and glasses, with very little of me to be seen but my nose and bare toes. I didn't look directly toward my own bungalow, but I didn't see any sign of

Terry Cole. Hopefully, he'd given up and had gone away.

I did pass a young couple and a waiter who tried hard not to stare at me, but other than that, the back paths were empty.

The burgundy limousine was waiting discreetly by the side entrance. I wondered what Cass would say when he saw me dressed up like this.

"Hi, Steve. Is it Halloween already?" he asked while he came around to open the door for me.

That's the trouble with being a comedian: No one takes you seriously.

But I'd show them.

chapter 53

I was sitting at the bar in Giorgio's sipping on a Perrier water, with extra lemon and lime, watching two Arab playboys at the pool table taking a break from their intensive shopping. I had come here from the Beverly Hills Post Office after mailing my stolen photograph to myself, special delivery, care of Chasen's restaurant.

Giorgio's is not a club; it's a clothing store on Rodeo Drive, with a cocktail bar and pool table for the amusement of shoppers who may have grown weary accumulating jewelry and clothes. Beverly Hills these days sometimes reminds me of the imitations of the towns that used to exist on the back lots of the movie studios. You can get a feeling here that if you walk through the wrong door, you'll come out upon bare wooden beams holding up all the *papier-mâché*.

I was in Giorgio's buying clothes, having decided I did not want to spend the rest of the day barefoot, with a floppy hat and a borrowed trench coat. Cass had suggested we merely return to the bungalow and he would personally make certain Terry Cole didn't bother me any more, but I said no. I wasn't quite ready to confront Terry and didn't want to waste my ammunition, so to speak, until I was completely prepared.

Thus Giorgio's. I had bought some jaunty soft white loafers, a pair of matching white trousers, and a pink-and-white-striped shirt. I would probably emerge onto Rodeo Drive looking like an Arab playboy in search of additions to his harem. Right now, the trousers were being altered to fit properly. One thing about the stores on Rodeo Drive—you can buy the same clothes downtown for half the price, but here they give you service galore.

"Another drink, Mr. Allen?" asked the handsome Italian bartender, pointing to my empty Perrier.

"One's my limit," I told him,

"Yes, sir."

They agree with everything you say at a place like this. That's what you're paying for. Actually, my mind was far away. I was thinking I'd been overly optimistic to set up my final confrontation at Chasen's for tomorrow night. There were still several details to wrap up, and of course the small matter of providing proof. But at least it all would be over with, for better or worse, and I could get on with my life.

The rhythmic clack of the pool balls had me half hypnotized and for a brief click of time I hardly registered the moment I saw Terry Cole walk into the store from Rodeo Drive. He was dressed in white running shorts and a blue-and-white-striped polo shirt, looking very athletic. I don't think he saw me and I turned around quickly so that my back was to the store. I found I could see him by looking up at the mirror above the bar. Terry remained in the front section among the accessories, near the big windows to Rodeo Drive. I watched him buy a pair of thin black leather gloves and a walking stick with a silver handle.

I was intrigued by his purchases. Why buy gloves in the warm California spring? And why a walking stick with a heavy silver handle?

Sinister, I thought.

"And here's your package, Mr. Allen," said my salesman, coming up to the bar.

I jumped. "Shh!"

"Of course," he whispered back, still smiling. You can see what I mean by service.

"Is he gone yet?"

"Who, sir?"

"Mr. Cole. He's up by the accessories, the guy in the white shorts. I don't want to run into him."

"Ah, I see! He's just signing his bill. There he goes now."

"Thanks."

I took my package and hurried after him. Terry took a left on Rodeo and began walking leisurely up the street, peering into the expensive shops along the way. Cass was parked just to the right of Giorgio's, posing in front of the burgundy limo for some Japanese tourists who wanted a photograph of the real Beverly Hills.

"Quick," I told him, "follow me."

"Where are you going?"

"I don't know."

Hoping Cass would be able to make a U-turn with the car and keep me in sight, I followed Terry on foot as he ambled up Rodeo Drive. It seemed ridiculous playing cat and mouse with both of us toting Giorgio shopping bags, but I was determined to find out what he was up to.

Terry turned right on Dayton Way and walked the crosstown block toward Beverly Drive. I stayed about thirty yards behind him. I lost him for a moment when we were temporarily separated by a small group of beefy West Germans coming out of Van Cleef and Arpels jewelry, but I found him again as soon as they crossed the street to their waiting limousine. Terry crossed Beverly and made another right turn down the street.

He didn't quite seem to know where he was going. He strolled down Beverly to the Israel Bank, which is shaped, bizarrely, like a mosque. Its owners have not become Muslim converts; the Israel Bank used to be a movie theater.

Terry himself seemed not to know what to make of the movie-theater-to-bank conversion. He stopped walking and stared at the ornate building for a moment, apparently deep in thought. Then he turned around and walked back toward Maison du Caviar, a few doors up the road. I had to do some intense window-shopping to keep from being seen during his maneuver. When Terry stepped into the store, I was able to amble up to the edge of the window and check on what he was doing.

Maison du Caviar is one of Beverly Hills' more recent additions. It is a high-ceilinged room, which looks more as if it should be a bank than the bank down the road, and is a place where you can buy every kind of caviar you've ever dreamed about, from Beluga to *Brut d'escargot*. I watched Terry at the counter picking out a variety of gourmet goodies, which were packed for him in small plastic containers. He put his Maison du Caviar bag into his Giorgio bag and for all appearances looked like your average millionaire out for a stroll. I still couldn't imagine what he was up to, though my curiosity had been tremendously aroused.

Terry took himself and his purchase out of the store and into a dark blue Mercedes Benz limousine that had apparently been waiting for him at the curb. I wondered if this had been the vehicle from which shots had been fired at me last week, and with which someone had tried to run me down in the Malibu fog, but it didn't seem dark enough, or fuzzy. I wished my eyesight were better, because I really wasn't sure.

The Mercedes swung out into the traffic and began heading up Beverly toward Wilshire Boulevard. I looked about frantically for Cass, and there he was—like magic—pulling up to the curb.

I stepped into the front seat of the Cadillac and pointed to the retreating dark blue Mercedes.

"Follow that limo," I commanded. And we were off on the chase, through the gaudy perils and delights of Beverly Hills.

chapter 54

The long blue Mercedes limousine cruised down Santa Monica Boulevard at a stately pace. It wasn't an easy car to miss. We followed half a block back, with several cars between us. Unfortunately, we were not an easy car to miss either. Somewhere in the detective's manual there must be a footnote that says when trailing suspects, one should *not* be riding in a burgundy-colored Cadillac stretch limousine.

Still, we did our best not to be seen, staying as far back as we dared. If Terry and his chauffeur had spotted us, they gave no sign. They continued at a sedate speed, which allowed them to hit the lights just as they were turning green.

Santa Monica Boulevard is one of those L.A. streets that goes on in an almost straight line forever, gas station after gas station, past small stores, motels, fast-food stands with blazing neon chickens advertising their delights, past big supermarkets and little apartment houses. On and on.

There is a somewhat seedy section after Beverly Hills, and then you come to the grandiose Mormon Temple, which looks like a pillar of salt rising above a

Sodom of used-car lots, shops, and small karate studios. Keep going west, and you come to Santa Monica itself, which used to be fashionable in the forties, then fell into a state of disrepair, and now has become "in" again. We followed the Mercedes clear to the end of land, and then down the ramp from the Palisades to the Pacific Coast Highway, where the lead car settled comfortably in the right-hand lane heading north. By this time, I had a feeling I knew where we were going. I wasn't sure what the heavy walking stick and black gloves were for, but the caviar could be a small offering for his most expensive ex-wife.

Cass seemed born for this kind of work. He drove without a word, two fingers of each hand lightly on the wheel, his concentrated gaze far ahead of the Mercedes and the turns of the highway. The traffic thinned out as we approached Malibu, and Cass let a greater distance fall between the two cars. We passed the pier where I had been nearly run down, which now sat innocently in the late morning sun. At the intersection to the Malibu Colony, the Mercedes cruised through on the yellow light and left us cooling our heels, stopped on the red. We watched the car disappear over the crest of the long grade out of Malibu before the light changed green. Cass put his foot down, and the powerful Caddy engine took us quickly to eighty without any sound of strain.

"Keep it at fifty-five," I told him.

"We'll lose 'em, man."

"I don't think so," I said. Besides that, I really didn't want to see the inside of the Malibu sheriff's station one more time.

After the Malibu Colony, the coast highway goes up

and down along the rounded hills, a long roller coaster ride. I caught sight of the Mercedes far ahead, then lost it again. I wasn't worried. If Terry or his driver had noticed us earlier, it was best for them to think we were no longer on their trail.

On the last stretch of the way, from Zuma Beach to Trancas, we didn't see them at all. But I was willing to bet they had turned off onto Broad Beach Road. We made the left turn from the main highway and then traveled slowly past the colony of expensive beach houses toward Kathleen's place.

I didn't see Terry's car parked on the road by her house. Had I misjudged the situation? Maybe Terry was on his way back to Santa Barbara, taking the longer but more scenic coast route.

"Keep going slowly past the house," I told Cass. I was whispering, which was silly. Cass made a slow run past Kathleen's driveway, and I saw I had not been wrong. The dark blue Mercedes limousine was parked in the courtyard before the front door. There was another car there as well: a jet black BMW that sat glistening in the sun. When I saw it, my stomach gave a lurch.

We pulled over onto the shoulder of Broad Beach Road a few doors past Kathleen's house. I was turned around in my seat, wondering what to do next, when I saw the black BMW come quickly out of Kathleen's courtyard and head away from us back in the direction of the main highway.

But could this really be *the* black car? I took off my glasses and looked at it retreating down the road through our rear window. The car certainly looked fuzzy, but I couldn't tell if it was the fuzzy car I sought. I had to make a decision fast.

"I'm getting out," I told Cass. "You follow that BMW, find out who's driving and where he goes. I want to see what Terry and Kathleen are up to."

"But how will you get back to Beverly Hills?"

"I'll call a cab. You'd better get going, Cass."

I stepped out of the Cadillac and watched Cass turn around in the first driveway, then race off down Broad Beach Road after the black BMW. As soon as I lost sight of his taillights, I had a lonely sense of being very much on my own. But it was a little late to be having qualms.

It was time to think hard and make the right decision. Each time I had visited Kathleen Cole, we had ended up in the front of the house overlooking the ocean. I had a feeling my best bet, if I wanted to spy on Terry and his ex-wife, was to get myself located in that direction.

The backs of the houses along Broad Beach Road formed a solid line separating me from the beach, but a few houses to the north I spotted a vacant lot— probably one of the last unbuilt spaces along this chic little colony. Removing my glasses in case someone was watching me—some disguise—I inspected the empty land as though I might be a prospective buyer.

There was nothing here but a strip a hundred feet wide of rolling sand dunes and some hearty-looking weeds that probably would be here long after man had vanished. The lot was bordered on one side by a gray Cape Cod house and on the other by a Mediterranean villa. It looked as though some local kids had set up an impromptu pitcher's mound amid the sand dunes, but there was no one around at this moment. An old and skimpy barbed-wire fence as well as a NO TRES-PASSING sign urged one to respect private property.

I gazed at the empty lot thoughtfully, as if trying to decide where the house would go. With an appropriate scowl, I climbed between the loose strands of barbed wire with no more difficulty than a boy crossing into a farmer's field to steal an apple. I walked onto the empty sand dunes as though I had every right to be there, surveying my future domain with a buyer's eye. Then I kept walking toward the ocean, feeling the sand spill into my new Giorgio loafers. Expensive neighborhoods like Trancas are more sensitive to trespassing than the poorer parts of town, but since I was well dressed no one stopped me or raised a cry. I breathed easier once I got myself down toward the hard, wet sand. The property laws of California wisely assume that no one can own the Pacific Ocean.

I walked down the beach toward Kathleen's house, which was half hidden behind the dunes. Two joggers passed by, a young couple in matching running clothes with earphones on their heads, presumably so they could listen to their favorite rock music instead of the roll of the breakers upon the shore and the lonely cries of sea gulls. I waved at the young people, but they did not wave back. Maybe I looked too old, or not healthy or rich enough to be part of their crowd.

I watched their bright, trim shorts disappear down the beach. There was no one else around except, to my surprise, a sea lion, whose head appeared in the middle of a wave. I started walking up toward the private property, where I did not belong. There was a sign near the high-tide mark, just so I would make no mistake about the offense I was about to commit:

PRIVATE PROPERTY BEYOND THIS LINE

NO TRESPASSING

I kept going past the sign, into the barrier of dunes that separated the houses from the shore. There was another sign, more strongly worded, closer to Kathleen's house:

WARNING! NO TRESPASSING!

ARMED RESPONSE

It was enough to scare away a lesser man. Once I was in the sand dunes, I sank to my hands and knees and began crawling toward Kathleen's house. From this point on, I could no longer pretend I was a prospective buyer or innocent stroller on the beach. Staying on my belly, I slithered to the top of a dune—feeling like a large lizard—and gazed out onto the front of Kathleen's house through a protective shield of wild dune grass. From this position, I could see my guess had been correct: I caught sight of Kathleen through the half-opened sliding glass door to her breakfast room, the very place we had had brunch a few days earlier. She was sitting at the table with Terry pacing the floor behind her. He seemed to be talking angrily, gesturing with his hands. From where I was, naturally I couldn't hear their conversation.

I decided to move closer. Perhaps this was unwise,

but it was unbearable to have come this far—to actually see Kathleen and Terry together—but not be able to overhear what they were conspiring.

It looked to me as if they were up to no good.

I judged my chances. Directly in front of Kathleen's house there was a stretch of level white sand where I would find no place to hide. But the series of dunes in which I was now ensconced wound toward the side of her house. Probably they had been left standing to give her some additional privacy. I saw I might make my way cautiously along these small hills and valleys closer to the open door to the breakfast room.

I suppose I never would have done all this if I had thought about it in advance. But each step of the way seemed possible—stepping through the barbed-wire fence to the beach, and then from the beach up to the house—leading me on to every new step. In this way, one sinks to becoming a Peeping Tom and trespasser not in one sweeping motion, but through a series of small decisions, as when traveling the road of corruption.

So there I was, crawling on my belly, remembering again my infantry basic training, moving toward the beach house, getting an occasional mouthful of sand. I forced myself to go slowly, except in the few places where I was visible from the house, and these spots I scurried across, quick as a sand crab.

Terry and Kathleen were shouting at each other now and I began to make out individual words and phrases.

"Damn blackmailer," Terry was saying. "I told you . . . never listen . . . all these years!"

A large breaker hit the shore behind me, covering the rest of his sentence. When the wave rolled back, I could hear Kathleen: ". . . have to keep your nerve . . . we'd still be safe . . . to the grave with Bobby. . . ."

I was getting enough to whet my appetite, but not enough to make much sense out of the conversation. I decided to crawl closer, alongside the front of the house, so as to be underneath the open door.

I didn't get very far. I saw the shadow first—a dark and elongated shape cutting across my path—before I saw the man. I spun around to see a very large pistol pointing down at me from a few feet in front of my nose. The pistol had a bluish metallic color and the empty circle at the front was as dark as the hole to kingdom come.

It was hard to look beyond the gun to the man who was holding it. (If you've ever been in a situation like this, you will know what I mean.) I forced my eyes up past the wrist and arm and found myself looking at a well-built black man in a chauffeur's uniform.

By way of further description, I'd wager that if this story were ever made into a film, there would be a tendency, on the part of the director, to cast a former NFL defensive lineman in the part of the chauffeur. Actually, had I met the fellow on the street without his uniform, I might have taken him for a mayor of an Eastern city, a college-level teacher, or a lawyer. Even his manner of taking control of the awkward situation that brought us together was gentlemanly. "My, my," he said, "what do we have here?"

I stood up slowly to show him I was not as dangerous as I looked. I tried to smile.

"Hi," I said. "I bet you don't know what's Irish and stays out all night!"

I didn't have a chance to tell him about Paddy O'Furniture. Terry Cole appeared in the open doorway.

"What do we have here, Paul?" he asked his driver.

"Is it a Peeping Tom, dear?" Kathleen asked, coming up beside him.

Terry smiled in a way that made my blood turn cold.

"Not a Peeping Tom," he sneered, "but the very son of a bitch I've been looking for!"

chapter 55

The chauffeur urged me toward the house with his pistol, poking me in the back once with the hard barrel. We walked up the wooden steps from the sand to the sun deck, then past the sliding glass door to the breakfast room. There was no cracked crab or Moet et Chandon to greet me this time. Kathleen and Terry Cole were regarding me with cool detachment, as if I were a spider they might have to crush.

"Well, well," I said brightly. "Here I was just taking a nice stroll down the beach from Zuma—had a meeting a bit earlier at Irwin Allen's house—and . . . uh . . . thought I'd drop in and say hello!"

"Don't be ridiculous," Kathleen said with a snort

of contempt. "We saw you sneaking up the dunes, crawling on your stomach. Now shut up and sit down."

I missed her flirtatious manner. "I'd rather stand, thank you." I tried, but the chauffeur shoved me forcibly into a chair.

"I think we should tie him up, darling," Kathleen said to her ex-husband. From her tone of voice, she might have been discussing whether to have key lime pie or chocolate *mousse* for dessert.

"Whatever," Terry replied. They seemed a model of domestic bliss.

"Hold on here! I'm flattered, I really am, but I'm afraid I'm expected back in town by Sergeant Walker. And, if I'm not back by two, he'll know just where to look."

"He's lying," Kathleen said to her ex-husband.

"Yes, I believe so," said Terry.

"I'm not," I insisted. "You can call the sergeant, if you like. He'll tell you."

They didn't even smile at my comic attempt to get help. One thing I've noticed: thievery and murder really rob people of their sense of humor. Terry took the gun while the chauffeur went to get some cord from the kitchen. From the way Terry held the pistol, he seemed to know what he was doing. I decided against a momentary impulse to charge at him, kick him in the groin, and keep on running out of the breakfast room onto the beach.

The chauffeur came back from the kitchen and tied my hands in back of me behind the chair.

"This isn't funny," I told the Coles.

"You should have minded your own business," said Kathleen.

"But *your* business is so fascinating," I insisted, "though deadly. A pity you had to kill Bobby Dyer, though. They'll probably send you to the gas chamber for that."

Terry narrowed his eyes, regarding me thoughtfully. I was emboldened to continue.

"Bobby knew how you got your start on television, and he's been blackmailing you all these years. You finally decided it was safer to get rid of him. But I still don't understand why you had him put the poison in the bottle of vodka. At first I thought you were trying to make it appear that someone wanted to kill you. But now I think maybe you were trying to kill me. That's it, isn't it? You were afraid I might end up stealing your goddamned show."

Terry's expression hadn't changed. He seemed almost hypnotized by my words.

"So you had Bobby put a little rat poison in the vodka, knowing I'd find it and that I'm so eternally curious I'd probably give it a try. Bobby's done all sorts of odd jobs for you in the past, hasn't he, and some of them none too savory. When you went down to his apartment, he was expecting you to pay him off—but *not* the kind of payoff you arranged."

Terry smiled. "You're not as smart as you think you are, pal."

"Smart enough to have found *you* out, Terry," I said. But I noticed his body had relaxed and he turned to Kathleen with an easy wink. That bothered me. I still didn't know everything, and Terry knew I was bluffing. My guesses might have been close, but it was still no bull's-eye. He turned to me with a jaunty look in his eye.

"Let's stop playing games. I want the photograph you stole."

"Photograph?"

"You know what I mean. No one takes anything from me, you bastard, so give it back."

I smiled with an assurance I didn't at all feel. "The photo's in a safe place. You'll never get away with this, Terry. That picture tells the whole story."

"You think so?" Terry asked. "Well, I don't, actually. That is, not if you're not around to explain it."

I didn't like the way he was looking at me. In fact, I decided maybe it was time to shout for help. Perhaps the maid was nearby or a neighbor walking on the beach.

"He-e-e-elp!" I shouted suddenly. "Po-lee-ece!"

I have strong lungs from years of singing and a bit of halfhearted trumpet playing, but it was no use. Paul, the chauffeur, stuck a napkin in my open mouth and then finished the job with tape. I wanted to tell them this was not *my* idea of a gag, but I couldn't say a word.

Kathleen walked around me, as though circling a new lamp she might buy.

"You know, I think we're going to have to kill him," she said.

"Mmmm!" I objected vehemently, shaking my head.

"We can say we thought he was a burglar," Terry suggested, eyeing me speculatively. "He came in through the window and I shot him before I realized who it was. It happens all the time."

Kathleen seemed to consider this. "I don't know, Terry. I think it would be best if we could just make him disappear. We could pretend he was never even here."

They discussed this for a while, how to get rid of Steve Allen. It was not a conversation I was pleased to hear.

"We could drown him in the bathtub," Kathleen offered, "and then toss his body into the surf later on tonight. People would think he had had an accident swimming."

"Don't be naive," Terry interrupted. "Someone tried that on *Quincy* and Jack Klugman saw right through it. There'd be fresh water in his lungs, you see."

"We could send Paul down to the ocean with a pail, don't you think? Fill the tub with salt water?" Kathleen proposed.

"It would take too many trips." Terry sighed. "And then what would the neighbors think? The main point about murdering someone," Terry philosophized, "is not to get caught. Do you have any vodka? I'm feeling slightly stressed out by all this."

"I could use a drink myself," Kathleen said.

"So could I," I mumbled, but they didn't understand.

I watched Paul, the chauffeur, step to the sideboard and pour a few fingers of vodka into a silver shaker. He added ice from a small bucket and shook vigorously. I was fascinated by his movements. Meanwhile Kathleen, perfect hostess that she was, had gone into the kitchen and had returned with two small, chilled martini glasses with green olives resting on the bottom. Paul poured out the drinks and Terry and Kathleen touched glasses.

"Maybe we can strap him to your exercise machine," Terry suggested, "and turn on the power full blast. Probably he'll have a heart attack after a while, or die of exhaustion."

"And just how will we explain his body in my exercise room?"

The two Coles were no longer even looking at me. I had ceased to exist except as some inanimate object they wished to dispose of.

"When it's dark, we'll carry him down the beach to Zuma and leave him in the sand. The police will think he had a heart attack while jogging."

"Wearing white Italian loafers and a sports coat?" Kathleen chided. "It's a good thing you always had me to do your thinking for you, or you'd still be back in a small radio station in Iowa, my dear."

"Knock off that crap right now!"

Terry was red in the face and I had a feeling they were about to come to blows over how best to murder me. But Kathleen turned my way, as if to remind Terry of my silent presence.

"We mustn't quarrel in front of our guest," she said.

As they regarded me silently, I tried to shrug my shoulders at the folly of mankind.

"I'll tell you what," Kathleen said. "For the time being we'll just stuff him in the wine cellar."

chapter 56

I was led downstairs to a part of Kathleen's house I had never seen. Houses like this were not built with cellars, so the wine room was actually a windowless, high-ceilinged closet next to a laundry area, about ten feet long by five feet wide. On one wall there were wooden racks with the wine bottles set on their sides, while the other wall was bare. The room was cold—refrigerated, I presumed, to keep the wine better—with a covered light fixture on the ceiling casting a harsh glow. All in all, it was not a place in which one would choose to spend a great deal of time.

"Paul, you'd better bring a chair from upstairs," Kathleen told the chauffeur.

"We don't need to make him comfortable," Terry grated. "After all, we're trying to kill him, aren't we?"

"He might as well die sitting down," she insisted. The lady was all heart. Still, I was glad when Paul appeared with a straight-back wooden chair, since the floor was unadorned concrete. My hands were still bound, and my mouth was gagged. Paul had some extra rope to tie me to the chair, just so I wouldn't go wandering about. I tried to express with my eyes all the contempt I felt for their nasty hospitality, but Terry, Kathleen, and their chauffeur seemed intent on not looking at me directly.

Terry was inspecting the thermometer on the wall near the door. "Forty-eight degrees," he announced. "I believe our uninvited guest could die of exposure after a time."

"Or hunger, I should think," Kathleen added. They both chortled at the thought.

"So long, Steverino," Terry said, mocking my stock TV salute gesture. He giggled as he closed the wine closet door. The light was turned off from outside and I was left in a darkness so complete that gray spots flickered in front of my eyes, and then were replaced by a black nothingness. The coldness only gradually became noticeable. Forty-eight degrees Fahrenheit does not immediately make itself apparent through a thin sports coat, but the longer I sat in the darkness, the more it penetrated.

The gag was biting into the corners of my mouth, my hands were becoming cramped behind my back, and the first tremblings of real fear were replacing anger. It occurred to me then that I might never make it out of the wine closet alive.

I tried to calm myself and think of some way out. I remembered books I had read in which people had gotten out of similar spots, hoping it might give me some plan for escape. In early Dick Francis novels, for example, it seemed the hero was often handcuffed in a dark stall with a wild horse nearby about to trample him to death and the villain due to return at any moment to finish what the horse might begin. By comparison, a dark, horse-free California wine closet seemed a fairly posh prison.

The longer I sat thinking, the colder I got. I realized I had to do something and that I'd better start with getting my hands free. The ropes were tight enough to cut off circulation. I tried to saw at them against the edge of the chair, hoping that even if I could not cut through the cord, at least I would be able to loosen it a little.

By shifting my weight, I found I was able to get a fairly good cutting angle against the sharp corner of the back of the chair. I wasn't able to pull my wrists up and down more than half an inch, but I felt if I kept at it long enough I might make some progress. There was nothing to lose, and at least I felt warmed by my exertions.

I lost track of time but tried not to become discouraged. The darkness was all-encompassing and the walls were so thick I could not hear a sound outside the closet—only my heartbeat and the rhythmic scraping of rope against a wooden corner. There came a time— perhaps an hour later—when my wrists felt looser, but I decided this was only because my hands had become too numb to feel much of anything.

Several times I lost hope, gave up, and then started again. In the boredom of all the endless darkness, I consoled myself by thinking of all the vengeful things I might do to Terry and Kathleen Cole if I ever got out of there.

I'm not sure how long it was before I felt the first piece of cord give way. I thought my hands should come immediately free, but apparently they were tied in a complex manner. Still, now that I knew it was possible to fray the rope against the chair, I worked with renewed energy and hope. When the next cord gave way, I was able to pull my hands out of the remaining loose rope. My wrists hurt and my hands throbbed as sensation gradually returned. It was bliss to be able to bring my arms to a comfortable position.

I massaged my wrists until they felt like part of my body again, and then removed the gag and the rest of the ropes attaching me to the chair. I tried standing up, but one leg had gone to sleep and I lurched sideways against the wine. After a moment, I was able to stand in my dark prison, feeling a little shaky but pleased I had managed to do something. To accomplish more, I needed light.

It seemed to me that whoever had designed Kathleen's beach house would have put a light switch somewhere inside the wine closet. I staggered around in the dark for a time, feeling with my hands against the smooth surface of the wall opposite the wine racks. Eventually it occurred to me that if there was a light switch, it would be located close to the door. The door was easy enough to find, and by feeling my way around the perimeter of the wooden frame, I came upon it: an electric switch.

I said a short prayer and flicked the switch upward. And there was light.

Blinding light. I had to close my eyes for a moment until I became used to the glare. When I opened my eyes and could finally see again, I felt totally elated— for all of five minutes. But the door to the outside was firmly closed, and I gradually realized that though I was free of my ropes and had light, I still wasn't going anywhere. I spent some time looking about the wine closet for some tool to help me escape—perhaps a corkscrew or a knife had been left behind. But there was nothing besides an extensive selection of mostly California wines, reds and whites, wooden racks, bare walls, and the one chair—upon which I sank back down, feeling cold and again depressed.

Looking upward to the ceiling, I noticed a screen that seemed to go to a ventilation shaft of some kind. This gave me a momentary hope, but when I stood up on the chair to try to reach the screen, I found it was still almost a yard away.

By now, I was beginning to feel painfully cold. I examined the thermometer by the door to see if there was a thermostat by which I could control the temperature. But if one existed, it was apparently outside. I hugged myself and began to pace my narrow prison, hoping exercise would keep me warm. Thinking bitterly of Saint Bernards with small casks of brandy around their necks gave me a pretty good idea. My prison, at least, was not without liquid refreshment.

I began foraging among the bottles, looking for something warming. When I drink wine—which is rare these days—I generally prefer the whites, but right now red sounded hotter. I picked out a 1984 Stag's Leap Cabernet Sauvignon from Northern California before I realized I had no way to open the bottle.

I was going to have to go out with champagne. It seemed a fitting end for my life.

The champagnes were in the far lower corner. I picked out the most expensive one I could find, a dust-covered bottle of Dom Pérignon. I brought it back to my chair, sat down once again, and worked the lead-and-wire wrapping off from around the cork. I pried the cork loose with my thumbs, making it fly like a rocket toward the ceiling. A small fountain of foam bubbled over the neck and down into my hands.

I made a whispered toast: "Here's to you, Jayne, and to our good life together, and all the wonderful laughs."

I brought the bottle to my lips and took a long swallow. It wasn't really as ice-cold as it should have been, but still it was welcome. I was about to take another slug when I noticed the discarded lead wrapper and wire still in my left hand. I took another swallow, tilting my head back, and caught sight of the screen to the ventilator shaft once again.

Was it possible?

I looked down at the lead and the wrapper, then up at the screen. If there had been anyone there to see me, they would have noticed a cagey smile crossing my lips.

It was time for action. I put the opened bottle of Dom Pérignon to one side and walked back to the champagne selection. I pulled out as many bottles as my arms could carry of some pleasant-looking plonk called Iron Horse, from Sonoma, and carried my stash back to the chair.

Then I sat down and opened the bottles one after another, sending the corks shooting upward to the ceiling.

Pop! . . . Fizz . . . Pop!

I hadn't had fun like this since the Fourth of July.

chapter 57

Chasen's is a restaurant of the old school, located on Beverly Boulevard on the southeastern edge of Beverly Hills. The red leather booths are deep and comfortable, the lighting dim. There is a masculine feeling to the place; you won't find edible flowers on the salads or sun-dried tomatoes in the pasta. Your best bet is to go for a piece of cholesterol-filled New York steak, or a slab of anti-Pritikin blood-rare prime rib, of the sort that probably put James Garner in the hospital. And though I've always found it too salty, their chili is highly praised, in case the prime rib doesn't give you the heart attack you've always been waiting for.

Chasen's has been a Hollywood tradition for as long as most people can remember, and you are apt to see the older Hollywood crowd there. It is said to be Ronald Reagan's favorite restaurant. (I'll let you decide whether that is a recommendation or not.)

I had chosen Chasen's for its central location and neutral qualities. I suppose it's like the Russians and the Americans meeting in Finland rather than Northern China or a *trattoria* in Rome. Basically, Chasen's seemed as good a spot for a dinner denouement as any.

Only, when the guests arrived, the host was not there. Still—aided by investigation after the fact—I can reconstruct what happened:

Detective Sergeant Walker was the first to arrive. He showed up at seven-thirty, a full half hour before everyone else. Perhaps he was afraid the kitchen might run out of food later in the evening; perhaps he wished to get a feel of the place. He came with two plainclothes cops, men from the homicide detail he had worked with before. W.B. was taking no chances. He stationed one of the detectives in an unmarked car by the restaurant's front awning and had the second wait around back in the alley where there was a door to the kitchen. The sergeant had a small, battery-powered beeper in his coat pocket by which he could call the two men to his aid.

W.B. took one more precaution before he entered the restaurant. He took his .38 Smith & Wesson service revolver out of his shoulder holster and spun the cylinder to make sure the action was free. A revolver does not have a safety, and normally W.B. leaves it with only five bullets inside, the hammer on an empty chamber. But tonight he took a small box of .38mm ammunition from the glove compartment of his car and inserted the sixth bullet. A detective sergeant rarely has to use his weapon, but he wanted to be ready if this was going to be one of those rare occasions.

After these details were taken care of, Walker slipped the revolver back into his shoulder holster and stepped out of his unmarked, inconspicuous American car into the restaurant. The parking man gave him a funny

315

look. A moment later the *maître d'*, having had vast experience in such matters, took one glance at the wrinkled brown suit and knew he was addressing a cop. Cops were people a *maître d'* needed to be polite to, but his expression was wary.

"May I help you, sir?"

W.B. knew he'd been "made"—as they say in the movies—but still flipped open his wallet to give the man a glimpse of the detective's shield. "I'm with Mr. Allen's party."

I trust the *maître d'* raised an eyebrow upon discovering that a guy dressed like W.B. Walker was in my group, but he gave a little bow, a weary smile, and said only: "Certainly, sir, won't you come this way?"

W.B. Walker was led through the dining room proper to the private room I had reserved. He had told me once, when we were talking of other matters, that swank places were often a letdown for him. People might expect a place like Chasen's or the Bistro to have some nearly luminous glow, as though the celebrities who had wandered in and out of these rooms over the years might have left behind part of their personal glamour. W.B. may have been disappointed that Chasen's looked a bit like a steak house in the Valley, a very normal sort of place—just a lot more expensive. At this hour of the night, he didn't catch sight of a single famous face.

The private dining room was off toward the rear of the restaurant, and there W.B. found a long oval table set for eight with white linen and silver. The room was as dimly lit as the main part of Chasen's with a candelabra casting a warm glow against the dark pine walls. A waiter in a short red jacket was still preparing the scene, setting wineglasses carefully above every knife.

W.B. was tempted to sit at the head of the table but chose a spot somewhere in the middle.

"May I get you a drink, sir?" asked the *maître d'* before departing.

"I'll take a root beer," replied W.B.

The *maître d'* did not betray a smile: Hollywood is a town built for and by the newly rich.

"I'm afraid we don't have root beer, sir."

"How about a diet Dr. Pepper?"

"We don't have that either, sir."

W.B. sighed, not understanding how a place with such a reputation could not stock items he could find in any local coffee shop. "Coffee, then," he said imperiously. "A big pot, and you can keep the cream."

The sergeant was on his second cup by the time the first guest arrived, at five minutes past eight. W.B. likes to make guesses about people, and he had been thinking Sonny Melnik would be first, as a man who had spent his life pleasing others. But Winston Dane was the first to arrive, ushered into the private dining room by the *maître d'*.

"Why, hello, Sergeant. We're the first, are we? I suppose you know what this is all about."

W.B. shrugged. "I'm in the dark, same as you. Mr. Allen is the only one who knows what he's up to—and even he may not be totally sure."

Winston ordered a whiskey sour, but before it arrived, Sonny Melnik and Kathleen Cole were ushered into the room. They said they had arrived separately, but had met at the front of the restaurant. Kathleen, a practiced Hollywood hostess, seemed to take over at this point, kissing cheeks, making small talk, and making sure everyone got a cocktail. Terry arrived five minutes later, giving everyone a sour look—particularly Detective Sergeant Walker.

"I want you to know, I'm here under protest, Sergeant. I was damn near tempted to bring my lawyer along, and I can have him here in five minutes if I need to."

"Oh, Terry, don't be such a grouch," said his exwife. "This is rather fun to see everyone like this, after all."

Winston Dane and Terry Cole shook hands without much enthusiasm.

"Do *you* think this is fun, Winnie?" Terry asked.

"Who knows? We'll have to see what Steve has in mind for us."

"Yeah? And where is Allen anyway?" a glowering Terry demanded as he looked about the room.

"He's not here yet, Mr. Cole," Sergeant Walker told him. "Why don't you sit down and relax? You can have one of your famous Cajun vodkas while you wait."

"I'm off the damn stuff," Terry grumbled, turning to the waiter. "Gimme a vodka martini, straight up with a twist and no goddamn olive. And it better be dry, buddy, if you expect to get any tip."

Winston shook his head with a faraway smile. "Always such a charmer, Terry," he said quietly.

"And how about you, Winnie? I hear you're living in Rome, no less. Do you get to bugger all the Italian boys in the ruins of the Colosseum? Or is the Villa Borghese where all the action is these days?"

"Terry!" cried his ex-wife, apparently truly shocked.

318

Winston turned to her. "Don't pay him any attention, my dear," he told her. "I certainly never have."

Sergeant Walker sat back in his chair and carefully watched the interaction among the different people. He made no comment, holding the fingertips of his two hands together on the table, close to his coffee.

"Waiter! Where's the damn waiter?" Terry cried. "If I'm going to be here against my will, I'd just as soon not die of thirst! Sonny, why don't you go out there and see what's keeping the guy?"

Sonny Melnik, in his most familiar role of Step-'n'-Fetchit, was about to do what Terry told him. But Sergeant Walker raised a hand.

"I think we should all remain here, if you don't mind, Mr. Melnik. I'm sure the waiter will be here soon enough with Mr. Cole's martini."

Sonny sat down again, looking a bit sullen. W.B. noticed that he seemed unusually quiet.

The door opened and all eyes looked up to see Tessa Moore making a late entrance, dressed in a glimmering silver dress that seemed to be made from aluminum foil. Her hair was a new color, part orange, part green.

Kathleen was first to greet her. "My, I didn't realize this was a costume party, Tessa."

"Hello, darling Kathleen!" Tessa cried. "But have you been ill? You're looking slightly unwell."

"I'm feeling just fine, my sweet," Kathleen said grimly.

W.B. could hardly believe what a viper's den he'd entered. Everyone sat down, leaving two empty places around the oval table. Kathleen took the liberty of ordering a few *hors d'oeuvres*, some caviar, a *pâté de foie gras,* as well as some iced prawns to be shared around the table.

"I'm certain Steve would want us to make ourselves comfortable," she insisted. "He's such a dear!"

Winston was consulting his watch. "It's a quarter to nine," he said. "I wonder what's keeping him."

The door opened once again, but it was not I. Cass came into the private dining room looking forlorn and uncomfortable, his hair slicked back against his forehead and his chauffeur's cap in his hand.

"Where's Steve?" Winston asked him.

"I don't know. The last time I saw him was yesterday afternoon. I was waiting for him to call, but finally I thought I'd come over and see if he made it here without me."

"Well, he hasn't!" said Terry Cole with a sneer. "And personally I'm going to wait another ten minutes, and if Steve hasn't come, I'm leaving. Some of you may have time to waste, but I don't."

"Come sit down, Mr. Cassidy," Sergeant Walker suggested, gesturing to the empty seat by his side. Cass seemed unhappy with the situation but did what he was told.

"Tell us about the last time you saw Mr. Allen," the sergeant requested.

"Well, I drove him to the beach—to Mrs. Cole's house. We were following Mr. Cole's blue Mercedes from Beverly Hills."

"And then what happened?"

"As soon as we arrived, we saw a black BMW leaving Mrs. Cole's driveway. Steve thought maybe it was the same car from which someone tried to shoot him last week, so he got out to follow Mr. Cole, and he told me to follow the BMW and see who was inside."

"And?"

Cass looked miserable. "I lost it in Westwood, cutting over from Santa Monica up through the campus to Sunset. I came to this intersection, you see, and there were three black BMWs that all looked exactly the same. I must have followed the wrong one—it took me halfway to San Diego before I realized my mistake. So I drove back home and waited for Steve to call, but he never did."

The room had grown quiet while Cass told his story. Sergeant Walker turned toward Kathleen and Terry Cole. "Well?" he asked.

"I don't know what he's talking about," Terry said. "I haven't been in Trancas for ages. I guess the BMW wasn't the *only* wrong car you followed yesterday."

"Hey, wait a minute," Cass objected, but Sergeant Walker took hold of his arm.

"What about you, Mrs. Cole? Did you see Mr. Allen yesterday?"

"Why, no," she lied. "Goodness, I was gone most of the afternoon taking a long walk on the beach."

"Did anyone see you?" asked the sergeant.

"Just the sea gulls," she said. "Is it important? I was communing with nature, you see."

"More likely she was taking on the lifeguards up at Zuma, on her back in one of those funny little shelters on stilts," Tessa Moore said in a loud aside that everyone heard.

Kathleen turned beet red. "I'm always tempted by those good-looking boys," she told Tessa, "but I'd be afraid of catching one of your unmentionable venereal diseases.''

It looked briefly as if the two women would come to blows, but Sergeant Walker rose to the occasion and told everyone to relax. The room grew quiet and tense. A waiter took orders for another round of drinks, but the festive atmosphere was gone. The seven people sat around the table in the dispirited manner of those waiting to board a plane that was three hours late.

And this is how I found everyone when I entered the scene around nine-fifteen. I'm sure they could smell me coming a football field away—the aroma of a thousand dollars worth of stale champagne.

There was a rip in the knee of my new Giorgio trousers, and my glasses were broken, held together in the center with the wire from around a champagne cork.

Seven faces looked up at me in stunned silence. The color in Terry's face, I noticed, rapidly disappeared. He looked from me to his ex-wife, but Kathleen only stared in my direction as though she were seeing a ghost.

"Hi, gang," I told them all. "Glad you could make it."

chapter 58

I was fascinated by the eyes and faces regarding me
so intently, each so different from the others.

There was Terry Cole, uncertain, looking at me
(yes!) with some fear; Kathleen, on the other hand,
refusing to be intimidated, challenged me with her eyes;
Sonny appeared anxious, waiting to see what I was up
to and how he might profit by it; Tessa seemed de-
lighted that someone was dressed as outrageously as
she; Winston regarded me with a chummy smile, as if
vastly amused by the entire situation. My friend Cass
was the only one with any concern in his expression
for what had happened to me that had prompted my
appearing in public in such a ragged condition.

And last of all, of course, there was Detective Sergeant W.B. Walker, whose *you-would* look suggested
that nothing I could do would any longer surprise him.

It was now time for us to play Which-One-Of-You-
Is-The-Murderer. As I've said before, I've gotten most
of my ideas about solving crimes through television and
detective fiction, and it seemed to me this was a situation worthy of an Hercule Poirot—though he might
have appeared for the occasion more suitably attired.

The waiter broke the tense silence. "A drink, sir?"

"No, thanks. I've had enough booze to last a lifetime."

Tessa giggled. "You smell like a wino, snookums. What have you been up to?"

"It doesn't matter," I assured her. "Has everyone ordered dinner?"

"We were waiting for you," Kathleen said in her dare-me tone.

"Then you were probably thinking you'd go hungry tonight," I teased. "Personally, I could eat a horse."

I wasn't kidding. It had been over twenty-four hours since my last meal and I was ravenous. I went through half a loaf of French bread while the waiter went around the table scribbling down on a pad what each person wished. When it was my turn, I kept it basic: a bowl of minestrone, a Caesar salad, the salmon steak without the fancy *béarnaise* sauce they tried to hide it in, and a pot of coffee.

I was seated on one side of Sergeant Walker, with Cass on the other. I think we were the only two people there with clear enough consciences to sit that close to the police.

"What are those marks on your wrists?" W.B. asked after the waiter had left.

"They're bruises," I said.

"We were getting worried about you, darling," Tessa shouted across the table. "Why were you so late?"

"I got tied up," I said—a terrible joke, but I had to do it. Terry turned a little paler and ordered a martini, a double this time.

"So what's this all about?" Sonny asked, his feral little eyes darting my way.

"Let's be civilized and eat first," I told him.

At the far end of the table, I noticed Kathleen had risen to the occasion. Trying to show how unconcerned she was, she had engaged Winston in a conversation about the Italian film industry, and the pluses and minuses of working at Cinecitta, the famous studio outside of Rome. Before long, the usual kind of industry chitchat took hold around the table: who was signed for this, who was canceled, or who, as *Variety* puts it, was ankling his pact. Deals and divorces, ratings and reviews, all came under scrutiny. I joined in with gusto between mouthfuls of food. I noticed Cass was discussing the inevitable return of the Western with Sonny Melnik. Only Sergeant Walker refrained from joining in, watching us all with a wry smile.

It wasn't until after the dinner dishes had been cleared and coffee, dessert, and cognac had appeared that I rose from my chair and tapped my water glass with a spoon.

"Ladies and gentlemen . . . as well as the cold-blooded killer in this group, who is neither of the above!"

This grabbed their attention. It was remarkable how fast the conversation died and I found every eye upon me.

"I've invited you here tonight because I have discovered *why* the rat poison was put in the bottle of vodka that killed Hal Hoaglund, and *who* shot Bobby Dyer. Since each of us has been a suspect in this case—excluding Cass and the sergeant, of course—I thought it would be interesting to bring us all together to explain how I've reached my conclusions."

There were a few coughs and anxious glances passing around the room. Sergeant Walker, I noticed, had closed his eyes and almost seemed to be falling asleep.

"There are certain things we know, and others we can only guess at," I continued. "We know, for example, that Bobby purchased a small package of Drop Dead rat poison two weeks before Hal Hoaglund's death, and that it was this particular brand of poison that killed Hal. Since it was Sonny's job to stock Terry's refrigerator each night before the show, and since Sonny, unbeknownst to Terry, had passed on this small chore to Bobby, we can safely infer that Bobby put the poison in the bottle—with or without the knowledge of Sonny Melnik," I added with a nod to Sonny, who was staring at me with his mouth half open.

"The big question in this case, of course, has always been, Who was the rat poison intended for—Hal Hoaglund, Terry Cole, or me? After all, you can't solve a crime until you have a motive. And you can't find a motive until you've discovered who the victim was supposed to be."

"I can't understand a thing he's saying," Tessa whispered to Winston, who was sitting on her left.

"Not too many ideas at once, old boy," Winston said. "This isn't *Meeting of Minds.*"

"Let's suppose for a moment that Hal was the intended victim, and therefore the murder went off as planned. Poor Hal, of course, led a fairly blameless life, pursuing his violin and the goal of perfect biceps—with or without steroids—and it's difficult to imagine a motive for his death. But maybe there's something

326

we don't know. Hal and Bobby belonged to the same health club, and though there's no indication they ever had anything to do with each other, we can't be certain of it. However, it is difficult to see what anyone would gain by Hal's death, which makes it unlikely he was the intended victim. And there's one more factor that indicates his death was accidental: How would anyone know I would give Hal a glass of the poisoned vodka? The event was entirely spontaneous. Hal was nervous—I had the bright and terrible idea that a shot of booze would relax him, and so he met his death. A murderer would hardly be able to plan that sequence of events. And so we must conclude that Hal Hoaglund was not the one who was supposed to die."

I looked around the table to see how I was doing. Sergeant Walker was frowning and rubbing his chin. Some of the eyes looking at me seemed slightly dazed. I continued, undaunted.

"That means someone was trying to kill either me or Terry," I said. And then I added with a cunning smile: "Or perhaps Terry, for reasons of his own, was trying to make it appear that someone was trying to kill him. Those are the three possibilities."

"Er, wait a moment, Steve," objected Winston Dane. "To be entirely fair here, and logical, you would have to add the possibility that *you* were trying to make it appear someone was trying to kill you."

"Why would Steve do that?" Cass objected, coming to my defense.

"Please, I'm not trying to put you on the spot, old man. I'm only trying to mention *all* the possibilities. So to answer your question, Mr. Cassidy, Steve could have planted the poison as a publicity stunt."

"That's ridiculous!" Cass said hotly.

"Is it? An actress I knew once arrived at the Venice Film Festival on water skis, stark naked. People in our profession are always trying to draw attention to themselves."

"But, Winston, come on," Tessa said. "An entertainer—any actor in the world, I suppose—might dream up some crazy stunt like that, but he'd hardly let an innocent man be killed as part of the scam."

"Right," Cass said. "He might offer the poor guy a drink of the poisoned stuff but then maybe take a sniff of it himself, act like he was suspicious, and slap the drink out of the guy's hand or something. He'd still get a lot of publicity that way and nobody would be dead."

"Thank you, Cass," I said, "but for once I don't need your help."

"Not so fast," Kathleen said, narrowing her eyes at me in a perfect imitation of a speculative manner. "Maybe your driver is right. Maybe that *is* what you planned, but the plan went wrong. Hoaglund took a quick drink before you could stop him. Come to think of it," she suddenly sputtered, raising her voice, "maybe this whole thing—including the phony investigation and the goddamned dinner party we were all stupid enough to take part in—is the real payoff to the publicity stunt."

Cass stood up from his chair, pushing aside his chocolate cake. "I'm not going to sit here and listen to this kind of crap," he shouted.

Everyone began talking at once. I was dismayed to watch the disintegration of my carefully planned party. It was embarrassing, really. When Hercule Poirot accosted his suspects at the end of an Agatha Christie novel, when he summed up the case with stunning logic, no one accused *him* of being the murderer.

Tessa Moore was rubbing her temples with her hands. "This is all giving me a terrible headache, darlings. Can't we think of some more amusing game to play?"

chapter 59

It was Sergeant Walker who saved the situation. In his best Napoleonic style, he stood up from the table and raised his arms. "Shut up!" he commanded. And the clamor of voices ceased.

"Let's allow Mr. Allen to continue. At the end, everyone will have a chance to speak."

"Thank you, W.B.," I said with a grateful nod. "Now, to return: Either I was the intended victim, or Terry Cole. *Or* Terry—or I—wanted the world to think someone was trying to murder us, in which case the field of suspects is wide open."

Tessa moaned at the thought, rolling her eyes.

"However," I continued quickly, "there is another consideration: the history of *The Terry Cole Show,* how it came into being in 1963, and the rather tangled re-

lationships among Bobby Dyer, Terry, Kathleen, Sonny, and Winston Dane."

I had everyone's close attention again.

"We have a scenario here involving ambition, greed, and blackmail—which eventually, as I will show, led to murder. But first, let's talk about our cast.

"In the center, we have a talented but at the time naive young comic named Terry Cole, fresh from a small radio station in Iowa, and whose possibilities of future stardom are apparent to two people: Sonny Melnik, and the never-naive Kathleen Donovan. I mentioned the word *ambition*. Both Kathleen and Sonny were greatly stricken with it, and both were wise enough to realize they themselves did not possess the necessary talents to rise very far on their own. They were looking for the coattails, so to speak, of a man on the rise."

"Now wait a second," cried Sonny, rising to his feet.

"Sit down, Mr. Melnik," Sergeant Walker told him firmly. "As I told you, you'll get your chance."

Sonny slumped back down into his chair. I noticed there were beads of perspiration on his forehead. I was glad, at least, that somebody was beginning to sweat.

"Thank you, Sergeant," I said again. "Now I don't mean to be critical, and I'm not trying to pass judgment. Both Kathleen and Sonny understood their limitations, which is more than can be said for many people in this town. They knew they needed a Terry Cole to make their mark.

"Sonny, in fact, who was a producer of sorts on Terry's show back in Iowa, convinced Terry to come to Hollywood with him, where he had managed to set up a meeting to discuss the possibility of a network radio show. Terry had obvious talent. He impressed the right people, and it looked as though the radio deal was going to go through. And then one fateful night, he and Sonny went to the old Ciro's nightclub on the Sunset Strip to celebrate their good fortune in the big town, and at the next table there happened to be an extremely good-looking makeup girl by the name of Kathleen Donovan—and her lover of the moment, Bobby Dyer.

"Everyone was feeling high, on champagne, on success. I wonder who began the conversation between the two tables? Somehow I imagine it was Sonny and Bobby—the two small-time hustlers might have recognized a common bond. But it was Kathleen and Terry who cemented the new friendship, recognizing a deeper connection, and before long, the two tables had become one."

"How romantic," Tessa said with a sigh. "I never knew tables could do that."

I was annoyed but gave her a rim-shot noise. "Terry returned briefly to Iowa and in 1963 he moved west for good, taking up residence in the Chateau Marmont Hotel and doing a nightly, coast-to-coast radio show in which—to attract an audience—he interviewed celebrities. The show wasn't on the air long enough to become popular, but Kathleen, like Sonny, sensed its potential. She more or less moved into the small suite at the Chateau and she and Terry and Sonny began plotting how they were going to make the move from radio to the real money on big-time TV.

"Kathleen, you'll remember, was the only one of the three to have a connection with TV, though it was a small one. She did makeup for what was then called *Winston Dane Interviews*. Because she was pretty, and very bright, Kathleen had formed various relationships with some of the big shots in the network, and also with Winston himself. From these contacts, she knew two important facts: one, Winston's ratings were sinking—the show was considered too cerebral, too hip for the room—and some of the people on high had begun to consider ways to break Winston's costly two-year contract without paying him off; and two, Winston was secretly—and unknown to the network at this point— a practicing homosexual. As Winnie himself reminded me the other day, the age of sexual liberation—for better or worse—had not yet begun, and so his inclinations were a fact he had to keep in the closet.

"This is where the whole thing starts to get nasty. Kathleen had the idea she could use her insider's knowledge to get rid of Winston and install Terry in his place, and in the process hitch herself by marriage to a rising star.

"Terry and Sonny were only too happy to go along. And so the three of them arranged to expose Winnie's sexual proclivities to *Confidential,* getting photographs of Winnie in the undeniable act. Had the story been printed, it would have been a major scandal not only for Winston but for the network too. That's where Kathleen made a brilliant move. She went to the chairman of the board and told him about the story a week before it was to break, not mentioning her own part in the drama, of course. The chairman was able to make a deal with *Confidential.* For an undisclosed sum of money, the story was never printed, but Winston was forced to resign. At that point Kathleen had cleared, with her typical cleverness, one major obstacle to her future progress. But any number of women in this town might have done that much, and a hell of a lot of men, too. The next couple of steps only someone as brilliant as Kathleen could have put together.

"She probably wore one of her more revealing or form-fitting dresses to the meeting with Mr. Big. What normal man wouldn't be attracted to Kathleen? I'll confess to that crime right now," I added with a mockingly gallant nod in the lady's direction. "How quickly the chairman lost his head it's now not necessary to say, but he certainly did. Kathleen had been wise enough to know that it's in the early stages of relationships of that sort that men feel most desperate, most idiotically romantic. So let's sum up the situation at that point. Number one, Kathleen had just done an enormous favor to the network, and had saved them millions in the process. Secondly, the poor sucker was madly in love with our friend here.

"No doubt coaxed by the object of his affections, he granted her three wishes. Yes, like a genie coming out of a bottle, he either proposed such an expression of gratitude or was helpless to resist when Kathleen brought it up.

"The first wish is history: Kathleen asked that Winston's now vacant time slot go to Terry Cole.

"The second was that the deal be set up in such a way that Terry would only get it if he married Kathleen.

"And the third wish was that a paragraph be put into the contract that if Terry and Kathleen ever divorced, she would get the bulk of the money, not Terry.

"It took some incredibly fancy legal maneuvering

involving the network's lawyers to get these conditions on paper, but Kathleen's admirer had not become chairman of the board for nothing. I should mention here that when Kathleen and Terry *did* divorce several years ago, wish number three had to be modified slightly so that Kathleen would inherit the bulk of Terry's estate but not get it directly with the settlement. This condition had us all confused for a while, since it seemed to indicate that Kathleen had a motive to murder her ex-husband.''

I let this last statement hang in the air for a moment, feeling all eyes upon me, especially Kathleen's. She continued to regard me with a slight but malicious smirk.

A busboy came into the private dining room with a silver pot to offer more coffee. I waited until he had done his work before I continued. Those who were watching me carefully must have noticed that I whispered something into the young man's ear as he passed by my part of the table. Sergeant Walker gave me a sleepy though encouraging smile.

"Let's leave Kathleen for the time being and talk about her friend and sometime lover, Bobby Dyer. Who was this man and what was his part in the conspiracy?

"The way I see it, Bobby was a combination small-time hustler and big-time dreamer. Hollywood, as we all know, draws people like this around the fringes, people with no particular talent, who would be unable to survive in the 'real' world. Bobby was a big talker—possibly he had some charm and savvy, especially when he was younger—but he was too second-rate ever to have a big chance in this town. No, Bobby's environ-

334

ment would always be the street, or the beach, but never the boardroom.

"Now at the very least, we must assume Bobby knew the dirty details of Terry Cole's rise to television prominence. So he had to be taken care of. Terry gave him the nebulous position of 'associate producer'—one of those jobs that can mean a lot, or only a little. Bobby did little more than collect his inflated salary and strut about pretending to be important. Over the years, Terry and Kathleen threw him various bones—like the membership in the Beverly Hills Health Club—to keep him happy and in line. Doubtless, there were other favors as well—vacations in Mexico, cars, cash, the kinds of gaudy little favors a man like Bobby would seek.

"So why was he killed? Did he finally get too greedy, ask for too much? By this time the dirty deeds he knew about were far in the past, and maybe Kathleen or Terry felt it was time to cut their loss.

"But of course, there was a new element here, a new dirty deed, in fact, that Bobby was part of: He purchased the rat poison and poured some of it into the Cajun vodka in Terry's secret on-set refrigerator. And now at last we're at the crux of the mystery: What was Bobby trying to do?

"Was he acting on his own? Perhaps he had his reasons to wish to kill Terry Cole. Or more likely, he was being controlled by someone else. I say more likely, because I do not believe that Bobby had the kind of perverted strength or ambition to actually commit murder on his own. My guess is that he was only obeying instructions. Perhaps he was told that the rat poison would not kill whoever it was meant for, but simply make that person ill. Bobby, I repeat, was not very bright. But when Hal Hoaglund drank that poisoned vodka and died, Bobby Dyer had to be killed as well, because he knew the identity of the person behind the scenes.

"So who was controlling Bobby Dyer?"

I looked around the table at all the upturned faces.

"Was it Kathleen Cole, perhaps impatient to collect the bulk of her ex-husband's estate?

"Or was it long-suffering Sonny Melnik, who hadn't gotten much respect out of a lifetime of slavery to Terry Cole, and might have wished to free himself from what had become a hateful situation?"

I kept moving my glance around the table.

"Maybe it was Terry himself. This has always been a fascinating possibility. Terry could have faked his emotional breakdown to remove himself to Happy Valley in order to establish an alibi. Meanwhile, he was able to control events from afar."

Terry returned my direct stare. "Why the hell would I want to poison my own vodka?" he asked.

"Oh, the poison was meant for me," I replied. "Or whoever was signed to be guest host in your absence."

"That's ridiculous!" he snorted.

"Is it? You had been hearing the grumblings, Terry, from on high. It's true, your ratings were still good after all these years, but there was talk you were becoming unreliable, drinking too much, taking off too much time, and that your salary had become much too inflated for what you were really worth. A man like you could become a little paranoid, Terry. Your old friend Sonny was suggesting you take some time off. But what did he mean? A few names had been suggested as possible temporary replacements for you—but once they were installed behind your desk, would they stay there for good?

"So that was your motive, Terry, if indeed you were the man controlling Bobby Dyer: You were trying to insure your survival on TV by getting rid of the competition."

"Bullshit," he muttered.

"We'll see. Meanwhile there's Tessa Moore to consider."

"Not me, snookums," she objected.

"Oh, yes," I said. "And Winston Dane. Both of you were aware you were being considered as possible alternatives to Terry, should Terry be unable to continue. Of course, I was actually doing the show and so to you I seemed to have an edge in the competition. So for either Winston or Tessa, the motive would have been fairly the same as Terry's: To rid themselves of the competition in order to gain the prize that they sought—a secure and profitable place on late-night TV."

Winston smiled wryly and rolled his eyes at me. Tessa pursed her lips, pouting. The others around the table were watching me, in various stages of boredom and fascination.

It was time to bring this to a close.

"So who is our killer—Kathleen, Sonny, Terry, Tessa, or Winston? The envelope, please."

The *maître d'* appeared on cue—I had sent word through the busboy—carrying the manila envelope I had mailed to myself here yesterday from the Beverly Hills Post Office.

I tore open the envelope and pulled out the photograph inside.

"And the murderer is," I announced Oscar-or-Emmy-Award-Style, "Winston Dane."

chapter 60

Winston stood up halfway, then sank down again. It was as if a jolt of electricity had passed through his body.

"You're joking," he said.

I shook my head sadly. "Alas, I'm not."

I held up the 8X10 photo for all to see. The black and white picture apparently had been taken on a large sailboat. Winston was sunbathing on the deck, lying on a foam pad wearing nothing but a European-style bikini bathing suit. Next to him, sharing the towel—his head actually upon Winston's shoulder—was Bobby Dyer.

They both looked young, carefree, and playfully lustful.

"Your mistake, Winnie, was pretending you didn't remember Bobby Dyer. As soon as I found this picture in Terry's photo album, I knew you were the killer."

Winnie had a funny half smile on his face. He was

studying a crumb of bread left on the white linen tablecloth near his spoon. The tiny object seemed to absorb all his attention.

"I don't understand," said Sonny.

"Don't you? Actually, this photograph is from the infamous set that was given to *Confidential*. Winston was set up, you see. He had confided in his good friend Kathleen about his sexual preference, but she did not have the proof she needed to discredit him. Enter good-looking Bobby Dyer with his muscles and Malibu tan, whose job was to entrap Winston and arrange for these . . . uh . . . photo opportunities. Bobby, I suspect, was not primarily inclined toward the gay life, but he had no morals and was willing to do just about anything for a buck. So you see, Bobby was one of the key players in the conspiracy, and I imagine he never felt that his part was fully appreciated. As I've said, he was neither bright nor terribly ambitious, but I believe he was left with a vague and sullen feeling that he should have gotten more out of the deal."

I had arrived at the point where I was guessing, winging it as I went along. Watching the way Winston sat there with his strange half smile, looking only at the crumb on the table, gave me assurance I was on the right track.

"I think Winnie actually fell in love with Bobby, which made the betrayal all the more cruel. In one blow, he lost both his career and his heart. So he went to Europe, but he did not forgive and forget. For all these years he's been plotting revenge—and a big return to television."

Winston looked up at me, and there was a wild, lost look in his eye that would have frightened me had we been alone. Then he returned his attention to the crumb of bread, picking it up between two fingers and slowly pulverizing it to dust.

"I also suspect that Bobby, strangely enough, found his true self through Winston—perhaps he really became bisexual—and there might have been some small regret on his part that he had dealt with Winston in such a terrible way."

Again Winston's eyes came up to meet mine. Was there gratitude there that someone finally understood what he had gone through all these years? I rather thought so, and it emboldened me to give voice to my biggest guess of all.

"Whatever the reason, Winnie and Bobby stayed in touch, long-distance, over the years. Maybe Bobby even went to Rome once or twice. It was through Bobby that Winston learned of Terry's gradual disintegration, the drinking on camera, the long absences from the show, and most of all, the fact that the network was becoming concerned enough to consider the possibility of retiring *The Terry Cole Show* and hiring someone else. There was even a strange though unlikely rumor that Winston himself was being considered for his old job. It was at this point that he came back from Rome.

"Now I've done some checking with the dates. Winston flew into Los Angeles and checked into the Beverly Hills Hotel one week before Terry left for Happy Valley. This gave him time to reestablish his relationship with Bobby, who was all too glad to change loyalties, hoping there would be some gain in it for himself. And so Winston convinced Bobby to put the poison in the bottle, probably telling him it would only make Terry sick. Winston, however, knew differently.

"So who was he trying to kill? Me or Terry? The answer, I suspect, is actually both of us. The poison was probably put into the bottle Thursday night, intended originally for Terry the next day. But then Terry made an unexpected departure for Happy Valley, and Winnie decided to let the vodka remain in the refrigerator on the chance that I—or any other guest host, for that matter—might get curious and try a sip.

"His reason for wishing Terry dead is obvious—it was a matter of his desire for revenge, which had been building as he fantasized about it for over twenty-five years. Murdering me was more impersonal, I trust. Winnie had learned that he really was a contender for the job and he wished to rid himself of all competition.

"This is where it gets even nastier. Winnie made a date with Bobby to pay him off for his help—only the payoff was a lot more final than Bobby imagined. Bobby, after all, had been part of the original conspiracy that had sent Winnie into his long exile in Europe, and we may assume Winnie never forgave him. Also, by killing Bobby, Winnie effectively destroyed any link to himself.

"So now Winnie was free to concentrate on landing the host job for himself. Poor man, he was greatly deluded! Terry would never have allowed anyone to steal his show—would you, Terry? And if the network *did* manage to cancel him, the spot would not have been given to an old war-horse like Winston Dane—or Tessa Moore, or Steve Allen, for that matter—but to some rising young star. It's an eighteen-to-forty-nine business, gang.

"But Winnie didn't know this. He had been away from Hollywood too long, harboring his hatreds, and he really believed he had a chance to return to television bigger than before. He believed Terry was crazy and out of the picture, so now only I was standing in his way.

"Winnie and I were staying at the same hotel, and it was easy for him to keep track of my movements. He had, incidentally, leased a black BMW, license number 3J459, from Luxury Car Rentals of Beverly Hills. From this car he tried once to shoot me, and another time, in Malibu, to run me down. The Malibu occasion was spur of the moment. Winnie had been visiting at Kathleen's house when I called her that night, so he knew where I'd be."

I shook my head. Suddenly I wasn't enjoying any of this—not my own cleverness or poor Winston Dane's situation.

"This is the most absurd pack of lies and psychotic conjecture I've ever heard," Kathleen objected loudly.

"Is it, Winnie, old friend?" I asked softly. His eyes were still only on me, and I noticed that the corners of his mustache were quivering.

He was sitting close to the door. I think I knew what he was about to do, but I didn't try to stop him. Without a word—and quick as an eel—Winston Dane spun in his chair and made a dash for it, out of the private dining room and into the restaurant at large. There was part of me that hoped he would get away.

"Well, stop him, for Chrissake!" yelled Sonny Melnik.

Detective Sergeant W.B. Walker pressed a small buzzer in his hand and shrugged.

"Oh, I don't think he'll get too far," he said, almost as if he were embarrassed by his own efficiency.

chapter 61

I stepped out of the shower and into a robe, happy to have rid myself of the smell of champagne. Sergeant Walker was waiting for me in my living room, slumped way back on my sofa. There were dark circles beneath his eyes. He looked tired out but satisfied.

"Well, you'll be glad to know Winston Dane was still busy confessing when I left the station. Once he started talking, he couldn't stop. It must be a relief to tell people what he's been going through all these years."

I sat down at my rented hotel piano without answering and began to play a slow, bluesy version of "Georgia On My Mind." I felt Sergeant Walker's eyes upon me. I knew there were some big questions he wanted to ask me, but I wasn't about to make it any easier for him.

"You made some good guesses," he said finally.

I shrugged as if it were no great matter. "I have an old friend who works for the *Times*—he was able to help me with some background information. As for the guesswork, well, once I'd seen the photo of Winston and Bobby together, it was all pretty obvious. Terry was stupid to keep a memento of the dirty way he got his show, but he was too much of an egomaniac to think he'd ever get caught."

"What about the Coles, then?"

"What about them?"

"Do you want to prosecute them for locking you in their wine closet?"

I played through the bridge without answering: "Other arms reach out for me, Other eyes smile tenderly. . . ."

"What happens if I don't press charges?" I asked finally.

"Nothing," he said. "There'd be no case. The Coles will just walk free."

"Okay," I said.

"Okay *what?*"

"Let 'em walk. They were only trying to protect themselves. If the story of what they did to Winston Dane ever came out, they'd both be finished in Hollywood. Frankly, I'm sick of scandals and the whole bloody thing."

"Don't you think they should be punished, Mr. Allen?"

I shrugged. "They'll punish themselves, I guess. Why don't we leave it at that? From what I've seen, revenge is not so sweet."

I sang through the last verse: "Georgia, Georgia, no peace I find. Just an old sweet song of Georgia on my mind. . . ."

You rediscover songs according to your mood, and I realized tonight that maybe Hoagy Carmichael, the great man, had written another American masterpiece in this one. W.B. walked up alongside the piano as I played, and he applauded when it was done.

"Very good, Mr. Allen. That was lovely. Now maybe I can ask you one more question."

"Yes, W.B. ?"

"How did you get out of that wine closet?"

I turned around on the piano bench so I could look at him. "It was elementary, my dear Walker."

"Then perhaps you might explain."

"Well, I told you how I got free of my ropes and finally found the light switch, didn't I?"

"When you left the table you were telling me about opening up bottles of champagne."

"Oh, yes. I had an idea I could make a kind of cable out of all the wire and lead. It seemed fairly brilliant at the time, though I must tell you, it takes about six bottles of champagne per foot, and it's slow going. I discovered the French are a bit more generous with their wire wrappings than the Californians, incidentally, in case you're ever in a similar situation. I was lucky Kathleen had quite a few cases of Dom Perignon laid away in her closet."

"And how far was this wire cable supposed to reach?" the sergeant prodded.

"Oh, to the screen on the ceiling, which seemed as if it might go to a ventilation shaft. Didn't I explain that? I thought I might crawl out that way."

"It sounds a little athletic, for you."

"I was desperate."

"Well?" he asked.

"I finally made a wire hook about three-and-a-half feet long, from which I was able to snag the screen when I stood up on my chair. I was able to get the screen loose, but unfortunately I was wrong in my assumption—there was a fan up there, and *not* a ventilation shaft. It was all a waste of time, I suppose, except the exertion kept me warm."

"So then what did you do?"

"What *was* there to do? I sat down on my chair and tried to think of a new plan."

I turned away from Sergeant Walker back to my piano and started "Cast Your Fate To The Wind," setting up an A-flat drone in the left hand, sounding an open fifth, while playing the chords of the haunting melody in the right. A good tune, but Detective Sergeant W.B. Walker seemed unable to enjoy it.

"Okay, *then* what happened?"

"I waited."

"Yes? For how long?"

"It's funny, but I really don't know. You may find, if this ever happens to you, that time spent in a wine closet seems to stretch on forever."

"But eventually you got out," the sergeant reminded me. He was beginning to sound irritated.

"Yes, it sounds dumb, but I'd never tried to see if the door was unlocked. Eventually, I turned the handle—and it opened. That's really all there is to it."

"The door was unlocked?" Walker repeated, for the first time dumbfounded.

"Yep. Either the Coles were incredibly careless, or one of them came down to unlock the door sometime during the night. Either way, it made me realize that bad as they are, neither of them is particularly capable of murder."

"So that's it?" the sergeant asked, shaking his head

in amazement. I think he would have felt more satisfied if I had crawled out through the ventilator shaft—and so would I, if you want to know the truth. But this is the way it happened: a turn of the door handle had set me free in an empty house, allowing me just enough time to make a few phone calls to my friend at the *Times* and get myself to Chasen's.

Sergeant Walker offered his hand. "Well, sir, I can't say it hasn't been interesting."

I rose from the piano to shake hands and say goodbye. "Call me Steve," I suggested. "After all, we've been through a lot."

"Okay, Steve. You take care of yourself, you hear?"

"You too, Wishbone," I told him.

Sergeant Walker, who had been about to walk out the door, froze in dumb surprise. He managed a pained smile.

"You found me out," he said.

"Wishbone B. Walker. That's how you're registered with the Burbank Police Department."

"My daddy was fond of chicken," he said with a rueful grin. "I keep it sort of secret from my friends and colleagues."

"Gee, I don't see why, Wishbone. I think it's kinda cute."

"But, er, you never did find out what the *B* stands for, did you?"

"No," I admitted. "That I did not."

Wishbone B. Walker smiled more easily and punched me playfully on the shoulder.

"Well, keep on trying, boy," he said, "and maybe one of these days you'll be a real detective."

"No," I told him. "I think I'll quit while I'm ahead."

"Sure," he said. We shook hands and he was gone. I was soon in bed with the lights out, stretched out comfortably and glad to leave all this behind me.

But I couldn't sleep. Feeling for the Bible in the drawer of the bedside table, I sat up.

Balthazar? I wondered. *Boaz? Beelzebub?*

I was up all night, trying to figure out what the *B* stood for, and how I might start looking for the information in the morning.

God, I hate mysteries.

J.J. MARRIC MYSTERIES

time passes quickly . . . As *DAY* blends with *NIGHT* and *WEEK* flies into *MONTH*, Gideon must fit together the pieces of death and destruction before time runs out!

GIDEON'S DAY   (2721, $3.95)
They mysterious death of a young police detective is only the beginning of a bizarre series of events which end in the fatal knifing of a seven-year-old girl. But for commander George gideon of New Scotland Yard, it is all in a day's work!

GIDEON'S MONTH   (2766, $3.95)
A smudged page on his calendar, Gideon's month is blackened by brazen and bizarre offenses ranging from mischief to murder. Gideon must put a halt to the sinister events which involve the corruption of children and a homicidal housekeeper, before the city drowns in blood!

GIDEON'S NIGHT   (2734, $3.50)
When an unusually virulent pair of psychopaths leaves behind a trail of pain, grief, and blood, Gideon once again is on the move. This time the terror all at once comes to a head and he must stop the deadly duel that is victimizing young women and children — in only one night!

GIDEON'S WEEK   (2722, $3.95)
When battered wife Ruby Benson set up her killer husband for capture by the cops, she never considered the possibility of his escape. Now Commander George Gideon of Scotland Yard must save Ruby from the vengeance of her sadistic spouse . . . or die trying!

Available wherever paperbacks are sold, or order direct from the Publisher. Send cover price plus 50¢ per copy for mailing and handling to Zebra Books, Dept. 3063, 475 Park Avenue South, New York, N.Y. 10016. Residents of New York, New Jersey and Pennsylvania must include sales tax. DO NOT SEND CASH.

MYSTERIES TO KEEP YOU GUESSING
by John Dickson Carr

CASTLE SKULL   (1974, $3.50)

The hand may be quicker than the eye, but ghost stories didn't hoodwink Henri Bencolin. A very real murderer was afoot in Castle Skull — a murderer who must be found before he strikes again.

IT WALKS BY NIGHT   (1931, $3.50)

The police burst in and found the Duc's severed head staring at them from the center of the room. Both the doors had been guarded, yet the murderer had gone in and out *without having been seen*!

THE EIGHT OF SWORDS   (1881, $3.50)

The evidence showed that while waiting to kill Mr. Depping, the murderer had calmly eaten his victim's dinner. But before famed crime-solver Dr. Gideon Fell could serve up the killer to Scotland Yard, there would be another course of murder.

THE MAN WHO COULD NOT SHUDDER (1703, $3.50)

Three guests at Martin Clarke's weekend party swore they saw the pistol lifted from the wall, levelled, and shot. *Yet no hand held it*. It couldn't have happened — but there was a dead body on the floor to prove that it had.

THE PROBLEM OF THE WIRE CAGE   (1702, $3.50)

There was only one set of footsteps in the soft clay surface — and those footsteps belonged to the victim. It seemed impossible to prove that anyone had killed Frank Dorrance.

Available wherever paperbacks are sold, or order direct from the Publisher. Send cover price plus 50¢ per copy for mailing and handling to Zebra Books, Dept. 3063, 475 Park Avenue South, New York, N.Y. 10016. Residents of New York, New Jersey and Pennsylvania must include sales tax. DO NOT SEND CASH.

DORIS MILES DISNEY IS
THE QUEEN OF SUSPENSE

DO NOT FOLD, SPINDLE OR MUTILATE   (2154, $2.95)
Even at 58, Sophie Tate Curtis was always clowning—sending her bridge club into stitches by filling out a computer dating service card with a phony name. But her clowning days were about to come to an abrupt end. For one of her computer-suitors was very, very serious—and he would make sure that this was Sophie's last laugh . . .

MRS. MEEKER'S MONEY   (2212, $2.95)
It took old Mrs. Meeker $30,000 to realize that she was being swindled by a private detective. Bent on justice, she turned to Postal Inspector Madden. But—unfortunately for Mrs. Meeker—this case was about to provide Madden with a change of pace by turning from mail fraud into murder, C.O.D.

HERE LIES   (2362, $2.95)
Someone was already occupying the final resting place of the late Mrs. Phoebe Upton Clarke. A stranger had taken up underground residence there more than 45 years earlier—an illegal squatter with no name—and a bullet in his skull!

THE LAST STRAW   (2286, $2.95)
Alone with a safe containing over $30,000 worth of bonds, Dean Lipscomb couldn't help remembering that he needed a little extra money. The bonds were easily exchanged for cash, but Leonard Riggott discovered them missing sooner than Dean expected. One crime quickly led to another . . . but this time Dean discovered that it was easier to redeem the bonds than himself!

Available wherever paperbacks are sold, or order direct from the Publisher. Send cover price plus 50¢ per copy for mailing and handling to Zebra Books, Dept. 3063, 475 Park Avenue South, New York, N.Y. 10016. Residents of New York, New Jersey and Pennsylvania must include sales tax. DO NOT SEND CASH.